U0027421

喚醒你的英文語感！

Get a Feel for English !

喚醒你的英文語感！

Get a Feel for English !

IELTS之所以拿不到高分, 原因在於寫作/口說拉低平均

IELTS高點

雅思制霸
7.0⁺ 說寫通

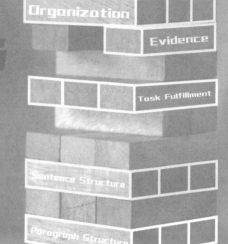

Ideas

Organization

Evidence

Task Fulfillment

Sentence Structure

Paragraph Structure

Writing 寫作強化篇

Score higher than 7.0

論證說服力

修辭活用法

組織邏輯性

用詞精準度

Why this book?

你之所以在看這本書，可能是因為你之前考過 IELTS 但分數不高；或是你即將第一次參加這項考試，需要得到超過 6.5 的分數。所以你可能正在找一本可以幫助你提升英語寫作和口說能力的書。

我的名字是 Quentin Brand，我從一九九〇年到現在一直在教英文。我先在英國倫敦一家頂尖的語言學校任教，教過來自世界各地的學生，並在一九九八年開始在台灣教英文。從此，我開始在台灣教 IELTS。當時，IELTS 第一次透過英國文化協會 (British Council) 引進台灣，這個機構創立並擁有 IELTS 測驗。後來我來到高點登峰美語 (Apex) 任教，在這段期間內也輔考過許多 IELTS 考生。

多年來，我注意到許多學生在寫作和口說部分所得到的分數常低於其他測驗項目。而本書正是根據我觀察中文母語人士在寫作 IELTS Tasks 和做口說測驗時經常遇到的困難點，並結合我多年來教導他們如何清楚、精準且有邏輯地撰寫英文及用英語進行對話的經驗，所歸納出的應試策略。若想在測驗中得到比 6.5 更高的分數，這些英語語言技巧和策略是你必須好好熟習的。

很高興能在本書與您分享我多年來所開發的教學和學習策略。希望藉此幫助我的學生和所有考生們成功克服這些困難，並在 IELTS 測驗得到更高的分數。

Quentin Brand

Why this book?

You are probably looking at this book because you have either done IELTS before and did not get a high enough score, or because you are going to take it for the first time in the future and need to get a score higher than 6.5. You are probably looking for a book that you think will help you to improve your writing and speaking in English.

My name is Quentin Brand, and I have been teaching English since 1990, first in the UK, where I worked in one of the top language schools in London, teaching students from all over the world, and since 1998 in Taiwan. I have been teaching IELTS in Taiwan since it was very first introduced into this country, first at the British Council, which is one of the owners and creators of the IELTS test, and then afterwards at Apex. I have also tutored many many IELTS test takers during that time.

Over the years, I have noticed many students getting a lower score on their writing and speaking than on the other papers. This book is based on my observations of the difficulties Chinese speakers have in writing IELTS tasks, and the difficulties Chinese speakers have in the speaking test. It will teach you the language skills and strategies necessary for getting a score higher than 6.5. in the writing and in the speaking test. It is based on all my years of experience teaching Chinese speakers how to write clearly, accurately and logically, and how to conduct conversations in English.

In this book I am happy to share with you the teaching and learning strategies I have developed over the years to help my students successfully overcome those difficulties to get scores in the higher ranges of IELTS.

Quentin Brand

CONTENTS 目錄

PART 1
雅思寫作任務一　IELTS Writing Task 1

PART 2
雅思寫作任務二　IELTS Writing Task 2

雅思寫作概論

About the IELTS Writing Test

寫作題型：雅思寫作任務一與任務二
Types of Writing: IELTS Task 1 and Task 2

IELTS 考生必須了解一個問題，那就是 Task 1 和 Task 2 之間的差異。它們是完全不同類型的寫作，徹底了解它們之間的差異有助於在測驗時有良好表現。

☑ Task 1

Task 1 基本上是一個**描述性寫作任務**。如果你要研究與技術或科學相關的學科，你就要會寫這種文章。在這類學科裡，能夠精確描述實驗、數據和圖片等是非常重要的。Task 1 的設計即是用來測驗你寫這類技術性文章的能力。

在這個寫作任務中，你必須證明你能夠準確描述事物。在中文裡，要做到精確是一件很困難的事，因為中文是一種很模糊的語言。而當你的母語不是英文卻要用英文寫作時，這個難度就更高了。

在這個任務裡，你**必須達到兩種精準度：訊息的精準度和語言的精準度**。

「訊息的精準度」是指你要能夠描述實際上看到的東西，同時不摻入自己的觀點、不表達自己的意見，或者不去詮釋你看到了什麼。你將在 Unit 1 和 Unit 2 學習如何做到這一點。

「語言的精準度」是指精準使用英文文法和詞彙，你必須努力使用不模糊的語言來寫作。在本書 Unit 3 到 Unit 7，將可學到更多這部分的知識。

☑ Task 2

Task 2 基本上是一種**論證型的寫作任務**。如果要研究人文學科，就必須要會寫這類文章。在此，詮釋和表達你對你的研究和讀物的意見非常重要。在這種寫作裡，你必須具說服力並合乎邏輯、必須展現出對主題的看法、必須對主題有見解，並且提出合理的理由和證據來支持你的意見。Task 2 的目的即是測試你寫作這種文章的能力。

Task 2 **有兩種類型的文章：論證／意見** (argument / opinion) 的文章，以及**問題／解決方案** (problem / solution) 的文章。

「論證／意見」的文章是要測試你檢驗雙方論點，並建立論證來支持一個意見的能力。

「問題／解決方案」的文章則是測試你描述問題及問題產生的原因、提出解決問題的方案，以及討論這些方案的預期和非預期後果。

在這兩種文章中，重點是建立論證，並且有說服力。你將在 Unit 11 到 Unit 14 學習如何做到這一點。

以我的經驗來說，許多考生認爲 Task 2 比較困難、也比較重要，因此他們在準備考試時會特別強調這個部分。然而，這樣做是不正確的。在我看來，Task 1 更難，因爲它需要完美的精準度。我強烈的建議，即使你沒有打算更認眞地看待 Task 1，也一定要把它看得和 Task 2 一樣重要。

常見問題：組織
Common Problems: Organisation

IELTS 考生之所以拿不到 6.5 以上的高分，常見的問題之一是文章缺乏組織。無論你的詞藻多麼華麗，用了多少晦澀的詞彙，也無論你運用了多複雜的句型文法，如果還是以中文的思維來組織想法，就得不到高於 6.5 的分數。除了使用高級用語，主考官也希望考生能用西方的思考邏輯來組織自己的想法。

用英文組織訊息的方式，和用中文組織訊息的方式有很大的不同，因爲它們的邏輯不同。這些差異一方面很大，但另一方面卻又非常細微。根據我的經驗，很多老師和學生都沒有意識到這種差異，所以他們不看重這個部分。我想在這裡特別強調這些差異。你將在 Unit 9 了解這些差異，而 Unit 10 至 Unit 14 有一些任務，也可以幫助你更加了解這些差異。

順便一提，了解西方人處理資訊的結構，對於閱讀測驗也有很大的幫助。

常見問題：語言
Common Problems: Language (the Leximodel)

在這個部分，我要向大家介紹 leximodel。Leximodel 是我看待語言的方式，它是以一個很簡單的概念爲基礎：

Language consists of words which are used with other words.
語言是由字串所構成的。

這個看法非常簡單易懂。它的意思是：與其把語言看成文法和單字，與其學習個別的單字，然後再學習句型，我們認爲語言是一群字或是字的組合，即語言是由字串所構成。

也就是說，有些字的組合比其他字的組合更容易預測。例如，我們可以預測到 listen 的後面永遠都會跟著 to，而不是 at 或 under 之類的其他字，所以我們可以說這個組合是完全固定的 (fixed)。另一方面，English 這個單字後面可接很多字，例如 gentleman、test、tea，所以很難預測接下來是哪一個字。我們可以說，這種組合是不固定的，它是流動的 (fluid)。

我們可以根據可預測度，把這些字串組合沿著以下的光譜來擺放：

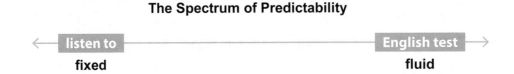

The Spectrum of Predictability

← **listen to** ─────────────────────── **English test** →
　　　fixed　　　　　　　　　　　　　　　　　fluid

知道哪些字串組合是固定的，哪些是不固定的，可以讓你更快學習和使用英文。如果你學習的是一群字，而不是單一一個字，你的學習速度會更快，也會知道如何使用它們，因為這些字從來都不是單獨使用的。

我們可以把所有字串（稱之為 MWIs ＝ multi word items）分為三類：chunks、set-phrases 和 word partnerships。由於中文裡沒有和這些詞相對應的概念，所以請直接記住它們的英文。讓我們更仔細看這三類字串，你很快就會知道，它們其實很容易理解和使用。

☑ Chunks

Chunks 通常被我們當成文法的部分。Chunks 通常很短，並且由 meaning words（有意義的字，如 listen、depend）和 function words（功能性的字，如 to、on）所組成。Chunks 包含了不固定元素和固定元素。例如，我們可以改變動詞時態 (was listening to / have not been listening to)，但不能改變後面的 to 這個字。

你知道的 chunks 可能已經很多，卻不知道自己知道！我們來進行一個任務，看看你是否明白我的意思。進行這個任務時，很重要的是不要先看答案，所以，請不要作弊！

A chunk is a combination of words which is more or less fixed. Every time a word in the chunk is used, it must be used with its partner(s). Chunks combine fixed and fluid elements of language. When you learn a new word, you should learn the chunk. There are thousands of chunks in English. One way you can help yourself to improve your English is by noticing and keeping a database of the chunks you find as you read. You should also try to memorize as many as possible.

現在，請把你的答案和下列語庫做比較。如果你沒有找到那麼多的 chunks，請再看看你能不能找到語庫裡所有的 chunks。

… a combination of n.p. …	… thousands of n.p. …
… more or less …	… in English …
… every time v.p. …	… help yourself to V …
… be used with n.p. …	… keep a database of n.p. …
… combine s/th and s/th. …	… try to V …
… elements of n.p. …	… as many as possible …

- 注意，語庫中的 chunks 是用原形 be 來表示 be 動詞，而不是 is 或 are。
- 記錄 chunks 時，會在 chunks 的前後都加上 …（刪節號）。
- 注意，有些 chunks 的後面會接著 V、Ving、n.p.（noun phrase，名詞片語）或 v.p.（verb phrase，動詞片語）。關於這部分，你很快就會學到更多。
- 學習大量的 chunks 可以提升在寫作上的文法精準度。你將在這本書學到很多 chunks。

☑ Set-phrases

Set-phrases 通常被當成組織或互動的部分。我們用 set-phrases 來完成工作，例如在餐廳點餐、在文章裡組織訊息。因為我們平常都用一樣的用語來做這些常見的事，所以 set-phrases 是更固定的 chunks。它們通常比較長，而且可能包含好幾個 chunks。Chunks 通常是沒頭沒尾的片斷文字組合；Set-phrases 則通常有個開頭或結尾，或是兩者都有，這表示有時候一個完整的句子也可能是一組 set-phrase。現在請看看下面的語庫並進行任務。

請想想以下的 **set-phrases** 你是否曾在哪裡見過？把認識的打勾。

- [ ] I disagree with the view that v.p. …
- [ ] There are many reasons why I think so.
- [ ] I do not believe that v.p. …
- [ ] It's my opinion that v.p. …
- [ ] There are many ways to solve this problem.
- [ ] I (dis)agree with this, and think that v.p. …
- [ ] This essay will look at some of the common problems and will then suggest two solutions.
- [ ] I can think of two solutions to this problem.
- [ ] There are two/three main reasons.
- [ ] I firmly believe that v.p. …
- [ ] There's no doubt in my mind that v.p. …

- 注意，set-phrases 通常以大寫字母開頭，或用句點結束。這三個點 (...) 表示句子裡不固定的部分要開始了。
- 你可能已經在 IELTS 文章中看過這些 set-phrases。它們通常用來表達對一個議題的看法。你將在 Unit 10 學習如何在寫作時使用它們。
- 由於 set-phrases 是三類字串中最固定的一種，所以在學習時，必須非常仔細留意每個 set-phrases 的細節。稍後對此會有更詳細的說明。
- 有些 set-phrases 以 n.p. 結尾，有些以 v.p. 結尾。這部分我稍後會談更多。
- 學習大量的 set-phrases 可以彰顯你在寫作上組織想法的能力。在本書中將可學到很多 set-phrases。

☑ Word partnerships

　　Word partnerships 是三類字串中最不固定，也就是流動性最高的一類。它是由兩個或更多的意義字（不同於 chunks 結合了意義字和功能字）所組成，通常是「動詞＋形容詞＋名詞」或是「名詞＋名詞」的組合。Word partnerships 會根據你寫的主題而改變，而 chunks 和 set-phrases 則可用於任何主題。現在，請進行下一個任務，藉此更清楚了解我的意思。

任務三 請看下列各組 word partnerships，並判斷它們來自於哪一種主題內容。請從主題列表中選擇。

主題
A. acting and theatre   B. psychological experiments   C. the environment   D. the history of cities   E. the law   F. the life of whales   G. social media

word partnerships ①

natural resources / environmental pollution

global warming / carbon dioxide emissions

主題是（　　　）

---

word partnerships ②

personal responsibility / conduct experiments / analyze results / collect data

主題是（　　　）

---

word partnerships ③

social networks / social withdrawal / virtual reality game / addictive behavior

主題是（　　　）

- 請注意，word partnerships 包含意義，由兩個字組合而成，有時候甚至由三個或四個字組合而成。
- 學習大量 word partnerships 可以讓你精確使用字彙和表達你的想法。

➡ 任務三答案：① C　② B　③ G

　　因此，我們最終版的 leximodel，現在看起來是這樣：

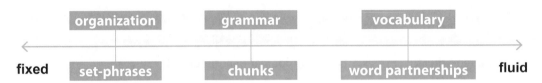

The Spectrum of Predictability

organization	grammar	vocabulary

fixed ←————————————————————————————→ fluid

set-phrases	chunks	word partnerships

這樣更接近語言在人腦中記憶和使用的習慣。如果你把重點放在學習 chunks，你的文法能力會提升，因為大多數的文法錯誤實際上是誤用了 chunks；如果你把重點放在學習 set-phrases，組織文章的能力會提升；而若是把重點放在 word partnerships，則使用詞彙的精準度會更高。

 ## 如何使用這本書
How to Use This Book

現在，我想各位應該會認為 leximodel 似乎是個不錯的概念，但可能還是有些疑問。讓我來歸納一下你可能會有的疑問是哪些，並看看能否幫忙解答。

問 請問這本書如何使用 **leximodel**？
答 本書會呈現出語言裡所有最常出現的固定部分（chunks、set-phrases 和 word partnerships，但大部分是 set-phrases 和 chunks），書中將告訴你如何學習並在 IELTS 寫作測驗的兩個 Task 裡使用它們。

問 有沒有什麼問題是我需要注意的？
答 有。這本書裡有許多練習，是設計用來幫你解決一些問題。學習 set-phrases 和 chunks 的主要問題是：

You must focus on the details of the set-phrase or chunk.
你必須把重點放在 set-phrases 或 chunks 的細節上。

在學習或使用 set-phrases 和 chunks 的時候，有四個部分的細節必須特別注意。

1. **小詞**（像是 a、the、to、in、at、on、and、but 之類的字）。這些字都非常難記，但難記還只是問題的一部分。如果你誤用了小詞，將會改變 set-phrase 或 chunk，而改變它們就表示出錯了。

2. **字尾**（有些字的字尾是 -ed，有些是 -ing，有些是 -ment，有些是 -s 或沒有 -s）。字尾改變了，字的意思也會隨之改變。如果弄錯字尾，會改變 set-phrase 或 chunk，也就等於是用錯了。

3. **set-phrases 和 chunks 的結尾**。在前面任務一和任務二中看到 set-phrases 和 chunks 可能以 v.p.、n.p.、V 或 Ving 結尾，我們把這些縮寫稱爲 codes。（V.p. = verb phrase 動詞片語；n.p. = noun phrase 名詞片語；V = verb 動詞，以及 Ving = Ving 動名詞。）

   把 set-phrase 和 chunk 加入句子之中時，可能出現許多錯誤。當你在學習 set-phrase 或 chunk 時，也請學習 code。弄錯 code 會改變 set-phrase 和 chunk，等於是寫錯了。稍後將在 Unit 3 學到更多這方面的知識。

4. **完整的 set-phrase 或 chunk**。你必須確定自己已學到並使用完整的 set-phrase 或 chunk。所以實際上，我們可以說 1、2 和 3 的錯誤，也同時是 4 的錯誤。對吧？

問 你會如何協助我？

答 我在後面許多單元設計了許多練習，讓你學習正確使用 set-phrase 和 chunk。你會進行一系列不同類型的練習，例如注意錯誤、注意 n.p 和 v.p. 之間的差異、訂正錯誤，並且根據 set-phrases 的意義將它們分門別類。所有這些練習，都是設計用來幫助你學習和記憶新的用語。我會給你正確的答案和詳盡的解析。另外，我會用範例文章告訴你許多正確使用這些用語的例子。也會告訴你，我在台灣教書多年來，看到人們最常誤用的狀況，並且分析到底錯在哪裡。

問 我該做些什麼？

答 你應該要確保自己徹底完成每一個單元。這些單元都經過精心設計，目的是幫助你學習，所以你不應該跳過任何單元、任何練習，或是在還沒完成練習前就直接看答案。請務必從頭到尾徹底學習所有單元，並利用每個單元最後的清單幫你追蹤自己的學習狀況。

問 我要花多久時間才能進步？

答 每個單元大約需要三個小時來完成。你應該爲每個單元保留這麼多的學習時間，

這樣在學習時才不會被中斷或干擾。此外，你應該花時間練習用英文及我教你的技巧來寫文章。除了我在每個單元裡已額外給你的練習題，你還可以在網路上找到許多範例文章來練習。

問 我如何得到回饋？

答 你可能會認為，除非有人給你回饋，否則練習寫文章的幫助不大。在某個程度上來說，這樣想是對的。但是，根據我實際的經驗來說，就算你沒有機會得到別人的回饋，盡可能多練習依然是非常關鍵的。你在本書學到的用語和思考方式，會幫助你的大腦記憶它們。

問 你還有其他祕訣可以教我嗎？

答 有。多閱讀。所有研究都清楚顯示，不管參加什麼考試，英文閱讀量較大的學生，分數都比較高，所以每天盡量多讀英文。此外，字彙量不足是妨礙你們在 IELTS 四個領域裡得到高分的一個大問題。大量閱讀可以讓你讀到更多字彙，並幫助你學會它們。

所以，你準備好要開始了嗎？

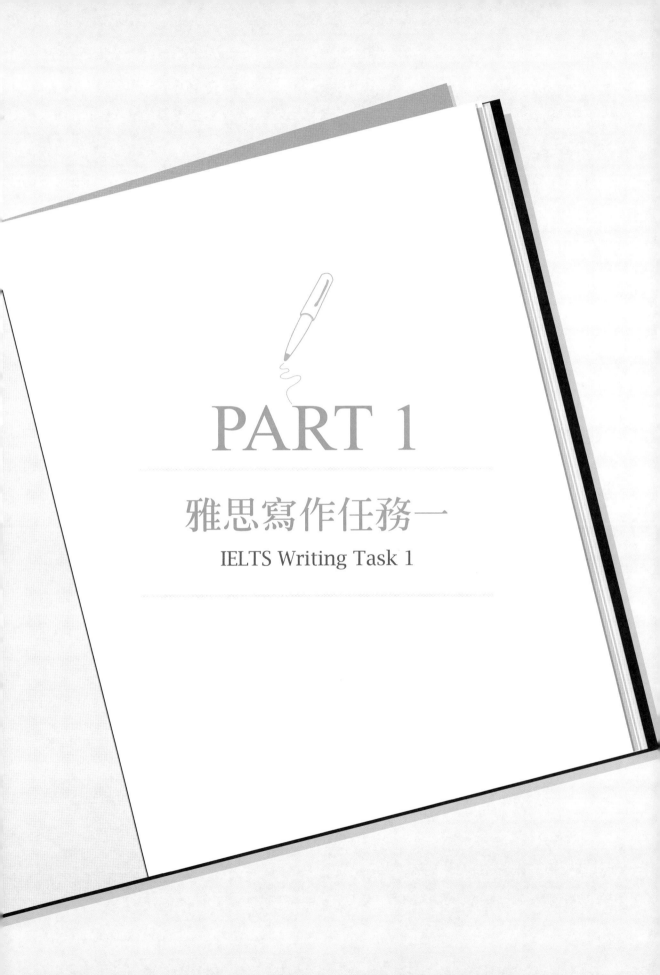

PART 1

雅思寫作任務一
IELTS Writing Task 1

Unit 1

寫作任務一介紹

Introduction to Task 1

任務描述 Task Description

　　在「雅思寫作概論」中，你已經知道 IELTS Task 1 和 IELTS Task 2 的差異，以及描述性寫作與論證性寫作的差異。在這個簡短的單元中，我會更詳細的介紹 IELTS Task 1 的測驗內容，並告訴你一些處理這個寫作任務的方法和策略。

　　正如我們在寫作概論中學到的，Task 1 基本上是個描述性任務。要求考生寫一段話來描述某一張圖片、長條圖、表格、地圖或圖表。這裡的重點是用語和資訊的精準度。

　　如果你以前做過 IELTS 測驗，就會知道 Task 1 的提示有三個部分。

1. 用像這樣的用語來描述圖片：

> This graph shows the demand for energy, and the amount of energy generated in Snowvania (measured in terawatt-hours) from January to December in any one year.

圖片描述的文字蘊含了非常有用的字彙。在下個單元中，我將告訴你如何分析它。

2. 像這樣的說明文字：

> Summarize the information by selecting and reporting the main features and make comparisons where relevant.

正式測驗中的說明文字雖然可能不完全相同，但通常相當類似。基本上，你必須用大約 150 個字來寫這篇文章，並盡可能精準地描述圖中的數據。

3. 像這樣的圖：

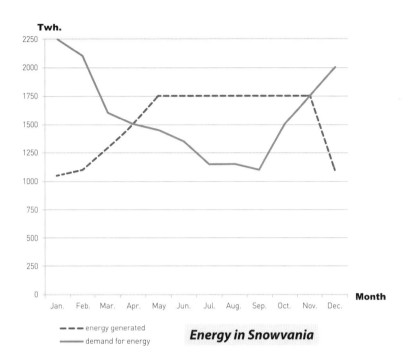

Energy in Snowvania

在下個單元裡，我將告訴你如何分析這種數據圖。

　　整個寫作測驗的時間只有一小時，所以你必須非常嚴格地控制時間。建議花在 Task 1 的寫作時間不能超過 15 分鐘，其中包括 5 分鐘用來分析圖片和規劃你的答案，7 分鐘用來寫作，3 分鐘檢查並修改文章。

高分寫作標準 Criteria for Success

根據 IELTS 官方考試中心提供的資訊，寫作測驗 Task 1 的評分標準有四個。

1. Task fulfillment 任務完成度

第一個是任務完成度，這也是最重要的標準。它的意思是你寫的文章有多符合圖片？你的描述能否精準說明圖片？這一點做起來比聽起來難。所以如果你一個不小心用字不夠精準，那麼你必須在 Task 1 使用的那些用語，它們的性質很容易會讓你的文章出現與圖片不太一樣的意義。在接下來的單元裡，我會請你把重點放在你即將學到的語言精確度上。

2. Organisation 組織

第二個標準是答案的組織。考生們在這個測驗裡常犯的錯誤，是想要描述他們在圖片裡看到的一切，但是，在 15 分鐘內必須寫下 150 個字的情況下，你不可能把所有看到的都描述出來，而且也不應該想要這麼做。相反的，你必須篩選資訊，然後把篩選出來的重要訊息寫出來。沒有所謂正確的方式來組織你的答案，但你的答案應該要有邏輯，並且讓主考官很容易閱讀。在下一個單元裡，我會告訴你如何做到這一點。

3. Vocabulary 字彙

這個標準和下一個標準強調的是用語。你要用的字彙和文法通常非常有限。舉例來說，你只有少數的方式可以用來描述表格，且這樣做對你反而有利，因為如果你能夠學會 Task 1 所需特定範圍內的字彙，而且能夠百分之百地正確使用它們，那麼就能夠完全達到這個標準。稍後在 Unit 3 至 Unit 7 將學到的內容，正是 Task 1 所需的關鍵用語。

4. Sentence structure 句子結構

這部分也和精準度有關，尤其是動詞的時態和句子的複雜度。在這裡，你必須表現出兩件事：「範圍」和「精準度」。如果你寫的句子結構簡單但完全精準 (S.V.O.)，得到的分數將會很低，因為你完全沒有證明自己有能力撰寫複雜的句子。反之，如果你寫的句子結構很複雜，但卻不是百分之百正確的，分數也會很低，因為你完全沒有證明你有精準的寫作能力。在 Unit 3 至 Unit 7，我會告訴各位如何擴大句子結構的範圍，但你可以自己決定是否要學習或完全正確使用它們。

記住，當主考官閱讀你的文章時，他或她會把重點放在以上四個要點，並根據它們來評斷你的表現。

寫作的過程 The Process of Writing

　　IELTS 寫作測驗成績低落最常見的原因之一，是考生只要想到什麼就一股腦把它寫下來。我猜他們之所以這樣做，是因為非常擔心時間有限，所以認為最好馬上開始寫、盡可能寫得快，並在一小時內盡可能多寫。但是，這種作法是大錯特錯。

　　以專業的作家來說，即使他們面臨緊迫的截稿日期，並且遇到急迫的工作，他們也從來不會用這種方式工作。專業的作家都知道，寫作是由三種不同的心理過程所組成，這些過程都會用到不同部分的大腦及不同類型的思考。我要告訴各位這三種不同的過程，以及如何把它們應用在 IELTS 寫作的 Task 1 之中。

　　這三個過程是：having ideas「產生想法」、organising ideas「組織想法」，以及 writing ideas「寫下想法」。

1. Having ideas 產生想法

　　這是寫作裡真正具創意的部分，奇特的是，此部分和寫作完全無關，而是和你的大腦思維裡使用創意力、想像力的部分有關，通常是你用想像力想出點子、畫面和例子等等。而在 Task 1 中，這部分則是和你所要分析的圖片有關。當你研究並分析圖片時，就會知道必須寫些什麼。你要選擇並比較數據，然後決定要寫哪個部分的數據。在此過程中，你甚至不應該想到用語或寫作，而是專注於讓你的腦海中（或在 IELTS Task 1 裡，是你的眼睛）產生想法。在此階段，你要做的是把想法記下來、做筆記，並且試著想出更多想法。

2. Organising ideas 組織想法

　　當你認為自己的想法夠多了，就該往第二個過程邁進。這個過程是組織答案，它會用到和上一個過程很不一樣的思考技巧。在此時，你要用的不是創意和想像力，而是必須運用你的邏輯思維和分析能力。你必須去思考，如何將不同的想法連結在一起。有許多常見的方法可以將想法串連在一起，例如，你可以把一個特定的例子和某個整體概念連接起來。或是，你可以把兩個想法放在一起，創造出一個小的程序。或是，你可以把兩個相似的想法放在一起，或把兩個非常不一樣的想法放在一起，然後對比它們之間的差異。又或是，你可以把想法擺在一起，藉此表現出其中一個想法是

另一個想法的原因或結果。在第二個過程中，你也不應該考慮到用語或寫作，而是應該把資訊組織成有邏輯的模式。

3. Writing ideas 寫下想法

當你完成了產生想法與組織想法的過程後，就該往第三個過程邁進：把想法寫下來。只有在這個階段，你才終於開始使用大腦裡的語言過程。在此時，你必須決定使用哪些字彙、哪些句子結構、哪一種動詞時態等等。由於你的母語是中文，所以當你用英文寫作時，根據人類使用第二語言的規則來說，你的思考過程一定會超載，才能將某一種語言和概念翻譯成另一種語言。你的記憶會變得高度活躍，你會努力回想字彙的正確拼法、正確組合句子的方式，以及正確使用字彙的方式。你必須確定你寫的內容是正確的。當你完成寫作時，你還要編輯它，而在這裡你的大腦中和語言相關的部分也會十分活躍。

現在，你可以發現這些心理過程確實有很大的不同，它們用了三種思考模式：想像力思考、組織思考以及語言思考。這裡的問題是，如果不把這些過程分開處理，你的大腦會超載，因為有太多不同的東西在進行，但這些不同的過程會彼此牴觸，並且妨礙彼此順暢運作。舉例來說，專業的作家都知道，一旦你用組織思維來組織想法時，創意思維就無法適當地運作。同樣的，一旦你開始嘗試用語言表達想法時，你頭腦裡掌管組織的部分就會停止運作，因為大腦要專注於語言模式，而不是處理想法之間的模式。

無論在任何情況下，當你寫作的時候，很重要的是要把這些過程分開，這一點在 IELTS 測驗更是如此，因為 IELTS 測驗非常看重文章的結果。

所以，我給你的建議是，在 IELTS 測驗裡你必須花時間把這些過程分開。做過練習後，它可以幫助你得到最佳結果。在下一個單元裡，我會要你把重點放在創意／分析和組織思考上，而在 Unit 3 到 Unit 7，重點則要放在語言思考。

在你結束這個單元之前，請將下列的清單看過，確定你能將所有要點都勾選起來。如果有一些要點你還搞不清楚，請回頭再次研讀本單元的相關部分。

☐ 我已經了解 Task 1 的測驗內容以及我必須做些什麼。
☐ 我已經學到如何組織 Task 1 的時間分配。

□ 我已經知道主考官會用哪四個標準來評判我的文章。

□ 我已經明白在 Task 1 中，保持高精準度有多麼重要，這一點會表現在我對圖片的描述及我用的語言。

□ 我已經學到寫作的三個過程，以及當我在從事任何寫作時，很重要的是必須把這些過程分開。

□ 我已經學會 IELTS Task 1 裡的三種不同寫作過程。

□ 我現在已經準備好要開始更深入地進行 Task 1 的寫作練習。

EXAM TIP BOX

✓ 在 Task 1 裡，說明文字通常不會要你表達自己的意見，或是猜測數據的原因和意義，所以你一定要謹慎地閱讀說明文字。

✓ 在 IELTS 測驗中，你永遠都要有心理準備可能會遇到意料之外的事。

Unit 2

分析資訊並組織你的答案

**Analysing the Information and
Organising Your Answer**

在這個單元裡，你會學到如何分析圖片裡的資訊並組織你的答案。本單元有許多相關的練習，這些練習很重要，因為經過大量的分析圖片練習，能幫助你在考試時更快速、更輕鬆地完成它，不但節省了時間，也會讓你更有自信地進行接下來的寫作。你先前之所以無法在考試取得高分，原因之一可能就是因為未能正確地分析資訊。接下來，我們將從你在 IELTS 寫作 Task 1 可能產生的問題開始。

Practice 1

請研究這張圖表和題目敘述，列出你在理解資訊時可能產生的問題，並規劃你的答案。

Topic | 文章標題

This graph shows the demand for energy, and the amount of energy generated in Snowvania (measured in terawatt-hours) from January to December in any one year.

Summarize the information by selecting and reporting the main features and make comparisons where relevant.

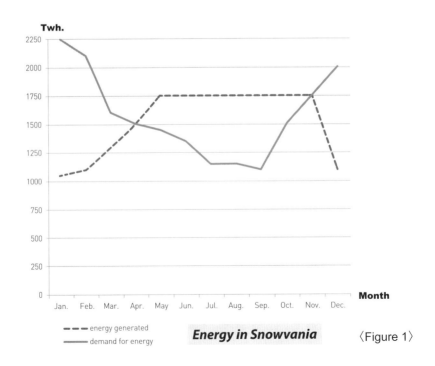

- - - energy generated
—— demand for energy

Energy in Snowvania

〈Figure 1〉

我當然不知道你寫了什麼,但是這裡有一些考生們常見的問題。

Q1 「我不理解在題目敘述裡所使用的字彙」,或是「我不懂圖片裡的用語」。

Q2 我不知道我該做什麼。我該針對資訊提出自己的看法嗎?我該描述所有資訊嗎?我該解讀資訊嗎?我該評判資訊嗎?我該推測資訊嗎?

Q3 我不確定圖表裡的時間點,不確定該用什麼時態來描述它。

Q4 我不清楚圖片裡的單位是什麼?是單數、以十為單位,還是百分比?我要描述它嗎?」

Q5 我不確定圖例的意思,它到底在說什麼?

Q6 圖片裡的資訊好多,我真的不知道該如何讓它們言之有理,該從哪裡下手,以及我必須涵蓋多少資訊,還有該如何把它們組織起來。

　　接下來看看該如何處理這些問題。首先,我們會把重點放在分析資訊,然後是組織你的答案。

分析資訊 Analysing the Information

分析題目和說明文字

1. **請將圖例的字彙畫上底線**。你要確保自己知道圖例中字彙的意思。這裡幾乎不太可能出現你不認識的字彙，如果有的話，你只能藉由常識和圖片裡的其他資訊來幫助自己理解它們。舉例來說，在 Practice 1 裡，你可能不認識 terawatt-hours 這個字，但也許想得到這應該是一種度量單位，用來測量非常大單位的能量。當你把字彙畫上底線後，就要把重點放在 word partnerships 和 chunks。這一點很重要，因為你必須在答案裡重複使用這些字彙。舉例來說，在上述的 Practice 1 裡，你可以把 the demand for 和 measured in 畫上底線，並且確定你有在答案裡正確使用這些 chunks。

2. **請確定你知道該做些什麼**。說明文字通常會要求你單純地描述你看到什麼。例如，在 Practice 1，題目要求你 summarize、select、report，並且 make comparisons，所以你必須確定自己有做到這些事。說明文字不太會要求你表達自己的意見，或是推測資料的原因或結果。你可能還記得我們在寫作概論和 Unit 1 提過的，IELTS 寫作 Task 1 的目標在於準確的描述性寫作。然而，在 IELTS 測驗裡，你永遠都要有心理準備可能會遇到意料之外的事。

分析圖表

3. **時間的間隔是多少**？這部分通常顯示在水平軸。這一點很重要，因為它會決定你應該用哪一種時態。一般來說，時間間隔是過去的時間，但請不要預設永遠都是這樣。如果它是在過去的時間，這表示你必須使用過去簡單式。例如，有些時間間隔可能從過去開始，但一直持續到未來。在這種情況下，你必須使用過去簡單式和表達未來的 will 或 might。或是，它可能把重點放在現在，這時你就必須用現在完成簡單式來說明結果，或是用現在進行式來說明整體趨勢。最有可能的情況是用過去簡單式，但不管怎麼樣都要小心，要確定你知道該用哪一種時態。舉例來說，在 Practice 1，水平軸表示一月到十二月，而且題目說明提到這是 in any one year，可以得知這是「平均一年」的意思。所以在這個 Task 中，你必須在答案裡用到現在簡單式，因為你要描述的事實每年都不太會有變化。

4. 再來，**請看看並找出垂直軸的單位**。它的單位是什麼？是百分比嗎？是以十、百或千爲單位嗎？請確定你了解這一點。舉例來說，在 Practice 1 中的單位是 terawatt-hours，即使你不知道這是什麼意思，還是可以用這個字，或是使用圖表上方顯示的符號：Twh。你也可以看到單位是以每 250 爲間隔來衡量的，從最低的 250 Twhs 到最高的 2,250 Twhs。

5. 接下來，我們**來看圖例**。圖例通常是放在圖表旁邊或下方。你要確定自己知道圖表中不同顏色或不同的線代表什麼。請注意這裡的字彙，因爲你可以把它們用在答案裡。舉例來說，在 Practice 1 中，實心線表示「能源的需求量」(demand for energy)，而虛線則代表由 Snowvania 鎮上多個發電廠「產生出來的能源」(energy generated)。

6. 現在，你必須**找到重要特徵** (significant features)。這個重要特徵是指圖片裡你馬上就注意到的特徵，亦即圖片中有哪些東西映入你的眼簾？這些都是你要寫的內容，所以請試著至少發掘兩項或三項特徵。例如，在 Practice 1 中，你可以馬上注意到「能源需求量」在冬季的月份達到最高，在夏季的月份最低，在春季和初夏月份則持平。人們在冬季和夏季的能源消耗量明顯有很大的落差，差異幾乎達到 1,150 Twhs。此外，你可能也很快注意到夏季月份產出的能源比冬季月份來得多。

7. 現在，來**看看整體趨勢** (general trends)。這些是你不會馬上注意到的趨勢，你必須在稍微研究過圖片後才能看出一些較細微的趨勢。舉例來說，在 Practice 1 中，你可以看到一整年產生能源的變化大約落在 650 Twhs 左右的小範圍裡，且一整年的供應量差不多都很穩定。

8. 最後，我們來**看看有什麼東西是可以比較的**。你可以找到哪些重要特徵來進行比較？你可以在整體趨勢中找到什麼來比較？如果有兩張圖，你可以比較它們之間的哪些部分？例如在 Practice 1 中，你可以比較兩條線的兩種形狀：在夏季的月份裡，能源產量較多而消耗較少，而在冬天裡能源的消耗則大於生產。

綜合以上，我們把分析資訊需注意的要點整理成一個清單。

1. **關鍵字彙**：把題目說明裡的關鍵字彙畫上底線。
2. **摘要提示**：把說明文字告訴你該怎麼做的部分畫上底線。
3. **時間**：請確定你知道圖表裡顯示的時間是什麼。
4. **主要變化**：請確認你看到的主要變化。
5. **次要變化**：請確認其他次要變化。
6. **重要特徵**：找到 significant features「重要特徵」。
7. **整體趨勢**：找到 general trends「整體趨勢」。
8. **比較內容**：找到可比較的地方。

　　現在，我們一起用 IELTS Writing Task 1 需注意的「分析數據清單」來進行練習。

Practice 2

請利用「分析數據清單」來練習分析以下三道題目及圖表。

Topic 1

The graph below shows the average hours per week of unpaid work done by males and females from different income brackets. (Unpaid work refers to such activities as childcare in the home, housework and gardening.)

Summarize the information and offer some reasons for it.

Unpaid Work by Gender and Income

〈Figure 2〉

Topic 2

The graphs below show the number of male and female workers in 1990 and 2010 in several employment sectors in Bolivia.

Summarize the information by selecting and reporting the main features and make comparisons where relevant.

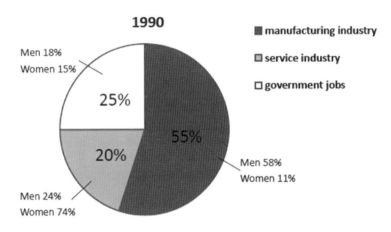

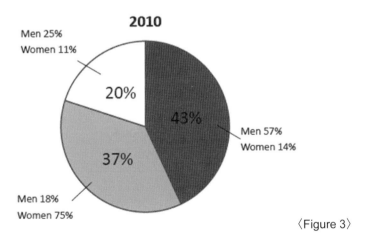

⟨Figure 3⟩

The table below shows the number of drink related driving accidents and other factors which contribute to the possibility of a drink related accident in the UK.

Write a report for a university professor summarizing the information and speculating as to what it might mean.

Number of drink related accidents (total 3000)	Factors
	Roads:
61	Motorway
609	Urban roads
330	Rural roads
	Seasons:
280	Winter
136	Spring
155	Summer
25	Autumn
	Time of day:
18	9 am – 5 pm
386	5 pm – 9 am
	Age of driver:
611	under 45
389	over 45

〈Figure 4〉

🔑 範例答案

我們來看看你分析的清單應該包含哪些內容吧！

Topic 1

	分析項目	參考內容
1	關鍵字彙	你應該畫上底線的字彙包括 the average hours per week、unpaid work、income brackets，以及在括號裡的字彙。還要注意的是，你在這裡要用的動詞是 do。
2	摘要提示	必須先將資訊摘要出來，然後用你的常識解釋它的原因。例如，你可以提到收入落在較高收入族群中的人，會花錢請別人做家務、照顧孩子，而在較低收入族群中的人則無法負擔這筆錢。你還可以提到傳統上仍認為女性應該比男性負擔更多無報酬的工作，例如操持家務和帶小孩，這個特徵表現在所有的收入階層之中。
3	時間	這裡沒有時間間隔，它確實沒有提到任何時間，所以你在這個 Task 裡應該用現在簡單式。
4	主要變化	這裡的計量單位是每週的小時數，時間間隔是兩小時。
5	次要變化	圖例說明男性和女性在三種不同收入階層的狀況：低、中、高。
6	重要特徵	在這裡，我希望你有注意到以下幾個重要特徵：在所有收入階層中，女性從事的無報酬工作比男性多；位於較高收入族群的男性和女性，他們從事的無報酬工作比較低收入族群的人少很多。
7	整體趨勢	這部分有點細微，但是你有看到收入階層越低的地方，男性和女性之間的差距越大嗎？
8	比較內容	這裡有很多東西可以比較。你可以比較所有收入階層裡的男性和女性，或是只比較女性或男性，也可以比較性別之間日益擴大的落差。你必須思考並判斷哪一種比較內容對你來說最簡單，且最能表現出你的英文寫作能力。

分析項目	參考內容
1 關鍵字彙	請　將 the number of、male and female workers、several employment sectors 畫上底線，其中 sector 這個字特別重要又有用。另外，請把圖例中的字彙也畫上底線：manufacturing、service 和 government jobs。
2 摘要提示	你必須選擇資訊、說明重要特徵並且加以比較。基本上，你必須做摘要。你絕對不能表達自己的看法或是推測數據，只要描述它就可以了。
3 時間	這兩個數據圖有 20 年的時間間隔，但是因為兩個年份都是過去的時間，所以當你在描述和比較兩者時，必須使用過去簡單式。
4 主要變化 5 次要變化	圖例的重點是三個主要產業別：製造業、服務業和政府部門。然後，每一個類別旁都分別標示出男性和女性的人口比例。
6 重要特徵	整體來說，這裡的重要特徵是製造業和政府部門的工作在這 20 年期間萎縮了，而服務業則成長了。還有一個很容易看出來的特徵是，在這兩個年度裡，只有服務業的女性佔比高於男性，其他產業則一直都是男性佔比高於女性。
7 整體趨勢	製造業和服務業的整體趨勢是，女性在 2010 年有更多就業機會，而男性則失去更多就業機會。在政府部門裡，男性在 2010 年擁有更多就業機會，而女性則失去就業機會。
8 比較內容	在這裡，你可以進行的比較有很多，所以必須慎選。舉例來說，你應該在各別年度之中進行比較，然後再進行一些橫跨兩個年份的比較。

分析項目	參考內容
1 關鍵字彙	你應該把 drink related driving accidents、other factors、contribute to、possibility of 畫上底線。這張表格也有很多字彙是你必須記下來的，例如 urban 和 rural。請注意，這兩個字是形容詞，所以後面一定要有名詞：urban roads、rural areas。
2 摘要提示	你必須把資訊摘要出來，所以請不要陳述你自己的意見或加以推測。
3 時間	這裡也沒有提到年份或時間間隔，所以你可以假設應該用現在簡單式來寫這則資訊。
4 主要變化	計算單位是樣本數 (3000) 中的事故總數，以及因酒駕和其他綜合因素造成的事故數量。
5 次要變化	這裡沒有圖例，所以必須把重點放在其他因素上。你必須確定自己知道它們的意思。
6 重要特徵	在撰寫重要特徵時，可以關注特別高的數字。例如：在冬季的下午和晚上，年紀在 45 歲以下的駕駛在都市的道路上發生的事故特別多。你也可以把重點放在最低的數字上。例如：超過 45 歲的駕駛較少在秋季的早上和午後於公路上發生事故。
7 整體趨勢	處理整體趨勢會稍微困難一點，但在這裡你可以把重點放在非常接近的數字上。例如，發生在春季和夏季的事故數非常接近。
8 比較內容	這裡有很多東西可以比較。你可以比較酒駕時容易發生意外事故的是怎樣的人：他們可能是年齡低於 45 歲，並在冬季的夜晚在城裡開車的人。你也可以比較每一個因素的數字：例如比較冬季和秋季，或是比較公路和都市的道路。

　　了解如何分析資訊後，我們接下來要看看如何運用你分析過的資訊來組織你的答案。

組織你的答案 Organising Your Answer

規劃和組織答案有四個要點：

1. **不用寫太多**。一般來說，**150 個字**大約是五或六個句子，這取決於句子的長度。不要把你看到的東西都鉅細靡遺描述出來（這種錯誤很常見），而是應該把重點放在你已經完成的分析上。

2. 不要按照想法產生的順序來寫下你的想法，而是要有**邏輯地組織**這些**想法**。

3. 沒有所謂「正確」的方式來組織你的想法，但你應該讓想法有邏輯，而且要容易懂。不要從一個想法跳到另一個想法，而是要**照著圖片來描述**。

4. 首先，**用緊扣題目的句子寫下開頭的第一句**（我會在下一個單元告訴你如何做到這一點）。然後，用幾個句子來說明重要特徵，再用幾個句子闡述整體趨勢。如果你認為還有其他重要特徵，那就再寫幾句描述它們；如果你認為還有其他整體趨勢，那也再寫幾句陳述它們；如果是必須進行比較的圖表類型，那就寫一些比較的句子。

我們來看看範例。

Practice 3

請搭配 **Figure 1** 閱讀以下的範例文章，然後用編號的句子完成下方表格。我們來看看範例。

❶ This line graph displays how much energy is used, and how much is generated over one typical year in Snowvania (measured in terawatt-hours).

❷ Significantly, the graph shows that demand for energy is the highest, at around 2,250 Twhs during the winter months, and the lowest in the summer months, at roughly 1,100 Twhs, a very great difference of almost 1,250 Twhs. ❸ On the other hand, the energy generated in Snowvania peaks at approximately 1,750 Twhs during the summer months, from April to the beginning of December. ❹ The lowest amount of energy generated is during the winter months, at only 1,100 Twhs. ❺ This means that more energy is generated during the summer and less in the winter, while more energy is consumed during the winter than in the summer.

❻ Another point to notice is that, generally, the range of energy generated is much smaller – only around 650 Twhs – than the range of energy consumed, which is huge, at roughly 1,150 Twhs.

General topic sentence	❶
Sentences about significant features	
Sentences about general trends	

🔑 範例答案

在這篇文章中，第二句到第五句和重要特徵有關，因為這張圖表中的重要特徵比整體趨勢多。而第六句則和整體趨勢有關。

☆ 第一句和題目密切相關。你會在下一個單元裡學到如何寫好第一句。

☆ 第二句描述能源需求的重要特徵，這是我們在解說 Practice 1 的時候提過的。第三句和第四句談的也是重要特徵，但這裡說的是能源生產量，其中第三句說的是最高點，第四句說的則是最低點。第五句透過清楚地比較，摘要了兩個重要特徵。所有的重要特徵都彼此相關卻組織清晰。

☆ 第六句描述整體趨勢，我們在 Practice 1 的回饋中說過它的範圍。

☆ 請注意，你可以使用像是 significantly 或 generally 這樣的字，讓讀者清楚知道你在談這個句子。

☆ 請注意這裡用的是現在簡單式，因為這個圖表並沒有告訴我們資料屬於哪一個特定的年份。

到目前為止，請不要擔心你使用了什麼用語，因為你會在接下來的單元裡學到必須使用哪些用語。但是請注意，你不應該寫出這樣的句子：From the graph we can see, … / We can see from the graph, … / We can understand from the diagram, … / It's easy for us to see from the data, ….。這類把閱讀資訊的人寫進句子裡的作法，並不是英文學術寫作的習慣，你必須用客觀和去人格化的方式來寫作。這也有可能是你在之前的測驗裡得到低分的另一個原因。記住，請直接描述資訊而不要把重點放在我們可以看到資訊這件事上。

> ☒ 錯誤
> - We can see that demand for energy is highest …
> - We can understand from the graph that more energy is generated …

> ☑ 正確
> - The graph shows that demand for energy is highest …
> - This means that more energy is generated …

現在，我們來看看你是否能夠根據這些簡單的指示，組織出一篇範例文章。在你開始練習之前，請再把 Figure 2 看過一次。

✎ Practice 4

請將這些句子組織成 Practice 2 中 Topic 1 的答案，並寫出最適當的句子順序。

A. Also, in the highest income brackets, both men and women do much less unpaid work than both sexes in low income brackets.

B. Another thing to note is that as incomes go down, the difference in hours of unpaid work by men and women goes up, with women always doing more of the work than the men, one hour more per week for the highest incomes, and approximately 6 hours per week for the lowest incomes.

C. Significantly, in all income brackets, the women do more unpaid work than the men.

D. The bar chart represents how many hours of unpaid work on average are done by people from different income brackets of both sexes.

E. The reasons for this are clearly that in high income brackets people can afford to pay others to look after their house and children.

F. The reasons for this are unclear.

G. This suggests that women are still expected to take care of housework and childrearing in all income brackets.

句子順序：D → (   ) → (   ) → (   ) → (   ) → (   ) → (   )

🔑 範例答案

☆ 正確的句子順序為：D → (C) → (G) → (A) → (E) → (B) → (F)

☆ 到目前為止，請先不要擔心用語問題，因為我們這裡的重點還是組織答案。

☆ 句子 D 是介紹句，你會發現它和題目密切相關，在下一個單元裡，我會說明如何做到這一點。然後是句子 C，它從最明顯的重要特徵開始談。再來是句子 G，它是重要特徵的可能原因。接著是句子 A，它描述了另一個重要特徵，而後面所接的句子 E 則是說明這個特徵的可能原因。最後是介紹整體趨勢的句子 B，以及敘述可能原因的句子 F。

現在，我們來看看一些有用的用語，你可以用它來組織你的答案 (organising your response)，並且解釋數據 (interpreting the data)，或是推測數據的原因。

✏️ Practice 5

請將這些語句的用途分別選填至下方表格中。

- A possible reason for this might be that v.p. …
- Also, …
- Another point to notice is that v.p. …
- Another thing to note is that v.p. …
- Clearly …
- Generally, …
- On the other hand, …
- … respectively.
- Significantly, …
- The reasons for this are that v.p. …
- The reasons for this are unclear.
- This means that v.p. …
- This might be due to the fact that v.p. …
- This suggests that v.p. …
- What's interesting is that v.p. …
- … v.p. while v.p. …

organising your response	interpreting the data

🔑 範例答案

請仔細研究這張表格和底下的說明。

organising your response	interpreting the data
• Significantly, …	• This means that (clearly) v.p. …
• On the other hand, …	• The reasons for this are that v.p. …
• Another point to notice is that v.p. …	• The reasons for this are unclear.
• Generally, …	• A possible reason for this might be that v.p. …
• Also, …	
• Another thing to note is that v.p. …	• Clearly, …
• What's interesting is that v.p. …	• This might be due to the fact that v.p. …
• … v.p. while v.p. …	• This suggests that v.p. …

☆ 首先,請務必記住,如果文章的題目確實有要你推測數據的原因,你才該去進行推測。否則,只需專心描述數據即可。

☆ 請用 Significantly, ... 把焦點放在重要特徵上;用 Generally, ... 把焦點放在整體趨勢上。

☆ 請小心使用 On the other hand。只有當你要說明的數據與之前的數據有對比關係時,你才能用這個詞。如果沒有明顯的對比就不要用這個詞。

☆ 請注意,所有解釋的部分以 v.p. 結尾,所以請確定你有用 v.p.。如果你不了解 v.p.,請回到本書「雅思寫作概論」,再次閱讀該部分。我們也會在下個單元裡針對 v.p. 作更多說明。

☆ 如果你對呈現出來的數據沒有想法的話，直接寫 The reasons for this are unclear 也是沒有關係的。請記住，這裡的重點不是要把所有答案都寫對，而是用完全精準的英文妥善表達自己的看法。

☆ 這裡的 while 沒有時間的意思，卻有對比的意涵。你可以用相同的方式使用 On the other hand，但要寫一個長的句子，而不是兩個短句子。

☆ 請在句子的最後用 ... respectively，清楚呈現你在對照兩張圖和兩個因素。你會在稍後的範例中學習如何做到這一點。

✎ Practice 6

請完整閱讀 Practice 3 和 Practice 4 中的範例文章，並且把你能找到的有關組織答案或解釋數據之範例用語都畫上底線。請注意這些字的使用方式。

🔑 範例答案

你應該可以找到十個例子，說明如下。

Practice 3	Practice 4
• Significantly, …	• Significantly, …
• On the other hand, …	• This suggests that v.p. …
• This means that v.p. …	• Also, …
• Another point to notice is that v.p. …	• The reasons for this are clearly that v.p. …
	• Another thing to note is that v.p. …
	• The reasons for this are unclear.

☆ 請注意，在 Practice 3 中，This means that 不是要你真的說明數據的原因，只需評論不同數據所顯示的差異。你也可以在這種情況下使用 This means that ——當你不只要真正解釋數據的起因或原因，還要對實際顯示的數據加以評論的時候。

　　我們即將結束這個單元了，但是在你完成之前，我會再給你兩個範例答案，讓你根據在本單元所學到的內容來進行分析。

參照 **Practice 2** 的題目和圖片，閱讀以下兩個範例答案及提醒。請研究它們的組織，並注意 **Practice 5** 所強調的用語。

🔎 **範例答案**　　**Practice 2 / Topic 2 / Figure 3**

The pie charts below show the changes in the number of male and female workers in Bolivia in 1990 and 2010 in different employment sectors.

Significantly, the manufacturing and government jobs sectors shrank in the twenty years between 1990 and 2010. This means that in these two sectors there were less jobs for both men and women. Women still had fewer jobs in these two sectors than men, 15% in government jobs in 1990 and 11% in 2010, while men had 58% and 57% in 1990 and 2010 respectively in manufacturing jobs. What's interesting is that although the manufacturing industry sector decreased, the number of jobs done by women in this sector increased slightly over the twenty year period.

Another thing to note is that women had slightly more jobs than men in the service industry sector, in both years. In 2010 the number of women working in the service industries sector rose slightly, with a big fall in the number of men.

☆ 使用過去簡單式的時候請多加注意，因為所有資料都和結束時間有關。

☆ 請注意，不要描述數據，而是要有所取捨，其中要先寫重要特徵，然後再寫整體趨勢。

☆ 請分別注意 58% 和 57% 這兩個數字，看看它們如何牽涉到前面句子描述過的兩個類別：1990 年和 2010 年。請確定你在談到這些類別時，寫的順序是一致的：58% 對應到 1990 年，57% 對應到 2010 年。

☆ 請注意，this means that 不是要你解釋數據的意義，而只是評論看到的東西。

☆ 請注意 Practice 5 的用語在此是怎麼被使用的，尤其是 while。

☆ 請注意題目中的字彙如何在文章中重複使用。

☆ 請注意這些文字分成三個段落，這樣寫可以讓主考官更容易閱讀。

The graph represents how many drink related driving accidents occur in the UK in any one year, and the factors which contribute to them.

Significantly, most accidents happen on urban roads in winter in the evening when it is dark, and most of these accidents happen to people under the age of 45. Fewer drink related accidents occur on the motorway in the morning and early afternoon. Autumn is the season when the least drink related accidents happen. Also, people over the age of 45 are generally less likely to have drink related accidents during these periods.

Generally, the time of day is the least important factor which contributes to the possibility of a drink related driving accident, with only 404 accidents caused by this factor. On the other hand, the type of road and the age of the driver are the most significant factors, with 1000 accidents each caused by these factors.

☆ 請注意這裡用的是現在簡單式，因為題目和表格都沒有提到時間。
☆ 並非每個圖或每個因素都有被提到，只有部分關鍵資訊被選擇並呈現出來。
☆ 請注意重要特徵和整體趨勢的組織方式，以及段落的用法。
☆ 請注意 Practice 5 的用語在此是怎麼被使用的。

　　在你結束這個單元之前，請將下列清單看過，確定你能將所有要點都勾選起來。如果有一些要點你還搞不清楚，請回頭再次研讀本單元的相關部分。

☐ 我已經學會如何分析 Task 1 的題目說明文字和圖片。
☐ 我完全了解如何重複使用題目的說明文字和圖片中的關鍵字彙。
☐ 我知道如何根據圖表和題目，決定要用哪一種動詞時態。
☐ 我知道如何選擇並描述重要特徵和整體趨勢，而且我還知道我不應該試圖描述圖中的所有資訊。
☐ 我已經透過「分析數據清單」，大量練習了分析題目和圖片。
☐ 我已經學會如何有邏輯且順暢地組織資訊，以及如何使用段落讓主考官更容易閱讀。
☐ 我已經學會使用一些有用的範例用語來呈現想法的結構。
☐ 如果寫作題目要求我推測數據的原因，我已經學到一些可以派上用場的用語。
☐ 我已經學到很多 IELTS 寫作 Task 1 的範例。

EXAM TIP BOX

✓ 請將你的文章分成三個短段落,這樣可以讓主考官認為你的文章更有吸引力且更容易閱讀。

✓ 不要讓主考官閱讀「長篇大論」。他們可能會因為精神不濟而產生負面反應,這樣可能會影響你的分數。

Unit 3

寫下你的答案——
第一句

**Writing Your Answer—
the First Sentence**

在這個單元裡，你將學到如何重複使用題目的用語來寫出文章的第一句。同時，你也會學到英文裡構成句子的兩個主要部分：「動詞片語」和「名詞片語」。對後面的單元來說，這單元的練習都很重要，你可以在 IELTS 寫作 Task 1 的其他部分和 Task 2 裡，使用你在這裡學到的內容。

✎ Practice 1

請看以下兩個句子，你可以找出它們之間的哪些差異？

作文題目說明

This graph illustrates the demand for energy and the energy available from fossil fuels in Asmallcountry from 1985 to 2005.

第一個句子

This bar chart shows how much energy was demanded, and how much energy was available from fossil fuels over a twenty year period in Asmallcountry.

🔑 範例答案

請研究這張比較表，並閱讀其後的說明。

	作文題目說明	第一句	筆記
1	This graph	This bar chart	字彙
2	illustrates	shows	字彙
3	-	how much	wh-
4	the demand for energy	energy was demanded	名詞片語和動詞片語
5	-	how much	wh-
6	the energy available	energy was available	名詞片語和動詞片語
7	from 1985 to 2005	over a twenty year period	日期／時間間隔
8	in Asmallcountry from 1985 to 2005.	over a twenty year period in Asmallcountry	詞序

一般來說，作文的題目說明會用比較多的名詞片語，實際寫作的第一句則會用比較多的動詞片語。而在這裡，你應該要找到八個差異：

1. 這是字彙的變化。Graph 是個一般性的字，它指的可能是任何一種圖。Bar chart 則更具體說明顯示的是某一種類型的圖。

2. Illustrates 和 shows 是同義字。

3. 在第一句裡，作者使用了 wh- 字彙或片語：how much。這樣做是必要的，因為它後面跟的是一個動詞片語。

4. 題目說明中用名詞片語 the demand for energy，你可以看到這裡沒有動詞。而在第一句中，作者則是把名詞片語改成動詞片語 energy was demanded，其中 was 是動詞。請注意，這個動詞片語是被動語態。

5. 作者在第一句又用了 wh- 字彙或片語，因為另一個動詞片語要出現了。

6. 在這裡，題目說明用名詞片語 the energy available，因為你沒有看到動詞。同樣的，作者在第一句中把名詞片語改成動詞片語 energy was available，其中 was 是動詞。

7. 這個題目用了兩個日期來確立時間區段，即開始的日期和結束的日期。第一句的作者則把它改成這兩個日期之間的時間間隔。

8. 在這裡，第一句的作者改變了字詞的順序，將 Asmallcountry 移到句尾的位置。

現在，我將告訴你如何使用和上述相同的方式寫出你的第一句。其中，7. 和 8. 的變化很容易看到和做到，所以不必把重點放在此處。首先我們要來看 1. 和 2. 的字彙變化，然後再看看在 3. 到 6. 中，你可以做哪些文法變化。

字彙變化 Vocabulary Changes

將 **specific** 欄位裡的字彙與插圖加以配對,並在正確的字旁邊寫出插圖的編號。我們來看看範例。

general	specific	
graphic	(⑥) bar chart	(　) diagram
graph	(　) flow chart	(　) line chart
illustration	(　) map	(　) pie chart
visual	(　) table	

①

	2012	2013	2014	2015	2016
Spring					
Summer					
Fall					
Winter					

②

③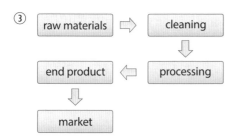

④

⑤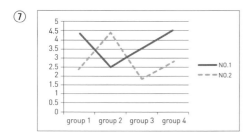

⑥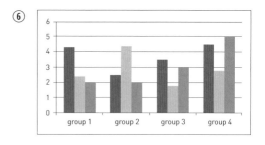

⑦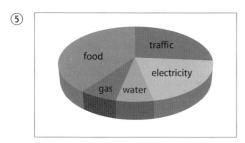

🔑 範例答案

② diagram ③ flow chart ⑦ line chart ④ map ⑤ pie chart ① table

現在，我們來看看主要動詞。

✏ Practice 3

請看看 shows 的同義字有哪些。

shows n.p. shows wh- v.p.	displays n.p. displays wh- v.p. illustrates n.p. illustrates wh- v.p. presents n.p. presents wh- v.p. represents n.p. represents wh- v.p.

☆ 請注意，所有的動詞都是以 s 結尾。請不要忘了這個 s。
☆ 你會發現有些動詞也有 wh-。以下列出有 wh- 的字彙和片語。

✏ Practice 4

請看看這些 wh- 的字彙和片語。

why	when
which	who
what	where
how	how often
how long	how soon
how much	how many

文法變化 Grammar Changes

　　接著我們要來看看文法部分。這部分比較複雜。首先，你需要徹底理解名詞片語和動詞片語的差異，這對你未來的所有寫作都很重要。在中文裡，名詞和動詞的差異不是很明顯，但是在英文裡，名詞片語和動詞片語是組成句子的兩個主要部分。你沒有在寫作測驗當中得到高分的原因之一，可能是未正確使用名詞片語和動詞片語。為了提高分數，你必須清楚地知道它們之間的差異，進而正確地使用它們。

> 動詞片語由一個主詞和一個動詞組成，例如：I go / It was raining / There is a problem。有些動詞片語還有受詞，例如：I read the book 和 The graph displays industrial development，但是受詞本身不是必要的。構成動詞片語的必要條件是一定有一個主詞和一個動詞。

> 名詞片語則是一群字彙，裡面有一個名詞，例如：a tax on private cars / weather patterns / increased productivity。名詞片語永遠不會有動詞，但它可以在動詞片語裡擔任主詞，不過如此一來我們會稱它為動詞片語，而不是名詞片語，例如：a tax on private cars has been implemented 是一個動詞片語，其主詞 a tax on private cars 即為一個名詞片語。

　　為了確定你了解這一點，現在請進行以下練習。

✎ Practice 5

請參考範例，在表格裡寫下 n.p. 或 v.p.。

renewable energy	*n.p.*
crimes were committed by young people	
male and female workers	
people emigrated to Canada	
carbon dioxide is found in the air	
popular scenic spots	
living standards have improved	
university subjects are popular	
exhaust emissions	

renewable energy	*n.p.*
crimes were committed by young people	v.p.
male and female workers	n.p.
people emigrated to Canada	v.p.
carbon dioxide is found in the air	v.p.
popular scenic spots	n.p.
living standards have improved	v.p.
university subjects are popular	v.p.
exhaust emissions	n.p.

PART
1

　　現在你應該已經清楚了解 n.p. 和 v.p. 之間的差異，接著我們來看看如何運用這個知識。Practice 3 裡的動詞後面都可以加上 n.p. 和 v.p.，但請注意，當你要使用 v.p. 時，必須先從 Practice 4 裡選出一個 wh- 的字彙或片語來連接動詞與動詞片語。如果你沒加上 wh- 的話就出錯了。

☑ 正確

- The graph displays how many people were employed. = wh- + v.p.
- This line graph displays how much pollution was in the North Sea. = wh- + v.p.
- This bar chart displays where different imports come from. = wh- + v.p.

☒ 錯誤

- The graph displays people were employed. = v.p. (wh- lacking)
- This line graph displays pollution was in the North Sea. = v.p. (wh- lacking)
- This bar chart displays different imports come from. = v.p. (wh- lacking)

　　我們來練習這部分的寫法。

請用 **Practice 5** 的 v.p. 完成以下的句子，並且加入 **Practice 4** 裡適當的 **wh-** 字彙或片語。

EX. The graph displays <u>what crimes were committed by young people</u>.

1. The bar chart shows _____

2. The line chart shows _____

3. The map shows _____

4. The pie chart represents _____

🔑 範例答案

1. The bar chart shows how many people emigrated to Canada ....
2. The line chart shows how much carbon dioxide is found in the air ....
3. The map shows where/how/how much living standards have improved ....
4. The pie chart represents which university subjects are popular ....

☆ 其實，你選了什麼 v.p. 並不重要，重要的是你用了哪一個 wh- 字彙或片語。
☆ 別忘了要思考意義和文法。

　　我們已經學了如何使用 wh- 和 v.p.，現在要學習如何使用 n.p.。在使用 n.p. 時也必須加上一個連接的詞。請看以下句子並思考它的意義。是否覺得看起來有點奇怪？

☒ 錯誤

• The line graph shows people in different occupations.

　　線條圖本身不會說明人的狀況，沒錯吧？這個句子確實有點奇怪，它並沒有顯示職業，卻顯示出做不同工作的<u>人數</u>，對嗎？所以，在動詞和 n.p. 之間，你必須要加上一個連接短語 the numbers of。

☑ 正確

• The line graph shows <u>the numbers of</u> people in different occupations.

這些連接短語有點複雜，因為你要思考它的意義和 wh- 字彙的意思如何匹配。

✏️ Practice 7

請參考範例，思考以下常用來和 **n.p.** 連用之連接短語的意義，並且把它們放入下方的表格中。

… the (different) period(s) of …   … the number of …
… the amount of …   … the origin(s) of …
… the categories of …   … the percentage of …
… the consumption of …   … the proportion of …
… the decrease of …   … the reasons for …
… the demand for …   … the relative importance of …
… the end of …   … the start of …
… the frequency of …   … the time(s) of …
… the increase of …   … the types of …
… the kinds of …   … the ways of …
… the location(s) of …   … the sources of …
… the methods of …   … the rate of …

why	where	when
		… the time(s) of …

how	how often / how soon	how much / how many
	… the frequency of …	

which / what

請仔細研究這張表格。

why	where	when
… the reasons for … … the relative importance of …	… the location(s) of … … the origin(s) of … … the source(s) of …	… the start of … … the end of … … the (different) period(s) of … … the time(s) of …

how	how often / how soon	how much / how many
… the methods of … … the ways of …	… the frequency of …	… the numbers of … … the amount of … … the percentage of … … the proportion of … … the demand for … … the consumption of … … the rate of … … the decrease of … … the increase of …

which / what
… the types of … … the kinds of … … the categories of …

☆ … the number of … 須與可數名詞一起使用；… the amount of … 須與不可數名詞一起使用。

☆ 請注意這些連接詞大多數會用 of，但 reasons 和 demand 不使用 of，而是用 for。

接著，我們來練習這個部分。

✏️ **Practice 8**

請用 **Practice 7** 的連接短語完成以下的句子。我們來看看範例。

EX. The graph displays the demand for renewable energy ….

1. The bar chart shows _____ male and female workers ....

2. The map shows _____ popular scenic spots ....

3. The line chart represents _____ exhaust emissions ....

4. The pie chart shows _____ main income among men and women.

🔑 範例答案

1. The bar chart shows <u>the numbers of</u> male and female workers ....
2. The map shows <u>the locations of</u> popular scenic spots ....
3. The line chart represents <u>the increase of</u> exhaust emissions ....
4. The pie chart shows <u>the source of</u> main income among men and women.

所以，到現在為止你學到了什麼？幫你彙整重點如下：

☆ 如果文章題目用 v.p.，那就在第一句用 n.p.。
☆ 如果文章題目用 n.p.，那就在第一句用 v.p.。
☆ 你必須將 wh- 字彙或片語和 v.p. 一起用。
☆ 你必須將連接短語 ... the _____ of ... 和 n.p. 一起用。

　　請用下一個 Practice 來練習這個部分。

✏️ **Practice 9**

請把這些句子從 n.p. 改成 v.p.，或是從 v.p. 改成 n.p. 以完成它們。例如：

This chart shows the number of people employed in different industries ....
→ *This chart shows how many people were employed in different industries ....*

1. This graph displays the amount of pollution in the North Sea ....

　　→ This graph displays _____

2. This diagram illustrates how much energy was used in three different countries ....

　　→ This diagram illustrates _____

3. The illustration shows the amount of fish consumed in 5 countries ….

   → The illustration shows _____

4. This bar chart displays where different imports come from ….

   → This bar chart displays _____

5. This table illustrates the proportion of fossil fuel consumed in three continents ….

   → The table illustrates _____

6. This pie chart shows how many people lived in three different cities ….

   → This pie chart shows _____

🔑 範例答案

請仔細看這些答案，並且將它們和原來的句子做比較。

1. This graph displays how much pollution was in the North Sea.
2. This diagram illustrates the consumption of energy in three different countries.
3. The illustration shows how much fish was consumed in 5 countries.
4. This bar chart displays the origin of different imports.
5. This table illustrates how much fossil fuel was consumed in three continents.
6. This pie chart shows the numbers of people living in three different cities.

所以，我們已經討論過如何把動詞片語改成名詞片語，以及把名詞片語改成動詞片語，並用這種方法寫出你的第一句。現在，我們要練習剩下的句子。

✎ Practice 10

請參考本單元 **Practice 1** 的範例。試著以改變字彙、文法、日期、時間間隔和工作順序等方法來改寫以下這些句子。

1. This bar chart illustrates the number of students studying different subjects at university level over a five year period.

   → _____

2. This graph shows the percentage of men and women employed in executive positions in

ASME Oil Company from July 1993 to July 1994.

→ _____

3. The graphs below present how many male and female workers were employed in different sectors in Atinynation over a one year period.

→ _____

4. The graphs below show the number of male and female workers in 1975 and 1995 in several employment sectors in Anotherplace.

→ _____

5. The graph below shows what part time jobs were performed by university students for a two year period in the UK.

→ _____

🔑 範例答案

比較看看你的答案和以下範例答案及原來的句子有何差異？請確定你有看出它們所有的差異，以及它們是怎麼來的。

1. This graph shows how many students studied different subjects from 2000 to 2005 at university level.
2. This bar chart displays how many men and women were employed by ASME Oil Company in executive positions over a one year period.
3. The pie charts below show the number of male and female workers from January 2010 to January 2011 in several employment sectors in Atinynation.
4. The pie charts below show how many male and female workers were employed in several employment sectors in Anotherplace over a twenty year period.
5. The pie chart below displays the kinds of part time jobs of university students in the UK from 2001 to 2003.

　　在你結束這個單元之前，請將下列清單看過，確定你能將所有要點都勾選起來。如果有一些要點你還不清楚，請回頭再研讀本單元的相關部分。

□ 我已經學到如何利用作文題目說明內容，藉由改變文法和字彙以及進行其他改變（例如文字的順序），寫出文章的第一句。

□ 我了解名詞片語和動詞片語的差異。

□ 我了解文章的第一句一定要用有動詞片語的 wh- 字彙或是片語。

□ 我了解文章的第一句必須將含有 ... the ___ of ... 的連接短語來和名詞片語一起使用。

□ 我能夠把動詞片語改成名詞片語，反之亦然。

□ 我已經學到許多有助於寫出第一句的字彙。

□ 我已經做過根據作文題目說明寫下第一句的練習。

EXAM TIP BOX

✓ 如果題目說明中使用一般性的字眼描述圖片，那麼就在第一句使用具體的字眼；如果題目說明使用具體的字眼，那麼就在第一句使用一般性的字眼。

✓ 如果題目說明中使用名詞片語，那麼就在第一句使用動詞片語；如果題目說明使用動詞片語，那麼就在第一句使用名詞片語。

✓ 這樣做可以讓主考官知道你能夠掌握基本的語言，也可以幫助你得到更高的分數。

Unit 4

寫下你的答案——
描述圖片裡的變動
Writing Your Answer–
Writing about Movement in Graphs

前言與暖身練習 Warm Up

在 Unit 2 中,你學到應該透過研究圖表以找到重要特徵 (significant features) 和整體趨勢 (general trends)。這些特徵和趨勢往往和某種變動有關,亦即某一個趨勢可能上升或增加,而同一時間另一個趨勢則可能下降或減少。在這個單元裡,你將學習如何使用動詞片語和名詞片語來描述這些變動。你還會學到如何在文章裡寫數字。我們會從描述變動的動詞片語開始,因為它們比較簡單又容易使用。

✎ Practice 1

請看以下作文題目說明並研究圖表,然後閱讀範例文章。

> The graph below shows the immigration rates for 4 European countries from 2002 to 2012.
>
> Summarize the information by selecting and reporting the main features and make comparisons where relevant.

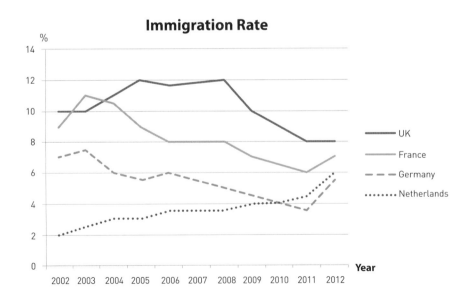

The line graph shows how much immigration there was over a ten year period in 4 different countries in the European Union.

In the Netherlands immigration rose steadily from around 2% to 6% over the ten year period. The UK had the highest rate of immigrants. Immigration in the UK saw a marked rise from 10% to 12 % during the first four years. It remained steady at 12% for a few years. After 2008, immigration in the UK fell significantly by 4% to just over 8%.

Immigration in Germany experienced a gradual fall of 4% from 2003 to 2010. In 2011 there was a noticeable increase in immigration of approximately 2%. Immigration in France followed a pattern similar to Germany's. There was a rapid rise during the first two years, and it reached a peak at 11% in the middle of 2003. After that it went down and troughed in 2011 at roughly 6%.

描述變動的動詞片語 Movement Verb Phrases

當你使用動詞片語時，首先要考慮的是時間和時態。在 Unit 2 裡有學過該如何分析圖表中的時間，現在你將了解爲什麼這一點很重要。你可能會有兩個選擇：如果圖表裡包含今年的訊息，那麼它就是未結束的時間 (unfinished time)；如果圖表裡不包含今年的訊息，那麼就是已結束的時間 (finished time)。舉例來說，前面的 Practice 1 圖中沒有和今年相關的訊息，也沒有和現在有關的時間，所以你必須用「過去簡單式」來描述所有變動。

✎ Practice 2

請研究以下表格、例句和下方的說明。

unfinished time	adverb	sample sentences
has increased	dramatically	• Student numbers increased noticeably
has decreased	rapidly	from May to June in 2001.
has risen	sharply	
has fallen		• The number of young people in full time
has dropped	significantly	work has fallen steadily over the last 5
has gone down	considerably	years.
has gone up	enormously	
has remained steady		• Consumption of hamburgers has
has stabilized	noticeably	dropped tenfold in the US over the last 2
	markedly	decades.
finished time		
increased		• Vehicle emissions rose markedly in the
decreased	gradually	years between 1999 and 2004.
rose	steadily	
fell		• The demand for energy has remained
dropped	modestly	steady over the last five years.
went up	slightly	
went down		• The amount of CO2 in the atmosphere
remained steady	fivefold	stabilized during that period.
stabilized	tenfold	

☆ 請注意例句裡的詞序完全依照表格從左到右。

☆ 注意不同的時態。如果你是用現在完成式，請確定已根據主詞而正確使用 have 或 has。

☆ 請注意，-ly 結尾的副詞是根據動作的種類，例如大動作或小動作，而放在一起。

☆ 如果某個事物真的已經增加了五倍或十倍，請用 fivefold 和 tenfold。

☆ 請注意，你必須小心處理動作的主詞，善用常識並把重點放在意思上。如以下所示，減少的不是漢堡，而是消費量；減少的不是年輕人，而是年輕人的人數。你可以用 Unit 3 中 Practice 7 裡的用語來當作主詞。

☒ 錯誤

- Hamburgers dropped tenfold in the US over the last 2 decades.
- Young people in full time work have fallen steadily over the last 5 years.

☑ 正確

- Consumption of hamburgers has dropped tenfold in the US over the last 2 decades.
- The number of young people in full time work has fallen steadily over the last 5 years.

✎ Practice 3

請回到 Practice 1 的範例文章，並且將所有描述變動的動詞片語畫上底線。

🔑 範例答案

你應該找到四個例子：

- immigration rose steadily
- It remained steady
- immigration in the UK fell significantly
- it went down

請看下面的圖，並用四個句子描述你看到的不同變動。

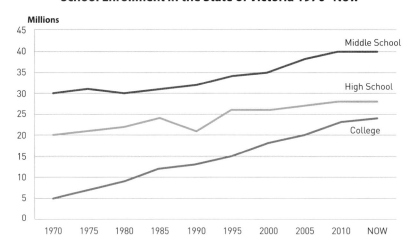

1. _____

2. _____

3. _____

4. _____

🔑 範例答案

以下是一些建議的句子：

1. The number of middle school students increased rapidly from 2000 to 2010.
2. The number of high school students fell slightly in the early 90s.
3. The number of college students has risen markedly over the whole period.
4. The number of middle school students has stabilized gradually over the last 5 years.

我當然不知道你寫了什麼句子，但根據我的經驗，有些常犯的錯誤請特別留意：

☆ 請檢查你的句子的主詞。記得要寫 the number of high school students「高中生的人數」，而不只是寫 high school students「高中生」。

☆ 請確定你的動詞時態是正確的。在第一句和第二句裡，動詞時態是過去簡單式，因為兩句話的時間區間皆已結束（第一句是 2000 to 2010，第二句是 in the early 90s）。而在第三句和第四句的動詞時態則須用現在完成式，因為它們的時間區間包括現在，所以是尚未結束的時間（第三句是 over the whole period，第四句則是 over the last 5 years）。請非常小心你的動詞時態！

☆ 請仔細檢查 -ly 副詞的拼字。

描述變動的名詞片語 Movement Noun Phrases

現在，我們來看看如何用名詞片語描述一樣的變動。這部分會比較困難，所以我們要進行一些練習。

✏️ **Practice 5**

請研究以下表格、例句和下方的說明。

verb	adjective		movement noun
be	a dramatic	a modest	increase (of # in s/th)
have	a rapid	a slight	decrease (of # in s/th)
experience	a sharp	a small	rise (of # in s/th)
see	a sharper	a smaller	fall (of # in s/th)
show			drop (of # in s/th)
enjoy	a significant	a steady overall	
suffer	a considerable	an overall	
	an enormous	a net	
	a major		
		a fivefold	
	a noticeable	a tenfold	
	a marked		
	a gradual		
	a steady		

sample sentences
• Car ownership enjoyed a steady overall increase from 78% to 83% in 2001.
• In 2000 there was a modest fall of around two per cent.
• There was a sharper rise in 1996.
• Taiwan had a noticeable drop in earthquakes during this period.

☆ 首先，看看這個表格和 Practice 2 裡的表格有哪些相似處。請注意，Practice 2 裡的動詞在這裡已經變成名詞，而副詞在這裡已經變成形容詞：increased slowly 已經

變成 slow increase，rose modestly 已經變成 a modest rise。

☆ Practice 2 裡大多數的動詞在 Practice 5 裡都有對應的名詞，除了 go up、go down、stabilize 和 remain steady 之外。遇到這類變動，你不能用描述變動的名詞片語，你只能用動詞片語。

☆ 請注意你必須在形容詞之前用 a。

☆ 請注意在 Practice 5 中，哪些形容詞在 Practice 2 裡沒有任何對應的副詞。

☆ 在 of 後面要加上一個數字：there was an increase of 20%。

☆ in 的後面你可以寫任何時間或主題：There was an increase in three years【時間】／ there was an increase in the number of homeless people【主題】。你將在本單元後面詳細了解如何寫數字。

　　現在，我們來探討可以和名詞片語一起使用的動詞。有七個動詞可以用：be、have、experience、see、show、enjoy、suffer。

☆ 在使用這七個動詞時，請記得使用正確的動詞時態。

☆ 如果主詞是 There，則用 be 動詞，例如：there was a slight increase.

☆ 如果主詞是名詞，請用 have、experience、see、show，例如：the consumption of fast food *had* a slight increase／the consumption of fast food *experienced* a slight increase／the consumption of fast food *saw* a slight increase／the consumption of fast food *showed* a slight increase。這些動詞的意義是空的，它們並不是真的 see、show 或 experience，只是我們拿來和描述變動的名詞片語一起用的動詞。

☆ 如果你想要強調變動有負面的影響，請用 suffer，例如：the pound suffered a fall against the dollar；如果你想強調變動有正面的影響，請用 enjoy，例如：the unemployment rate enjoyed a fall；如果變動的影響是中性的，或是你不想強調正面或負面，請用 saw。

　　接下來，我們來看看用 be 動詞和其他動詞的差異。

Practice 6

請比較這兩個句子。你看得出兩者的訊息結構有哪些差異嗎？

There was a marked drop in the number of people using private cars.
The number of people using private cars saw a marked drop.

🔑 範例答案

這兩個句子傳達的都是「私家車使用人數明顯下降」這個訊息。如果你用 There was，主題 the number of people driving cars 會移到句子最後面，就像第一句那樣；如果你用其他動詞，則主題會移到句子前面作爲動詞 saw 的主詞，就像第二句那樣。

✏️ **Practice 7**

請改寫句子，使其具有相同的意思。我們先來看看範例。

EX. The amount of pollution in the air experienced a noticeable increase.

→ *There was a noticeable increase in the amount of pollution in the air.*

1. The amount of plastic in the ocean saw a marked rise.

→ There _____

2. There was a sharp fall in the number of people studying maths.

→ The _____

3. The volume of magazines sold showed a significant drop.

→ _____

4. There was a significant increase in the number of private schools.

→ _____

🔑 範例答案

1. There was a marked rise in the amount of plastic in the ocean.
2. The number of people studying maths saw a sharp fall.
3. There was a significant drop in the number of magazines sold.
4. The number of private schools experienced a significant increase.

✏️ **Practice 8**

請回到 Practice 1 的範例文章，並且將所有描述變動的名詞片語畫上底線。

🔑 範例答案

你應該找到四個例子，兩個是 there was，另外兩個是前面那七個動詞裡的動詞。

• immigration in the UK saw a marked rise
• immigration in Germany experienced a gradual fall
• there was a noticeable increase in immigration
• there was a rapid rise

　　在我們討論數字之前，必須先看兩種類型的變動：一個是描述變動中的最高點，另一個是描述變動中的最低點。

✏ Practice 9

請研究表格、例句和下方的說明。

type of movement	verb phrase	noun phrase
⋀	peaked (at #)	reached a peak (at #)
⋁	troughed (at #)	reached a trough (at #)
—	stabilized (at #) remained steady (at #)	- -
sample sentences		
• The number of cars on the road reached a peak at 3.4 million in 2005. • The consumption of hamburgers troughed at 300,000 units in that year.		

☆ 請注意，這些類型的變動使用的動詞一定要用過去簡單式。永遠不要在這些類型的變動使用現在完成式。

☆ 請注意介系詞 at 後面要有一個數字。

✏ Practice 10

請回到 **Practice 1** 的範例文章，並且將所有這些類型變動的例子都畫上底線。

🔑 範例答案

你可以找到兩個例子：

• it reached a peak at 11% ＝名詞。　　　• troughed (in 2011) at roughly 6% ＝動詞。

數字 Figures

在本單元稍早前，我曾在 Practice 5 的說明部分提到如何把數字和描述變動的名詞片語一起用，並提醒一定要在數字前面加上 of。現在我們就來看看該如何在描述變動的句子中加上數字。這部分有點複雜，因為我們可用兩種方式來思考數字：

1. 你可以只考慮變動中的一個點 (point)，例如：The number of people studying overseas remained steady at 34%.
2. 你可以思考兩個點之間的距離 (distance)，例如：The number of people studying abroad rose by 3%.

我們用不同的語言來描述 point 和 distance。

Practice 11

請研究表格、例句和下方的說明。

distance		point	
X points/units	by X percent/%	to X	be at X
X percent/%	from X to Z	from X	at X
by X points/units	of X %		
of X points/units			

sample sentences
• The number of people studying social sciences increased to 156.
• The amount of plastic rubbish in the oceans increased by 38%.
• Pollution in the soil saw an increase to 134 units.
• There was an increase of 10% in pollution.
• The number of women in paid employment rose from 56% to 58%.

☆ 第一個句子說的是 point。156 指出變動的結束，它是最高點。

☆ 第二個句子說的是 distance。38% 是變動的起點和終點之間的距離。

☆ 第三句指的是 point。134 單位是變動的結束，它是最高點。

☆ 第四句說的是 distance。10% 是涵蓋了變動起點和終點的距離。

☆ 第五句是包含兩個 point (from 56%) (to 58%) 所形成的一段 distance。

☆ 請注意哪些句子使用了變動的動詞片語，而哪些使用了變動的名詞片語。

　　Point 和 distance 之間的差異對精準度來說非常重要。若介系詞寫錯了，句子的意思就會改變。而你之前考試分數不高的原因之一也很可能是因為介系詞寫錯，混淆了 point 和 distance。

　　當你在描述數字的時候，可能沒有足夠的空間或時間精準掌握百分比，而且我也不建議你浪費時間算數學！相反的，你可以用「模糊標記」(vagueness marker) 讓數字模糊化。請看下一張表格，了解如何做到這一點。

✎ Practice 12

請研究表格、例句和下方的說明。

preposition	vagueness marker	number
	roughly around just over just under approximately	
sample sentences		

• Unemployment rose from roughly 2% to just over 4%.
• The birth rate fell from around 23%.

☆ 請注意，模糊標記出現的位置在介系詞和數字的中間。

☆ 你可以用這種用語來描述 point 或 distance，兩者都可以。

Practice 13

請回到 Practice 1 的範例文章，將所有描述數字的部分畫上底線，並注意 Practice 11 和 Practice 12 提到的描述用語。

範例答案

你應該找到共九個例子。

- from around 2% to 6% (combined points and distance)
- from 10% to 12 % (combined points and distance)
- at 12% (= point)
- by 4% (= distance)
- to just over 8% (= point)
- of 4% (= distance)
- of approximately 2% (= distance)
- at 11% (= point)
- at roughly 6% (= point)

　　為了確定你真的了解這個觀念，並且可以完全精準使用這些用語，下一個練習會要求你特別把重點放在數字上。

Practice 14

請研究以下的題目說明和圖表，並且將 Practice 11 的用語填入段落裡的空白處。

The graph shows the number of students studying two languages in the language department of the University of Somewhere over a 5 year period.

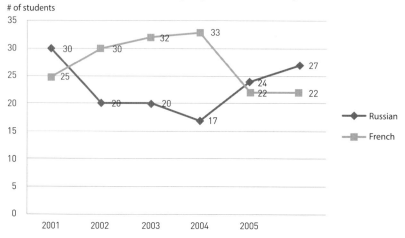

Number of Students in Department of Modern Language in X University

The number of students studying French rose (1) _____ 25 (2) _____ 32 during the first 3 years. It reached a peak (3) _____ 33 in 2004 and then dropped (4) _____ 11 students in 2005.

The number of students studying Russian dropped gradually (5) _____ 30 students (6) _____ 20 students in 2002. It remained steady (7) _____ 20 students until 2004, when it fell again (8) _____ 17. The number of students taking Russian troughed (9) _____ 17 in 2004, but after that it rose significantly (10) _____ 10 students at the end of the period.

🔑 範例答案

你應該找到共九個例子。

1. from (= point)
2. to (= point)
3. at (= point)
4. by (= distance)
5. from (= point)
6. to (= point)
7. at (= point)
8. to (= point)
9. at (= point)
10. by (= distance)

☆ 請注意，這**不是** IELTS Writing Task 1 的標準答案寫法。

☆ 我不建議你用這種方式描述圖片裡的每一個變動。

☆ 我的建議是，你只需要用這麼詳細的程度寫下一個或兩個句子即可，讓主考官知道你能夠把點和距離寫得很精準。

描述變動的動詞片語和名詞片語
Movement Verb Phrases and Movement Noun Phrases

那麼，就 IELTS 考試而言，描述變動的動詞片語和名詞片語，兩者之間的意義和風格有什麼差異呢？一般來說，相較於動詞片語，學術寫作更常使用名詞片語。然而，在平常說話的時候，我們用的動詞片語則比名詞片語多。如果在寫作時多使用名詞片語，得到的分數將會比較高，因為你的文章會更具學術性。當然，最好的情況是能夠善用一系列的動詞片語和名詞片語，讓主考官知道你可以掌控好這兩種結構。因此，為了讓你使用這兩種結構時更有信心，我們將會進行一些練習，幫助你培養出從其中一種結構輕鬆變換到另一種的能力。如果知道自己能夠用這種方法掌握語言，將讓你在寫作時更有自信。

✐ Practice 15

請於下欄中找出意思完全相同的語句填入下列各題。

1. has increased steadily = _____

2. dropped sharply = _____

3. have risen slightly = _____

4. has increased noticeably = _____

5. rose considerably = _____

has experienced a slight rise	saw a steadily increase
has seen a noticeable increase	showed a considerable rise
has seen a steady increase	there was a sharp drop
has shown a considerable rise	there was a slight rise
saw a noticeable increase	

🔑 範例答案

1. has increased steadily = has seen a steady increase
2. dropped sharply = there was a sharp drop

3. have risen slightly = has experienced a slight rise

4. has increased noticeably = has seen a noticeable increase

5. rose considerably = showed a considerable rise

☆ 請特別把重點放在動詞的時態。

☆ 如果你答錯了，請確實了解錯在哪裡。

✎ **Practice 16**

請改寫下面的句子，將描述變動的動詞片語改成名詞片語，反之亦然。我們來看範例。

EX. There was a considerable drop in the number of students doing maths in the 5 year period.

→ *The number of students doing maths dropped considerably in the 5 year period.*

1. They enjoyed a steady overall increase from 78% to 83% in 2001.

→ _____

2. In 2000 there was a modest fall of around 2% in sales.

→ _____

3. There was a sharper rise in profits in 1996.

→ _____

4. Taiwan had a noticeable drop in earthquakes during this period.

→ _____

5. Student numbers increased noticeably from May to June in 2001.

→ _____

6. The number of young people in full time work has fallen steadily over the last 5 years.

→ _____

7. Consumption of hamburgers has dropped tenfold in the US over the last 2 decades.

→ _____

8. Vehicle emissions rose markedly in the years between 1999 and 2004.

→ _____

🔑 範例答案

1. They increased steadily from 78% to 83% in 2001.
2. In 2000 sales fell modestly by 2%
3. Profits rose more sharply in 1996.
4. The number of earthquakes in Taiwan dropped noticeably during this period.
5. Student numbers saw a noticeable increase from May to June in 2001.
6. The number of young people in full time work has seen a steady fall over the last 5 years.
7. Consumption of hamburgers has seen a tenfold drop in the US over the last 2 decades.
8. There was a marked rise in vehicle emissions in the years between 1999 and 2004.

☆ 當你檢查答案時,請把重點放在描述變動的動詞片語和名詞片語之間的相異或相似處,以及用於含括數字的語言。

　　在你結束這個單元之前,請將下列清單看過,確定你能將所有要點都勾選起來。如果有一些要點你還不清楚,請回頭再研讀本單元的相關部分。

☐ 我知道如何利用描述變動的動詞片語和名詞片語來撰寫圖片的重要特徵 (significant features) 和整體趨勢 (general trends)。

☐ 我知道如何將描述變動的動詞片語改成描述變動的名詞片語,反之亦然。這樣做可以讓主考官知道我有能力掌握自己使用的語言。

☐ 當我把數字放進句子時,我能夠了解 point 和 distance 的差異。

☐ 我知道如何模糊地描述數字。

□ 我知道當我使用描述變動的動詞片語時，必須特別注意它的動詞時態，如果變動發生在過去已結束的時間，要用過去簡單式；如果發生在尚未結束的現在，則要使用現在完成式。

□ 在使用描述變動的名詞片語時，我知道在使用 There was 或其他七個動詞時，該如何調整句子裡的訊息結構。

□ 我已經學到許多有助於 IELTS 寫作 Task 1 的字彙。

□ 我已經進行了很多寫作練習。

PART
1

EXAM TIP BOX

✓ 不要只用動詞片語或名詞片語。

✓ 如果你能夠在文章裡善用名詞片語和動詞片語，這表示你能夠適當掌握這些語言，並能幫助你得到更高的分數。

NOTES

Unit 5

寫下你的答案──
描述比較

Writing Your Answer–
Writing about Comparison

前言與暖身練習 Warm Up

在 Unit 4，你學到如何描寫重要特徵 (significant features) 和整體趨勢 (general trends) 的變動。在這個單元裡，我們將繼續學習如何用比較形式（比較級和最高級）來描述重要特徵和整體趨勢。這類用語是出了名的刁鑽，所以主考官會想知道你如何處理它們。在使用這類比較形式時，你必須著重在精準度，我們將從用於比較的用語開始練習，然後再看如何描述最高級。

Practice 1

請看以下作文題目說明並研究圖表，然後閱讀範例文章。

> The chart shows how many male and female students were enrolled in different undergraduate departments during the academic year 2005 - 2006 at Averygood University.
>
> Summarize the information by selecting and reporting the main features and make comparisons where relevant.

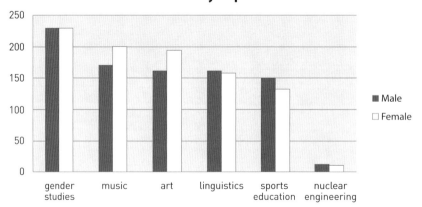

The chart shows the number of undergraduate students of both sexes enrolled in different departments at Averygood University during the academic year 2005 - 2006.

The department of gender studies had the most students, with just as many male students as female students. The department of nuclear engineering had the lowest number of students of both sexes, although there were slightly more male students than female students in this department.

In the music department there were significantly more female students than male students, and the art department was also significantly more popular with females than with males. There were almost as many male students in the art department as in the linguistics department. However, in the linguistics department, the number of male students was 4% higher than the number of female students.

Likewise, the sports education department had many more male students than female. In most other departments, the number of male students was more or less the same as the number of female students.

比較 Comparison

進行「比較」的寫法有兩種，首先是把重點放在兩件事的相異處 (difference)，其次是把重點放在相似處 (similarities)。我們將從相異處開始談起。

 Practice 2

請研究表格、例句和下方的說明。

describing differences 1			
be have do	much slightly x%	higher (n.p.) lower (n.p.) more (n.p.) less (n.p.) fewer (n.p.) ___ er (n.p.)	than n.p. than v.p.
sample sentences			

- The number of people in paid employment was slightly higher than the number of unemployed people.
- Lille University had 20% more.
- The number of people owning cars was lower than the number of people owning bicycles.
- France had more tourists in 2005 than in 2006.
- In 2004 Australians did less work than in 2008.
- People had fewer part time jobs at that time than they do now.
- The department of gender studies had more boys than girls.
- The government did more to help single mothers in 2006 than they did in 2016.
- New houses now are much smaller than they were 20 years ago.

☆ 請注意句子的主詞，並確定你使用的動詞具有正確的人稱和時態。

☆ 你可以使用任何動詞，但是 have、be 和 do 是最常見的。

☆ 如果你想強調一個很大的差異，可以用 much；如果想強調微小的差異，可用 slightly；而若你想精準地描述差異，請使用百分比。注意，這些強調詞會緊跟在動

詞的後面。另外，即使你用了 much，後面還是要加 more。因為 more 才是關鍵字，much 不是。

☆ 請注意形容詞的比較級以 -er 結尾。如果你用的形容詞有三個或三個以上的音節，則必須在形容詞前面用 more，而不是在字尾加上 -er。

☆ 遇到不可數名詞時請用 less，例如 less work；遇到可數名詞則用 fewer，例如 fewer part time jobs。

☆ 你可以在 -er 的後面接名詞片語，但並非必要。

☆ 請特別注意 than 的拼字，千萬別誤寫成 then 或 that。

☒ 錯誤
- There were <u>less people</u> living below the poverty line in 1995 than in 2005.
- The Red Team scored more goals <u>then</u> the Blue Team, but the Blue Team had more fouls <u>that</u> the Red Team.

☑ 正確
- There were <u>fewer people</u> living below the poverty line in 1995 than in 2005.
- The Red Team scored more goals <u>than</u> the Blue Team, but the Blue Team had more fouls <u>than</u> the Red Team.

除了 Practice 2 的用語之外，你也可以用 there is / there are 來比較相異處。它們和先前說過的用語具有相同的基本規則。

✎ **Practice 3**

請研究表格、例句和下方的說明。

describing differences 2			
There were/was	much slightly x%	higher (n.p.) lower (n.p.) more (n.p.) less (n.p.) fewer (n.p.)	than n.p.

sample sentences
• There were more people living in poverty in France than in Germany.
• There was less pollution in rivers than in the atmosphere.
• There were fewer homeless people in London than in Manchester.

☆ 你必須非常注意可數名詞和不可數名詞，並且判斷該用 were 或 was。

☒ 錯誤
• There <u>were</u> less work for the staff of A Company in 2005 than in 2004.
• There <u>was</u> less boys than girls in the last 2 years of high school in Rottenham High School in 2006.

☑ 正確
• There <u>was</u> less work for the staff of A Company in 2005 than in 2004.
• There <u>were</u> fewer boys than girls in the last 2 years of high school in Rottenham High School in 2006.

Practice 4

請回到 **Practice 1** 的範例文章，並且將所有強調相異處的比較範例畫上底線。

範例答案

你應該找到以下三個例子：

• art department <u>was also significantly more popular with females than</u> with males
• the number of male students <u>was 4% higher than</u> the number of female students
• the sports education department <u>had many more male students than</u> female

以及兩個用 there were 來比較的例子：

• <u>there were slightly more male students than female students</u>
• <u>there were significantly more female students</u> than male students

✏️ Practice 5

請修正下列句子裡的錯誤，有些句子包含一個以上的錯誤。

1. Germany had many immigrants in 2006 than in 2004.

2. In 2004 Americans ate fewer vegetarian food then in 2008.

3. There were a much bigger jump in the figures for 2011 than for 2010.

4. New houses now are much expensiver than they were 20 years ago.

5. People had less second cars at that time they do now.

6. The British Museum have 20% more visitors.

7. There was many more children in China in the year 1950 than old people.

8. The government passing more new laws in 2006 than they did in 2016.

9. The media studies department had more than other years applicants in that year.

10. The number of cars on the road was slightly higher in 2002 that in 2000.

11. The number of couples with children lower in 2005 than in 2000.

12. There were much more pollution in the world than then now.

🔑 範例答案

1. Germany had many <u>more</u> immigrants in 2006 than in 2004.
2. In 2004 Americans ate <u>less</u> vegetarian food <u>than</u> in 2008.
3. There <u>was</u> a much bigger jump in the figures for 2011 than for 2010.
4. New houses now are much <u>more expensive</u> than they were 20 years ago.
5. People had <u>fewer</u> second cars at that time <u>than</u> they do now.
6. The British Museum <u>had</u> 20% more visitors.
7. There <u>were</u> many more children in China in the year 1950 than old people.
8. The government <u>passed</u> more new laws in 2006 than they did in 2016.
9. The media studies department had <u>more applicants in that year than</u> other years.
10. The number of cars on the road was slightly higher in 2002 <u>than</u> in 2000.
11. The number of couples with children <u>was</u> lower in 2005 than in 2000.
12. There was much more pollution in the world then <u>than</u> now.

☆ 請參照前面幾個練習的表格、例句和說明，務必確認已經了解這些句子中的錯誤點。

根據以下條形圖所顯示的資訊，用四個句子來比較不同國家的成人識字率。請把重點放在相異處。

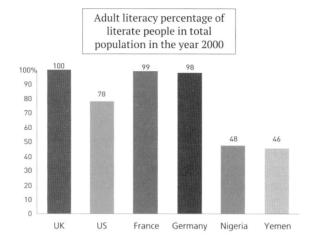

1. _____

2. _____

3. _____

4. _____

🔑 範例答案

以下是一些建議的句子：

1. There were fewer literate people in America than in any other Western developed nation.
2. France had slightly more adult literacy than Germany.
3. Adult literacy was 50% higher in Germany than in Nigeria.
4. There were many more literate people in France than in Yemen.

我當然不知道你寫了什麼句子，但根據我的經驗，有些常犯的錯誤請特別留意：

☆ 如果你用了 there was 或 there were，請檢查句子的主詞。
☆ 請確定你的動詞時態正確。
☆ 請參照 Practice 2 和 Practice 3 的表格，確認所有使用的比較用語都正確。

我們前面一直在討論如何把重點放在要比較的事物之間的相異處 (differences)。現在，我們來看看如何把重點放在要比較的事物之間的相似處 (similarities)。

✏ Practice 7

請研究表格、例句和下方的說明。

describing similarities 1			
be have do	(just) (almost) (not)	as much (n.p.) as many (n.p.) as (adjective) the same (n.p.)	as n.p. as v.p.
sample sentences			

- Adult literacy in France was almost as much as it was in Germany.
- Most respondents said that job satisfaction was just as important as a high salary.
- Gun crime in Louisiana was almost as common as it was in Chicago.
- Nigeria had as many unmarried women as Yuganda.
- In all sectors men did the same work as women.
- The developing countries of Africa did not have as much adult literacy as the developed countries of the West.
- New York does not have as many public parks as Paris.
- The city government in Tokyo did not do as much renovation of public buildings as the city government of San Francisco did.

☆ 請注意句子的主詞，並確定你用的動詞具有正確的人稱和時態。

☆ 比較相似處的句子一定要有兩個 as，除非你是用 the same。注意，請不要用 with。

☆ 如果後面要比較的名詞片語是不可數的，請用 as much；如果後面的名詞片語是可數的，請用 as many。

☆ 如果 as many 和可數名詞一起用，請記得要把名詞加上 s，讓它變成複數。

☆ 在第二個 as 後面，你可以用名詞片語或動詞片語。

☆ 雖然這類用語在文法上要表達的是相似處，但我們仍然可以用它來描述相異處，方法是使用 not。

☆ 請注意 not 和動詞 have、do 的位置。

> ☒ 錯誤
> - Adult literacy in the UK was almost <u>as much it was</u> in the US.
> - In all sectors men did the same work <u>with</u> women.
> - The city government in Tokyo did <u>not</u> as much renovation of public buildings as the city government of San Francisco did.
> - New York does not have as many public <u>park</u> as Paris.

> ☑ 正確
> - Adult literacy in the UK was almost <u>as much as it was</u> in the US.
> - In all sectors men did the same work <u>as</u> women.
> - The city government in Tokyo <u>did not do</u> as much renovation of public buildings as the city government of San Francisco did.
> - New York does not have as many public <u>parks</u> as Paris.

除了 Practice 7 的用語之外，你也可以用 there is / there are 來比較相似處。它們和先前說過的用語具有相同的基本規則。

✎ Practice 8

請研究表格、例句和下方的說明。

describing similarities 2			
There were/was	(almost) (not)	as much (n.p.) as many (n.p.)	as n.p. as v.p.
sample sentences			
• There was almost as much pollution in 2010 as 2012.			
• There were not as many respondents to the questionnaire in June as there were in August.			

☆ 當你使用這種句構時，請確保所有名詞、動詞和主詞的一致性，亦即必須都是不可數、單數可數或複數可數。

☆ 我們也可以用這種文法結構來描述相異處，只要加上 not 即可。

- ⊠ 錯誤
  - There <u>was</u> almost as many <u>attack</u> on immigrants in 2010 as 2012.
  - There <u>was</u> not as <u>much people</u> living in urban areas as in rural areas.

- ☑ 正確
  - There <u>were</u> almost as <u>many attacks</u> on immigrants in 2010 as 2012.
  - There <u>were</u> not as <u>many people</u> living in urban areas as in rural areas.

✎ Practice 9

請回到 **Practice 1** 的範例文章，並且將所有強調相似處的比較範例畫上底線。

✐ 範例答案

你應該找到以下三個例子：

- with just <u>as many male students as</u> female students.
- <u>There were almost as many</u> male students in the art department <u>as</u> in the linguistics department.
- the number of male students was more or less <u>the same as</u> the number of female students.

　　再說一次，使用這類比較的用語時，你必須非常注意細節。下一個練習會幫助你專注於這個部分。

Practice 10

請在以下方框中選出適當的字彙或短語填入句中。

There were	does not have	as much
as consumers	was not the same with	popular with
as many	with	There was
as much money	as	was not the same as
popular	much	as there were
as there was	much money	has not
consumers	popular as	many
		as many money

1. Adult education in the UK was almost as _____ it was in the US.

2. Chicago _____ as many night clubs as New Orleans.

3. Consumers in the developing countries of Asia did not have as much disposable income _____ in the developed countries of the West.

4. In all cities car ownership _____ bicycle ownership.

5. In all sectors men did the same work _____ women.

6. Nigeria had as _____ unmarried young men as Yuganda.

7. The city government did not give _____ to the arts as they gave to shelters for the homeless.

8. _____ almost as much traffic in 1995 as 2005.

9. There were not as many people doing office jobs _____ doing construction jobs.

🔑 範例答案

1. popular as
2. does not have
3. as consumers
4. was not the same as
5. as
6. many

7. as much money
8. There was
9. as there were

✏️ **Practice 11**

請再次回到 **Practice 6**，並根據條形圖所顯示的資訊，用四個句子來比較不同國家的成人識字率。請把重點放在相似處。

1. _____

2. _____

3. _____

4. _____

🔑 範例答案

以下是一些建議的句子：

1. There were almost as many literate people in Nigeria as in Yemen.
2. There was not as much adult literacy in Yemen as in the UK.
3. Germany had almost as much adult literacy as the UK.
4. Adult literacy in Germany in the year 2000 was almost the same as it was in France.

同樣的，有些常犯的錯誤請特別留意：

☆ 如果你用 there was 或 there were，請檢查句子的主詞。
☆ 請確定你的動詞時態正確。
☆ 請參照 Practice 7 和 Practice 8 的表格，確認所有使用的比較用語都正確。

最高級 Superlatives

我們已經學過如何針對事物的相異處和相似處來進行比較，現在要來看如何描述某樣東西是最好的、最大的、最了不起的。也就是文法上所謂的「最高級」。這部分比進行比較要容易得多，但還是有一些複雜問題須注意，尤其是規則變化的 (regular) 最高級，以及不規則變化 (irregular) 的最高級之間的差異。

✎ Practice 12

請研究表格、例句和下方的說明。

regular	irregular
the highest n.p.	the best n.p.
the lowest n.p.	the worst n.p.
the biggest n.p.	the most (adjective) n.p.
the most n.p.	
the least n.p.	
the fewest n.p.	
the smallest n.p.	
the _____est n.p.	

sample sentences
• Taiwan had the highest number of earthquakes during this period.

• Taiwan had the highest number of earthquakes during this period.
• The lowest employment rate was in Venezuela.
• Between gold and silver, the biggest increase was in gold.
• The island has the smallest number of species ever recorded.
• The brightest star in the solar system is Sirius.
• The most important result of the experiment was that they found a cure for cancer.
• In terms of rainfall, the best weather was between March and September, while the worst was between September and March.

☆ 如果是規則變化的最高級（形容詞是單音節或以 -y 結尾的雙音節字），只要在形容詞字尾加上 -est 即可。

☆ 不規則變化的最高級會用 best 表示 good、worst 表示 bad，而如果形容詞有三個以上的音節則必須用 most。注意，若形容詞少於三個音節，就不可以用 most 或是把 most 和 -est 結合。

☆ 這類用語一定會出現在關鍵名詞的前面，例如 the highest number of earthquakes，其中 earthquakes 是關鍵名詞。

☆ 不要忘記使用最高級形容詞時，必須加定冠詞 the，不要使用 a/an。

☆ 不要試圖比較已經是同類中最好或最大的東西。

PART
1

☒ 錯誤

• Japan had <u>the higher</u> number of typhoons during this period.
• The region has <u>a</u> smallest number of trees ever recorded.
• Jupiter is the biggest planet <u>than Saturn</u>.

☑ 正確

• Japan had <u>the highest</u> number of typhoons during this period.
• The region has <u>the</u> smallest number of trees ever recorded.
• Jupiter is <u>the biggest</u> planet.

✎ Practice 13

請回到 Practice 1 的範例文章，並且將所有強調最高級的比較範例畫上底線。

🔑 範例答案

你應該找到以下兩個例子：

• The department of gender studies had <u>the most</u> students,
• The department of nuclear engineering had <u>the lowest</u> number

　　和本單元前面說過的比較用語一樣，使用最高級用語主要的困難也是在於精準度。當你要做下個練習時，請把注意力集中在 Practice 12 的表格，特別留意用字的精準度。

 **Practice 14**

請修正下列句子裡的錯誤。

1. Australia is the smallest continent than Africa.

2. The galaxy has the smaller number of stars ever recorded.

3. The most big increase was in oxygen.

4. The most brightest star in the solar system is Sirius

5. The Philippines had lowest number of typhoons during this period.

6. The popularest course was economics.

7. The region has the smaller number of earthquakes ever recorded.

8. Venezuela had a lowest birth rate.

🔑 範例答案

1. Australia is <u>the smallest</u> continent.
2. The galaxy has <u>the smallest</u> number of stars ever recorded.
3. <u>The biggest</u> increase was in oxygen.
4. <u>The brightest</u> star in the solar system is Sirius.
5. The Philippines had <u>the lowest</u> number of typhoons during this period.
6. <u>The most popular</u> course was economics.
7. The region has <u>the smallest</u> number of earthquakes ever recorded.
8. Venezuela had <u>the lowest</u> birth rate.

Practice 15

請再次回到 **Practice 6**，並根據條形圖所顯示的資訊，用四個句子來比較不同國家的成人識字率。請把重點放在最高級。

1. ＿＿＿＿＿＿＿＿＿＿＿＿＿＿＿＿＿＿＿＿＿＿＿＿＿＿＿＿＿＿＿＿

2. ＿＿＿＿＿＿＿＿＿＿＿＿＿＿＿＿＿＿＿＿＿＿＿＿＿＿＿＿＿＿＿＿

3. ＿＿＿＿＿＿＿＿＿＿＿＿＿＿＿＿＿＿＿＿＿＿＿＿＿＿＿＿＿＿＿＿

4. ＿＿＿＿＿＿＿＿＿＿＿＿＿＿＿＿＿＿＿＿＿＿＿＿＿＿＿＿＿＿＿＿

以下是一些建議的句子：

1. Between Nigeria and Yemen, Nigeria had the highest adult literacy.
2. The UK was the best country in the world in terms of adult literacy.
3. The US was the worst country in the developed world in terms of adult literacy.
4. Yemen had the lowest adult literacy.

再次提醒，有些常犯的錯誤請特別留意：

☆ 如果你用 there was 或 there were，請檢查句子的主詞。

☆ 請確定你的動詞時態正確。

☆ 請參照 Practice 12 的表格，確認所有描述最高級的用語都正確。

在你結束這個單元之前，請將下列清單看過，確定你能將所有要點都勾選起來。
如果有一些要點你還搞不清楚，請回頭再研讀本單元的相關部分。

☐ 我知道如何根據相異處來比較不同的事物。

☐ 我知道如何根據相似處來比較不同的事物。

☐ 我知道如何使用最高級來描述事物。

☐ 我知道何時該注重精準度，以及當我使用比較級和最高級的用語時，必須避免哪些
常見的錯誤。

☐ 我已經學到許多有助於 IELTS Writing Task 1 的字彙。

☐ 我已經進行了很多寫作練習。

EXAM TIP BOX

✓ 不要只用一種文法。例如，不要只用 X is bigger than Y、Y is more
than Z。

✓ 在 Task 1 中，你至少應該使用兩個不同的比較結構來寫作，讓主考
官知道你懂得如何使用這類用語。這樣可以幫你得到更高的分數。

NOTES

Unit 6

寫下你的答案——
描述物體和地圖
Writing Your Answer–
Writing about Objects and Maps

在這個單元中，我們將把重點放在不同類型的任務，也就是描述地圖。這個任務的目的是測試你是否能夠精準描述事物的位置和變化。在之前的單元裡，你學到的大部分內容都和這裡彼此相關：名詞片語和動詞片語之間的差異、比較性用語、用正確的時態描述已結束／未結束的時間及沒有提到時間的時間。我們將先把重點放在分析資訊和組織你的答案上，然後再看看在這類型的任務中你必須使用哪些用語。

Practice 1

請先研究以下的題目說明及地圖，然後閱讀範例文章。

The maps below show the changes to the village of Wadhurst and its surroundings from 1970 to 2010.

Summarize the information by selecting and reporting the main features and make comparisons where relevant.

Wadhurst

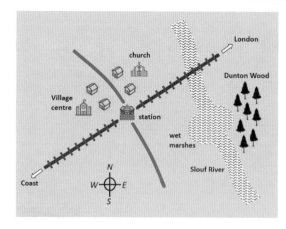

1970
Railway ┼┼┼┼┼┼
Road ▬▬▬

2010
Railway ┼┼┼┼┼┼
Road ▬▬▬

The village of Wadhurst underwent considerable changes during the 40 year period shown in the maps.

The biggest change was that a new water sports park was built to the south east of the village. Two new roads were constructed to link the water park to the railway and the existing road running from north to south through the village. Also, the old railway station in the middle of the village was converted into a visitor centre, and a new station was built outside the village, to the north east. The village itself expanded during that time and a suburb was added to the north west of the village.

The construction of the water sports park also had some negative impacts on the environment. The planners of the water sports park drained the wet marshes to the east of the village to make way for the park, and they also chopped down and cleared Dunton Wood.

1. 首先，分析題目和說明文字，就像先前在 Unit 2 說明的那樣。把關鍵字彙畫上底線，接著就可以把它們用在答案中。舉例來說，在上述 Practice 1 的題目說明中，你可以把 surroundings 這個字彙畫上底線，並且把它用在你的答案。從地圖來看，你可能會用到像 marshes、wood 和 suburb 這些字彙。這裡不太可能會出現你不知道的字彙，但為了避免這種情況發生，建議你最好大量學習與景觀或都市區域相關的字彙。

2. 題目說明要求你選擇、說明並進行比較。注意，除非說明中有特別要求，否則請不要提出你的看法，也不要推測變化的原因或影響。再次提醒，在 IELTS Writing Task 1 中，你的任務就是要進行精準地描述。

3. 請研讀地圖以了解地圖所傳達的時間訊息。了解地圖上顯示的時間非常重要，因為這會決定你必須用哪一種動詞時態。另外還要記得研究地圖上的圖例。你可能會遇到很多不同類型的地圖。這個地圖可能顯示出從過去某個時間到過去的另一個時間，或是從過去到現在，甚或是未來可能的改變。它也可能是一個沒有顯示任何變化的地圖，只有包含你希望能盡可能精準描述的資訊。首先，你必須判斷地圖是否有顯示任何變化。例如，在 Practice 1 的地圖裡，它顯示從已經過去的 1970 年到 2010 年之間的變化，這表示你在答案裡的動詞時態必須使用過去簡單式；如果地圖顯示的是從過去到現在的變化，你就必須用現在完成式；如果地圖顯示未來可能的改變，就必須用未來式；如果地圖沒有顯示變化，那你就要用現在簡單式。稍後我會在這個單元中說明更多相關內容。

4. 現在來看看你可以認出多少 major changes「主要變化」。這就像許多人小時候可能玩過的遊戲：看著兩張非常相似的圖片，然後找出它們之間的差異。請在這裡使用相同的方法。例如，在上述 Practice 1 中，你可以馬上發現五個差異：(1) 地圖二有一個郊區。(2) 地圖一的車站在地圖二中變成了遊客中心。(3) 村子外面蓋了一個新車站。(4) 有一個大型水上運動公園蓋在地圖一中原本有沼澤和森林的地方。(5) 地圖二中開通了兩條新道路，將水上公園連接至主要幹道和新車站。

5. 主要變化是馬上就可以看出來的變化，但還有其他變化是不容易發現的，所以接下來你應該找出這些變化。我們可以把這些較小或次要的變化稱為 minor, or secondary changes，因為它們的變遷取決於主要變化。例如，在 Practice 1 中有兩個次要變化：為了騰出空間蓋水上運動公園，沼澤已經被抽乾了，森林也被砍伐了。我們可以說這些都是負面的變化，或是因為主要變化而產生的變化。沒有主要變化，就不會發生這些次要變化。

　　這裡有一張分析地圖資訊的清單。

PART
1

✏️ Practice 2

請研究以下分析地圖資訊的清單。

分析數據清單：地圖
1. **關鍵字彙**：將題目、說明文字和地圖上的關鍵字彙畫上底線。
2. **摘要提示**：將說明文字中提到你該怎麼做的部分畫上底線。
3. **時間**：請確定你知道地圖顯示的整體時間。
4. **主要變化**：請辨認你看到的主要變化。
5. **次要變化**：請辨認其他微小、次要的變化。

✏️ Practice 3

請看下方的題目說明和地圖，並使用清單來分析顯示的資訊。想想看要如何組織答案。

The maps below show what changes have occurred to Anyold Town Centre.

Summarize the information by selecting and reporting the main features and make comparisons where relevant.

Anyold Town Centre (Then)

Anyold Town Centre (Now)

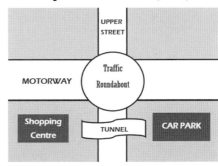

我們來看看你分析的清單應該包含哪些內容吧！

	分析項目	參考內容
1	關鍵字彙	題目和說明文字的字彙不多，但是兩張地圖裡面的字彙很多，你應該在答案裡使用這些字彙。
2	摘要提示	你應該只要選擇、說明和比較。不要就人們可能對這些改變有什麼看法而提出你的意見或進行推測。
3	時間	這裡有點刁鑽，它除了 Then 和 Now，沒有其他資訊。遇到這種圖，你要用現在完成式來說明過去的改變如何帶來現在的結果。我稍後會告訴你如何做到這一點。
4	主要變化	這裡有五個主要變化：(1) 有一條公路就蓋在市中心，還有一條新的 (2) 環形道路。(3) 一棟新的購物中心就蓋在公路旁邊，(4) 還有一個很大的停車場，購物中心和停車場之間有一條 (5) 隧道相連。
5	次要變化	這裡有四個次要變化：(1) Broad Street 被拓寬而且重新命名。(2) 市中心原本的舊建築都被清除，騰出空間蓋新的公路和環形道路。(3) 樹木都被連根拔起和砍掉，而且 (4) 公園被夷為平地，用來蓋停車場。

當你這樣分析資訊的同時，應該想一想如何把你對地圖的研究結果，組織成答案。

你應該從描述 general changes「整體變化」的句子開始寫。我很快就會告訴你如何做到這一點。接著，你應該用三、四個句子描述 major changes「主要變化」，再用另外三或四個句子描述 minor, dependent changes「次要、仰賴主要變化的變化」。組織資訊時沒有所謂「正確」的方式，但你應該讓資訊有邏輯，而且要容易懂。不要把在地圖上看到的一切都描述出來，應該把重點放在「變化」。

 **Practice 4**

請閱讀 Practice 1 的範例文章，並且判斷將其組織後會是下列 A、B 或 C。

A	B	C
Introductory general sentence	Introductory general sentence	Introductory general sentence
The water sport park	Major changes	Secondary changes
The station	Secondary changes	The suburb
The wet marshes		The water sport park

🔑 範例答案

希望你有看出這個範例文章組織後的結果是 B。

　　好的，了解如何分析這類圖像之後，現在我們來看看描述地圖時需要用到的一些用語。首先，我們要學習如何寫開頭的第一句，然後再把重點放在你要用的動詞時態。我會教你很多可以用在這種寫作的動詞，以及一些用來描述位置的字。

第一句：描述一般性的變化
Opening Sentence: Describing General Changes

在 Unit 3 已學過動詞片語和名詞片語的差異，以及如何將一個片語改成另一個片語，在這裡你也會用到這些知識。首先，我會先告訴你如何用動詞片語描述改變，然後再談如何用名詞片語描述改變。

✏ Practice 5

請研究以下表格、例句和下方的說明。

describing general changes: verb phrase		
finished time verb	**unfinished time verb**	**adverb**
changed	has changed	dramatically
was developed	has been developed	spectacularly
was transformed	has been transformed	considerably
		significantly
		radically
sample sentences		
• The island was significantly developed between the years 1960 and 2000.		
• The village of Waddington was transformed considerably during that time.		
• The Old Town has changed dramatically.		

☆ 首先，請注意這裡使用的主詞非常籠統，然後看表格時請從左到右。

☆ 請注意時態的使用。前兩句使用過去簡單式，因為改變已經發生了 (… was significantly developed ….)。2000 年是最新的日期，但從我們的角度來看，它仍然是過去的時間，所以 during that time 也是過去已經結束的時間。基本上，規則就是：如果你用的是表示已結束時間的字眼，就必須用過去簡單式。

☆ 第三句使用現在完成式。這句話的重點是「過去的變化造成現在的結果」，和我們在 Practice 3 中遇到的狀況一樣。你可以在未結束的時間使用 in recent years，但是在描寫過去的變化帶來現在的結果時，不一定要用這種字。

☆ 第一和第二句都用被動語態。但請注意，不要把 change 這個動詞加上被動語態，這個動詞在中文裡必須用被動態，但是英文不需要。你會在下一個單元學到更多被

動態。

☆ 請注意，在第一句中 significantly 可以放在助動詞和主要動詞之間，considerably 也可以出現在這個位置，但其他副詞則不行。事實上，把這兩個副詞放在兩個動詞之間會更自然。

☒ 錯誤

• The site has been developed in 2010.
• The city centre was transformed recently.
• The park was changed spectacularly during that time.

☑ 正確

• The site was developed in 2010.
• The city centre has been transformed recently.
• The park changed spectacularly during that time.

　　現在，我們來看看如何用名詞片語寫開頭第一句。

✎ **Practice 6**

請研究以下表格、例句和下方的說明。

describing general changes: noun phrase			
verb		**adjective**	**noun**
finished time	unfinished time		
saw	has seen	dramatic	changes
experienced	has experienced	spectacular	developments
underwent	has undergone	considerable	transformations
witnessed	has witnessed	significant	
		radical	
sample sentences			
• The island saw significant developments between the years 1960 and 2000.			
• The village of Waddington underwent considerable transformations during that time.			
• The Old Town has witnessed many dramatic changes.			

☆ 如果你比較 Practice 5 和這裡的例句，將對於如何把動詞片語改成名詞片語有個大致的概念。

☆ 首先，請注意這裡使用的主詞非常籠統，然後看表格時請從左到右。

☆ 相同的規則也適用於時態的使用。對於時間已經結束的變化，請用過去簡單式；對於時間尚未結束的變化，請用現在完成式。

☆ 如果用這些名詞片語，請不要使用被動語態。只要像表格和例句呈現的那樣，用主動語態就可以了。

☆ 請注意，你必須把副詞改成形容詞。

☒ 錯誤

• The site <u>has seen</u> dramatic changes in 2010.

• The city centre <u>underwent considerably</u> transformations recently.

• The park <u>was experienced</u> spectacular developments during that time.

☑ 正確

• The site <u>saw</u> dramatic changes in 2010.

• The city centre has <u>undergone considerable</u> transformations recently.

• The park <u>experienced</u> spectacular developments during that time.

✎ **Practice 7**

請再次閱讀 Practice 1 的範例文章，並且把你能在 Practice 5 和 Practice 6 看到的所有用語都畫上底線。

🔑 範例答案

文章作者使用了 Practice 6 中的這個名詞片語：

underwent considerable changes

✎ **Practice 8**

現在請根據 **Practice 3** 的地圖來練習寫兩個開頭的句子，一個帶有動詞片語，另一個帶有名詞片語。

🔎 範例答案

我不知道你寫了什麼，但我的例子在這裡。請注意要使用現在完成式，因為這裡的兩張圖分別代表 Then 和 Now，而且沒有指明結束的時間。

• Anyold town centre has been significantly developed.

• Anyold town centre has undergone dramatic changes.

接下來，我們要繼續討論，來看一些你可以用來描述改變的動詞。

PART
1

字彙：改變 Vocabulary: Changes

✎ **Practice 9**

請研究表格、例句和下方的說明。

verbs: changes					
constructive changes		**destructive changes**		**no change**	
English	**中文**	**English**	**中文**	**English**	**中文**
add (sth) to	添加	chop down	砍倒	remain as it is/was	保持原樣
build	建立	clear	清除	remain untouched	保持不變
construct	建造	cut down	降低	leave (s/th) untouched	保持不變
convert (s/th) into	轉換為	destroy	破壞	leave (s/th)	未開發
develop	發展	demolish	拆除	undeveloped	
establish	建立	divert	轉移	leave (s/th) alone	讓某人獨處
expand	擴大	drain	排出	spare	騰出
extend	延伸	flatten	整平		
modernize	現代化	knock down	擊倒		
open	打開	remove	移除		
plant	栽種	ruin	毀壞		
reconstruct	重建	pave over	鋪平		
relocate	搬遷				
renovate	修復				
replace	取代				
set up	建立				
turn (s/th) into	擴大				
widen					
sample sentences					

- A new sports centre has been opened in the centre of town.
- The city government has modernized the traffic system in the centre of town.
- The old forest to the north of the village has been chopped down.
- The developers demolished all the old buildings by the canal.
- The old church remained untouched.

☆ 首先，請確定你知道每個動詞的意思。

☆ 你會看到三類動詞。首先是用於描述正面或有建設性 (constructive) 的變化，以及事情已經形成或是新事物已經確立的情況。

還有一些動詞是用來描述負面或破壞性 (destructive) 的變化，也就是事物會消失。

最後，有些動詞可以用來描述沒有變化 (no changes) 的事物。

☆ 請注意，這裡彙整的動詞是基本的不定詞形式。你必須根據地圖顯示的時間來改變時態。

☆ 你還要決定是否使用主動或被動時態。

☆ 在第一組中，你會發現 add、convert 和 turn 這幾個動詞有點棘手，因為它們有從屬介系詞。看看這些例子：〈They added a suburb to the city / A suburb was added to the city.〉〈The builders converted the old factory into a coffee shop / The old factory was converted into a coffee shop.〉〈The city government turned the suburb into a city / A suburb was turned into a city.〉請注意受詞在主動和被動句子裡的位置。

☆ 第三組動詞用來描述沒有變化的情況，remain as it is/was 以及 remain untouched 不能用在被動語態。leave (s/th) untouched, leave (s/th) alone, 和 spare 可以用在主動或被動語態，例如：〈The planners left the old mill untouched / The old mill was left untouched.〉〈The planners left the old mill alone / The old mill was left alone.〉〈The planners spared the ancient tree / The ancient tree was spared.〉

☆ 請注意，這些動詞不能用在現在簡單式。因為它們用來描述變化，也因為變化永遠都與時間有關，所以用這些動詞描述變化卻沒有時間，是一件很不合理的事。

☆ 現在，我要告訴你如何正確使用時態。

PART
1

請研究以下表格、例句和下方的說明。

describing changes in the finished past time:	
active	**passive**
• The developers chopped down the trees in 2014. • The planners renovated the old mill in 2015.	• The trees were chopped down in 2014. • The old mill was renovated in 2015.
describing results in the unfinished present time:	
• The developers have chopped down the trees. • The planners have renovated the old mill.	• The trees have been chopped down. • The old mill has been renovated.
describing proposed future changes:	
• The developers will chop down the trees. • The planners will probably renovate the old mill.	• The trees will be chopped down. • The old mill will probably be renovated.

☆ 因為很重要,所以我再重複一次:如果地圖含有已經結束的過去時間,請用過去簡單式,就像上述 Practice 1 的地圖;如果地圖顯示未結束的現在時間,如前面 Practice 3 的地圖所示,請用現在完成式;如果地圖顯示未來可能的改變,則用 will。

☆ 請注意主動動詞的主詞。主詞通常會是像 the developers、the planners、the builders、the town council 以及 the city government 等等。在這些名詞當中,請注意哪些必須加上 s 表示複數。如果你想用被動語態,請確定助動詞 be 與主詞一致。

> ⊠ 錯誤
> • The city planner modernise the centre of town.
> • The wetlands has been drained and the trees has been chopped down.
> • The ancient forest has left alone.

☑ 正確

- The city <u>planners</u> <u>have modernised</u> the centre of town.
- The wetlands <u>have</u> been drained and the trees <u>have</u> been chopped down.
- The ancient forest <u>has been left</u> alone.

✎ Practice 11

請再次閱讀 **Practice 1** 的範例文章，把你在 **Practice 9** 看到的所有用語都畫上底線，並請注意時態的使用。

🔑 範例答案

希望你有在範例文章中看出這九個動詞：

- was built
- were constructed
- was converted into
- was built
- expanded

- was added to
- drained
- chopped down
- cleared

☆ 請注意它們全部都用過去簡單式，因為地圖清楚顯示時間已經結束。
☆ 也請注意哪些動詞是被動語態，哪些是主動語態。

✎ Practice 12

現在，請用四個句子描述你在前面 **Practice 3** 的地圖中看到的所有變化。

🔑 範例答案

在這裡提供一些範例。請注意範例中使用的時態，以及我用的主動和被動態。在句子三中，請注意我如何使用 used to 來強調當下狀態和先前狀態之間的差異。

1. The old Broad Street has been widened and turned into a motorway.
2. A roundabout has been built in the centre of the town.
3. The planners have chopped down all the trees and built new flats where the trees used to stand.
4. The park has been destroyed and paved over to make room for a car park.

字彙：時間字串 Vocabulary: Time Chunks

　　我們現在來看一下在這類任務中可能會使用的兩種字彙：撰寫和時間 (time) 有關的內容，以及和位置 (location) 有關的內容。先從時間開始看。

Practice 13

請研究表格、例句和下方的說明。

finished time chunks	unfinished time chunks
over the period	during this time
from X to Y	during the X year period
during that time	so far
during the X year period	recently
between X and Y	
X years ago	

sample sentences	

- From 1970 to 2010 the town underwent many changes.
- During the 10 year period, the town changed considerably.
- Recently the area has changed considerably.
- So far, the changes have focused on the north part of the area.

☆ 看到時間已經結束的字眼時，請用過去簡單式，就像 Practice 1 的地圖中已清楚說明在某個已經結束的時間裡，所有改變都已經發生了。

☆ 看到時間尚未結束的字眼時，請用現在完成式，就像 Practice 3 的地圖中只顯示 Then 和 Now。

☆ During the X year period 可以用過去簡單式，也可以用現在完成式。

☒ 錯誤

- From 1930 to 1960 the town <u>has undergone</u> many changes.
- Ten years ago, the town <u>has changed</u> considerably.
- The town <u>changed</u> a lot recently.

☑ 正確

- From 1930 to 1960 the town <u>underwent</u> many changes.
- Ten years ago, the town <u>changed</u> considerably.
- The town <u>has changed</u> a lot recently.

字彙：位置字串 Vocabulary: Location Chunks

✎ **Practice 14**

請研究表格、例句和下方的說明。

location chunks	
to the north/south/east/west	next to the X
to the north/south/east/west of the X	beside the X
to the north east/north west/south east/south west of the X	near the X
to the right/left of the X	by the X
in the north/south/east/west	… nearby.
in the north/south/east/west of the X	north
between the X and the Y	south
among the Xs	east
in the middle/centre of the X	west
through the middle/centre of the X	north east/north west
on the other side of the X	south east/south west
across from the X	by the edge of the X
opposite the X	at the edge of the X
on the north/south/east/west/side of the X	from north to south
	from east to west
	outside the X
sample sentences	

- The forest to the north east of the village has been chopped down.
- The buildings in the north of the city have all been renovated.
- A road has been built by the canal.
- A railway line running from north to south has been built.

☆ 說明位置時請使用明確的羅盤方位而不是 left 或 right，因為 left 和 right 的意義很模糊，它們會隨著觀察者的位置不同而改變。只有當意義完全清楚時，才可以使用 left 和 right。

☆ To the north of the town 表示有兩個東西，一個是城鎮，另一個是城鎮以外的某個東西。而 in the north of the town 也表示有兩個東西，其中一個東西在另一個東西裡面。

☆ 請注意是 beside，而不是 besides。

☆ 請注意 near 的後面不是接 to。

☆ 請將 nearby 放在句子或子句的結尾。Nearby 是副詞，所以它後面不接任何東西。

☆ between X and Y 的意思是，某個東西的位置只在兩個東西的中間。

☆ among the Xs 的意思是，某個東西的位置在兩個以上的東西之間。如果用這個字串，請不要忘記 X 要用複數名詞。

PART
1

☆ 請用 from north to south 或 from east to west 來描述道路、河流、鐵路和其他邊界的方向。

☆ 請格外小心這些字串裡的小詞，尤其要注意 the 及介系詞。這些用語很容易用錯，也是考生們在 IELTS Writing Task 1 裡得分很低的原因之一。

☒ 錯誤

• The old bridge nearby the mill has been renovated.

• A new bank has been built besides the park.

• A memorial has been built among the tree.

• A car park has been built next to shopping centre.

☑ 正確

• The old bridge near the mill has been renovated.

• A new bank has been built beside the park.

• A memorial has been built among the trees.

• A car park has been built next to the shopping centre.

請再次閱讀 **Practice 1** 的範例文章，並把你在 **Practice 13** 和 **Practice 14** 看到的所有用語都畫上底線。

🔑 範例答案

希望你有找到以下這些範例：

〈Practice 13 時間字串〉

during the 40 year period　　　　　　during that time

〈Practice 14 位置字串〉

to the south east of the　　　　　　to the north east

from north to south　　　　　　　　to the north west of the

in the middle of the　　　　　　　　to the east of the

outside the

Practice 16

以前面 **Practice 3** 的地圖為依據，再次閱讀以下範例文章。請注意你使用的時態和文章組織。然後從 **Practice 13** 和 **Practice 14** 中選擇適當的字串填入空格裡。

The town centre of Anyold Town has been dramatically transformed. In fact most of the old town has disappeared and been developed.

The biggest change is that the old Broad Street has been widened and turned into a motorway which runs right (1) _____. A roundabout has been built right (2) _____ old town centre and the old buildings which used to stand there have been demolished to make room for it.

Another big change is that a huge shopping centre has been constructed (3) _____ motorway, (4) _____ Upper Street. (5) _____ road an enormous car park has been built, connected to the shopping centre by a tunnel. The old park, which used to stand there, has been paved over, and the trees which used to stand (6) _____ Broad Street have also been cut down.

🔑 **範例答案**

首先，希望你有注意到這裡用了現在完成式、主動和被動態來描述這張地圖。其次，你有注意到文章組織嗎？文中的重點是兩個主要變化 (major)，也就是公路和購物中心，並且用兩個小段落來描述它們。這些小段落裡還有 minor, secondary，即微小、次要的變化。空格裡的答案如下：

(1) through the centre of the town
(2) in the middle of the
(3) to the south of the
(4) to the west of
(5) On the other side of the
(6) on the north side of

請注意 (4) 和 (6) 少了最後的 the。這是因為其後接的字是專有名詞 (Upper Street, Broad Street)，所以你不該在專有名詞前用 the。

在你結束這個單元之前，請將下列清單看過，確定你能將所有要點都勾選起來。如果有一些要點你還搞不清楚，請回頭再研讀本單元的相關部分。

☐ 我知道如何研究、理解地圖。
☐ 我知道如何把我的想法組織成 major changes 和 secondary changes。
☐ 我知道了解地圖上顯示的時間非常重要。
☐ 我知道我應該用過去簡單式描述已結束時間的變化，用現在完成式描述未結束時間下造成的目前改變，以及用 will 描述未來可能的改變。
☐ 我知道有時候當我在描述地圖時必須用被動態的動詞，有時候則用主動態的動詞。
☐ 我已經學到許多有助於寫作與改變及描述時間、位置有關的字彙。
☐ 我已經練習了很多寫作。

EXAM TIP BOX

✓ 在寫和地圖相關的內容時，請試著（以正確的時態）混用主動和被動態動詞。

✓ 這樣做可以讓主考官知道你能夠掌握這兩種動詞，也可以幫助你得到更高的分數。

Unit 7

寫下你的答案──
描述過程

**Writing Your Answer–
Writing about Processes**

在前面四個單元裡，你學到如何描述和圖表、柱狀圖、圓餅圖或地圖有關的內容；你學到如何描述可以從圖中觀察到的變動，以及比較這些圖。在這個單元裡，我們將把重點放在不同類型的任務上：你必須根據一張圖片或圖表描述一個過程。這部分做起來比看起來還簡單，因為你實際上只需要把重點放在三個領域的用字：序列標記 (sequence markers)、被動態動詞 (passive verbs)，以及目的和結果 (purpose and result)。稍後，我們將從如何分析圖片和組織你的答案開始談起。

✐ Practice 1

請看以下的題目、研究圖表，並閱讀範例文章。

The diagram illustrates the process of making cheese.

Summarize the information by selecting and reporting the main features and make comparisons where relevant.

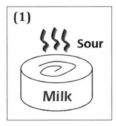
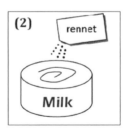
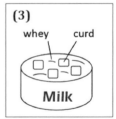

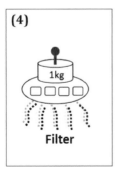
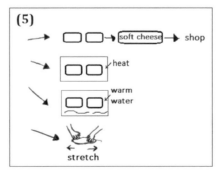
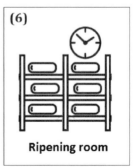

〈Figure 1〉

124

The process of making cheese starts when milk is allowed to go sour and rennet is added to it. By this method, the milk is separated into two parts: curds, a solid substance, and whey, a liquid.

In the next stage, the whey is pressed out of the curd, making it harder and easier to cut into squares. The curd cubes are heated during the next stage to make harder cheeses, or the curd cubes can be packaged and sold as softer cheeses. During this stage, there are also other processes which are done to produce different tastes and textures. For example, the curd is washed in warm water, resulting in a mild tasting cheese. Or it can be stretched and pulled about, making a softer cheese suitable for cooking.

During the final stage, the cheese is left to ripen for different lengths of time, the different lengths of time resulting in different flavours.

PART
1

分析圖片和組織你的答案
Analysing the Visual and Organising Your Response

在 Unit 2 裡有說明過如何分析圖片和題目。當時，我們把重點放在折線圖、柱狀圖和圓餅圖，但是對於圖表的著墨不多；在 Unit 6 裡，我們看過分析地圖的過程。而用你在這些單元中學到的方法，經過調整後，再加上大量的常識就可以用在分析圖表上。

分析題目和說明文字

1. 將題目和說明文字裡任何有用的字彙都畫上底線。試著在你的答案裡重複使用這些字彙。當然，如果你有自信可以改得正確的話，也可以改變其中的用字。例如，你可以將名詞改成動詞。

分析圖表

2. 請確定你知道圖表中，過程的起始點和結束點，以及不同的階段。在這個過程中，上面的任務從左上角開始，但從那之後可能會往任何方向走。不要把圖表的過程和過程的方向搞混了。

3. 現在，請找出有多少階段。在圖表中，你可以看到各階段的編號（如：Practice 1），但也可能不會有編號。如果它們有編號，那麼你的答案也應該要有一樣的階段號碼。如果他們都沒有編號，請用你的常識想一想，最好要有多少階段。請不要漏掉任何一個階段。

4. 圖表中應該有給你關鍵的詞彙。請看這個詞彙是名詞還是動詞，並確定你有在答案裡正確使用它。

5. 當你在研究圖表時，請思考你要用什麼 verbs 來描述這個過程。

6. 當你在研究圖表時，請思考你可以描述哪些目的和結果 (purposes and results)。

7. 如果你拿到一張看起來很複雜的圖表，請運用你的常識來看它。例如，你可能會看到兩個過程同時發生，然後合而爲一。你要怎麼形容這種狀況呢？這裡的原則和我之前描述過的方法一樣，所以最重要的是，別驚慌！

　　這裡有一張分析圖表資訊的清單。

✎ **Practice 2**

請研究下面的清單。

分析數據清單：圖表
1. 將題目和說明文字裡任何有用的詞彙都畫上底線。 2. 找到圖表中過程的起始點和結束點。 3. 注意並計算階段。 4. 把圖表裡的關鍵詞彙畫上底線。 5. 想一想你要用什麼動詞來描述這些過程。 6. 想一想你可以強調的目的和結果是什麼。 7. 如果圖表看起來很複雜，請運用常識來做判斷。

請看下方的圖表,並使用清單來分析圖中顯示的資訊。思考一下你要如何組織答案。

The diagram illustrates the process of refining iron from ore.

Summarize the information by selecting and reporting the main features and make comparisons where relevant.

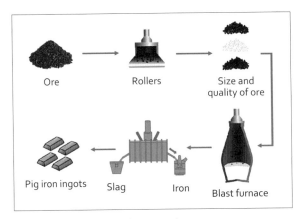

〈Figure 2〉

　　稍後在本單元裡,你會看到這個圖表的一篇範例文章,你可以把自己的想法與範例的答案相互比較。就組織而言,這種寫作任務的最大挑戰是如何把過程組織成不同的階段。在一般的開頭句之後,你必須將過程分成不同階段,並用我們稱為序列標記 (sequence markers) 的用語來清楚標記這些階段。

序列標記 Sequence Markers

✎ Practice 4

請研究以下表格、例句和下方的說明。

sequence markers	
The process of X starts with n.p.	in the next stage
The process of making X starts when v.p.	in this stage
First,	in the final stage
Second,	in the second stage
Next,	during the next stage
After that,	during the second stage
After this,	during this stage
Then,	during the final stage
Finally,	
While this has been happening, v.p.	
Meanwhile,	
At the same time,	
It's during this stage that v.p.	

☆ 在左欄中，你會看到用大寫字母開頭的表達用語。這些用語出現在句子的開頭。

☆ 在右欄中，你會看到它們沒有用大寫。這表示它們可以出現在句首或句中。如果你把它們放在句首，請確定你有用大寫並且加上逗號。例如：Sugar is added in the next stage to make it sweet. 也可以寫成 In the next stage, sugar is added to make it sweet.

☆ 你可以把階段數到第二階段，但在那之後，請使用像 next 或 then 這樣的字來描述，不要用 third、fourth 等字。

☆ 在被動態的字串裡，Then 也可以出現在第一個動詞後面。例如：The ore is then washed. 或 The beans are then dried.。

☆ 如果圖表顯示有兩個過程同時發生，或是有第二個過程在某個時間點融入第一個過程時，請使用 While this has been happening, v.p. / Meanwhile, / At the same time。

☆ 請注意逗號 (,) 和大寫。

☒ 錯誤

- <u>in</u> the next stage the beans are washed.
- <u>Finally</u> the final product is sent to the shop.
- The wine <u>then</u> is stored for a few years.

☑ 正確

- <u>In</u> the next stage the beans are washed.
- <u>Finally,</u> the final product is sent to the shop.
- The wine is <u>then</u> stored for a few years.

🖉 **Practice 5**

請回到 **Practice 1** 的範例文章，將任何序列標記例子都畫上底線，並注意這些字是如何使用的。

🔎 範例答案

你應該找到共五個例子。

- The process of making cheese starts when
- In the next stage,
- during the next stage
- During this stage,
- During the final stage,

被動態動詞 Passive Verbs

在上個單元裡，我告訴你可以用被動動詞和主動動詞來描述變化。但是在描述過程的任務中，你通常只能用被動態。所以，清楚了解被動語態的意義和用法非常重要。用 passive 這個字來形容這種動詞其實有點誤導，因為這種語法實際上沒有哪裡是「被動」的。

被動態的作用是把句子的重點轉移到曾被做過的事情，而不是做這件事情的人。這種語法的基本規則是：句子的第一個字——通常是動詞的主詞——是句子其他部分在談論的對象。

Scientists do research ＝（主動的動詞）強調科學家，他們是正在做這個行動的人。
Research is done by scientists ＝（被動的動詞）強調研究本身，而不是科學家。

很多時候，做動作的人並不重要，尤其當我們在描寫過程的時候，因為任何人、每一個人都可以做這個動作，重要的是行動本身以及被達成的事情。為了讓各位更明白我的意思，來看一些具體的例子。

✎ Practice 6

想想看這些句子是出自哪些文本內容？請將句子和它們的出處配對。

句子

1. Cows produce milk.
2. Milk is produced by cows.
3. Tobacco is grown in Brazil.
4. Brazil is one of the world's main tobacco growers.
5. Chocolate is made from the cocoa bean.
6. Chocolatiers make chocolate from cocoa beans.

原文內容

A. A text about Brazil
B. A text about chocolate

C. A text about cows

D. A text about milk production

E. A text about people who make chocolate

F. A text about tobacco production

🔑 範例答案

1 = C：這個句子的主詞是 cow，所以我們可以預期這個句子來自和牛有關的內容，與它們的用途、習慣和特徵有關。

2 = D：這句的主詞是 milk，所以我們可以預期原文的重點在於生產牛奶的不同階段。在這類內容中，牛不是重點。

3 = F：這個句子的主詞是 tobacco，所以我們預期原文的重點在於生產菸草的不同階段。

4 = A：這個句子的主詞是 Brazil，所以我們可預期原文的重點在於巴西經濟的不同面向，包括但不限於菸草生產。

5 = B：這句的主詞是 chocolate，所以我們可以預期原文內容是要告訴我們巧克力生產的其他不同階段。參與這個過程的人，他們的重要性不如過程本身，這就是為什麼我把 chocolate 放在句首，並且用被動態動詞。

6 = E：這個句子的主詞是 chocolatiers，所以我們可以預期這個句子出自於描述奇特、不尋常或有趣工作的一段文字，像是做巧克力的人，或是製作香水的人。這個「工作」出現在句首，因為它是句子其餘部分要說明的對象。

　　所以你現在明白了，被動態的目的是透過把訊息在句子裡移動，來強調不同的訊息。也就是把重要訊息移到句首，將不重要的訊息移到句尾，或完全省略。在強調機械或製造過程時，被動態是很常見的寫作技巧。在這類內容中，做這個動作的人並不重要，所以我們沒有提到他。

　　如果你在 IELTS 考試裡拿到這種任務，這是因為考官想刻意測試你是否了解被動態的目的，以及你是否知道如何正確使用它。

　　現在，你已經知道被動態的目的了，我們繼續來看它的形式。

請將 **Practice 6** 裡句子 **1-6** 的被動態動詞都畫上底線。

🔑 範例答案

1. Cows produce milk.
2. Milk is produced by cows.
3. Tobacco is grown in Brazil.
4. Brazil is one of the world's main tobacco growers.
5. Chocolate is made from the cocoa bean.
6. Chocolatiers make chocolate from cocoa beans.

你可以看到被動態是由 be 動詞所形成，主要動詞則是過去分詞：is produced / is grown / is made

　　在這些例子裡，be 動詞的動詞時態是現在簡單式 is，因為現在簡單式和時間無關。這種動詞時態最常用來描寫過程和程序。然而，這裡有一張表格比較了其他時態。

✎ **Practice 8**

請研究這張比較表，並且閱讀下方的說明。

passive verb chunks		
verb tense	**active**	**passive**
present simple	they make X	X is/are made
present continuous	they are making X	X is/are being made
present perfect	they have made X	X has been/have been made
past simple	they made X	X was/were made
past continuous	they were making	X was/were being made
past perfect	they had made X	X had been made
will future	they will make X	X will be made

☆ 為了保持時態一致，你必須隨時注意 be 動詞的時態。其他動詞永遠都是過去分詞。
☆ 在 IELTS Writing Task 1 中，你可能只需要用到過去簡單式、現在完成式或 will 來描述地圖裡的改變，就像我在前面單元所說明的。或是，你必須用現在簡單式來描

述過程,這是本單元的重點。

☆ 請小心處理主詞,要記住如果主詞是單數或不可數,則要用 is。

☆ 用 be made of + 一個物質 (ex. glass is made of sand.)。

☆ 用 be made from + 兩個或多個物質加在一起 (ex. chocolate is made from cocoa beans, milk, and sugar.)。

☆ 用 be made by + 某人做一個動作 (ex. drugs are made by chemists in a lab.)。注意,在被動態的句子裡,由於做動作的人(我們稱之為 agent)並不重要,所以這個資訊通常會省略。

☆ 用 be made by + Ving 來描述動作如何被完成 (ex. chocolate is made by adding milk and sugar to a mix of cocoa bean extract.)。

☆ 用 be made in + 地點 (ex. computer chips are mainly made in Taiwan.)。

☒ 錯誤

• Cheese <u>are</u> made of milk.

• Paper is made <u>by</u> wood.

• Perfume is made <u>from</u> perfumers.

• Cars <u>is</u> assembled on an assembly line.

☑ 正確

• Cheese <u>is</u> made of milk.

• Paper is made <u>of</u> wood.

• Perfume is made <u>by</u> perfumers.

• Cars <u>are</u> assembled on an assembly line.

　　除了上述的動詞時態之外,還有一些情態動詞 (modal verbs) 常被用於描述過程和程序。

Practice 9

請研究這張比較表，並且閱讀下方的說明。

active modal verbs	passive modal verbs
They **can** check X	X **can** be checked
They **have to** check X	X **has** to be checked
They **need to** check X	X **needs** to be checked
They **should** check X	X **should** be checked
They **allow** X to cool down	X is **allowed to** cool down

☆ 這裡的規則與 Practice 4 相同：在情態動詞的後面須用 be 動詞和過去分詞作爲主要動詞。

☆ 你可以看到，在這類被動態動詞中，通常在情態動詞之後的 V（have to V ＝ have to check），會成爲 be ＋ p.p.（have to be p.p. ＝ have to be checked）。

Practice 10

請再次閱讀 **Practice 1** 的範例文章，將所有被動態動詞以及 **Practice 9** 中的被動態情態動詞都畫上底線。

範例答案

你應該找到十個被動態的例子，包括 Practice 9 裡三個使用情態動詞的例子：

Passive verbs

- is added
- is separated into
- is pressed out
- are heated
- are done
- is washed
- is left

Modal passive verbs

- is allowed to
- can be packaged
- can be stretched

☆ 請注意動詞的主詞，必須使用和主詞一致的 is 或 are。

好的，我們繼續來練習被動態，將主動態動詞改成被動態動詞。

 **Practice 11**

請用被動態改寫以下句子。

1. Workers adjust the temperature so that the beans don't burn.

   → The temperature _____.

2. Workers allow the resulting mixture to cool for 12 hours.

   → The resulting mixture _____.

3. The company has already arranged the supply of raw materials in advance.

   → _____.

4. Workers assemble the machines in a few hours.

   → _____.

5. Technicians then broadcast the signal to the public.

   → _____.

6. Scientists have to check that nothing has contaminated the samples.

   → The samples _____.

7. Office workers collect the contact details and then store them in a database.

   → The contact details _____.

8. Machines first grind the sand into a very fine powder.

   → _____.

9. Workers then pump the mixture into molds.

   → _____.

10. Managers need to control the volume of goods passing through the store.

    → _____.

1. The temperature is adjusted so that the beans don't burn.
2. The resulting mixture is allowed to cool for 12 hours.
3. The supply of raw materials has already been arranged in advance.
4. The machines are assembled in a few hours.
5. The signal is then broadcast to the public.
6. The samples have to be checked that they have not been contaminated.
7. The contact details are collected and then stored in a database.
8. The sand is first ground into a very fine powder.
9. The mixture is then pumped into molds.
10. The volume of goods passing through the store needs to be controlled.

☆ 你可以看到在這些句子中，做動作的人被省略了，因為他們並不重要。

☆ 檢查你的主詞和動詞是否一致。

☆ 檢查你的動詞時態是否正確。舉例來說，第三句用現在完成被動態，第六句的第二個動詞也是。

☆ 請注意第二、第六和第十句的情態被動動詞。

　　在描述過程時，有一個問題是詞彙量不足，尤其是關鍵的名詞和動詞。題目通常會給你關鍵的名詞，如 Figure 1 中的 curd、whey，但題目往往不會給你任何動詞，因為你自己應該要知道這些動詞。

　　以下列出常見動詞字串，可用來描述許多不同的過程。

Practice 12

請研讀下表中的動詞和翻譯，並確實掌握它們的意思。

English	中文	English	中文
be added to	被加到	be lengthened	被加長
be adjusted to	調整為	be mixed together	被混合
be altered to	被改為	be mixed with Y	被與 Y 混合
be applied to	被應用於	be packaged	被包裝
be assembled	被組裝	be packed into	被包裝成
be bent (into X)	被彎曲成	be prepared	做好準備
be cast	被施放	be pressed	被按下

be chosen	被選中	be pumped out	被抽出來
be classified (into X)	被分類為	be put together	被放在一起
be combined with	與……結合	be released	被釋出
be cooled	被冷卻	be removed	被移除
be crushed	被粉碎	be rolled	被滾動
be cut into	被切成	be separated into X and Y	被分成 X 和 Y
be designed	被設計	be shipped	被運送
be developed	被開發	be shortened	被縮短
be discarded	被丟棄	be sieved	被篩過
be divided into	被分成	be sorted (into)	被排序成
be dried	被烘乾	be stored	被儲存
be evaluated	被評估	be stretched	被延展
be extracted	被提取	be transported	被運送
be flattened	被整平	be thrown away	被丟掉
be ground into	被磨成	be used to V	被用於
be hardened	被硬化	be washed	被洗
be heated	被加熱	be welded together	被焊接在一起
be inserted into	被插入	be left to V	被留給

✏️ **Practice 13**

請再次研究 **Practice 3** 的圖表，然後從底下選出 **12** 個被動態動詞字串填入空格中。

The process of making iron is very old, but essentially quite simple. First, rocks containing iron in mineral form, are mined from the ground. This ore (1) _____ by heavy rollers into smaller pieces, and the pieces (2) _____ according to size and quality. They (3) _____ and impurities (4) _____. Then, the stones (5) _____ to the blast furnace in preparation for the next stage. At the blast furnace the ore (6) _____ to extremely high temperatures, and it's during this stage that the iron (7) _____ from the rocks. The iron sinks to the bottom of the blast furnace, where it (8) _____. The unwanted slag can (9) _____, but the pig iron (10) _____ into ingots. The ingots of pig iron (11) _____ with other metal ores and minerals to make other metals. For example, pig iron (12) _____ to make steel, the commonest use for iron.

be cast	be heated	be sorted
be combined with	be packaged	be thrown away
be crushed	be removed	be transported
be dried	be separated	be used to
be extracted	be shortened	be washed

🔑 範例答案

1. is crushed
2. are sorted
3. are washed
4. are removed
5. are transported
6. is heated
7. is separated
8. is extracted
9. be thrown away
10. is cast
11. are combined with
12. is used to

☆ 我希望你非常小心你的 be 動詞。例如，在空格 (1) 中必須使用 is，因為 ore 是不可數。然而，在空格 (2) 中必須使用 are，因為主詞是複數：pieces。

☆ 你必須清楚知道哪些名詞是可數，哪些是不可數。

目的和結果 Purpose and Result

我們現在要看看如何描寫動作的 purpose「目的」──它為什麼會被完成，以及 result「結果」──動作的結果是什麼。

Practice 14

請研究以下表格、例句和下方的說明。

purpose	to V, in order to V
result	Ving, resulting in n.p.
sample sentences	• The mixture is left to dry. • In order to make it attractive to the customer, the product is packaged in a beautiful box. • The product is wrapped in plastic in order to protect it during the journey. • Carbon dioxide gas is added to the liquid, making it fizzy. • Salt is added, resulting in a stronger taste.

☆ 就 IELTS Writing Task 1 而言，目的和結果之間的意義沒有太大的差異。例如：Carbon dioxide gas is added to the liquid, making it fizzy (*result*). / Carbon dioxide gas is added to the liquid to make it fizzy (*purpose*). 這兩個句子的意思差不多。

☆ 然而，resulting in 不能被改成 to result in。這樣改是錯的。

☆ 請注意，purpose 可以在動作的前面或後面，但 result 永遠都在後面。

☆ 請注意，在你增加和 result 有關的資訊時，前面要使用逗號 (,)。但當你在描寫 purpose 時，不要使用逗號。

☆ 不要用 Ving 來描述 purpose 或 result。例如：Carbon dioxide gas is added to the liquid for making it fizzy. 這樣寫是錯的。

☆ 使用 V 時也要用 to，不管是在描述 purpose 或 result。

☒ 錯誤

- The fabric is left <u>for drying</u>.
- The products are organized on shelves, <u>make</u> it easier for customers to find them.
- Preservatives are added <u>to result in</u> a longer lasting product.

☑ 正確

- The fabric is left <u>to dry</u>.
- The products are organized on shelves, <u>making</u> it easier for customers to find them.
- Preservatives are added, <u>resulting in</u> a longer lasting product.

✎ Practice 15

請再次閱讀 **Practice 1** 的範例文章以及 **Practice 13** 裡的文章,並且把所有目的和結果的範例都畫上底線。

🔑 範例答案

你應該找到共七個例子。

Practice 1

- making it harder
- to make harder cheeses
- to produce different tastes
- resulting in a mild tasting cheese
- making a softer cheese

Practice 13

- to make other metals
- to make steel

✎ Practice 16

使用方框中的三個動詞以及給定的資訊將 **purpose** 或 **result** 加入各個句子中。請看範例。

leave / improve / make

EX. Preservatives are added / the product last longer

Preservatives are added to make the product last longer.

Preservatives are added, making the product last longer.

1. Sugar is added / sweeter taste

_____

2. Milk is added / a lighter chocolate

_____

3. The beans are roasted / the flavor

_____

4. The beans can be roasted longer / them easier to grind

_____

5. The husks of the beans are removed and discarded / the beans smooth and shiny

_____

🔑 範例答案

1. Sugar is added to make a sweeter taste.
   Sugar is added, making a sweeter taste.
2. Milk is added, making a lighter chocolate.
   Milk is added to make a lighter chocolate.
3. The beans are roasted to improve the flavor.
   The beans are roasted, improving the flavor.
4. The beans can be roasted longer, making them easier to grind.
   The beans can be roasted longer to make them easier to grind.
5. The husks of the beans are removed and discarded, leaving the beans smooth and shiny.
   The husks of the beans are removed and discarded to leave the beans smooth and shiny.

☆ 你可以看到，在大多數的句子裡，你可以用 purpose 或 result，兩者皆可。
☆ 請注意結果句子裡使用的逗號 (,)。

在你結束這個單元之前，請將下列清單看過，確定你能將所有要點都勾選起來。如果有一些要點你還不清楚，請回頭再研讀本單元的相關部分。

☐ 我知道如何研究並理解圖表。

☐ 我知道我必須特別注意不同的階段。

☐ 我知道如何用序列標記顯示過程的不同階段。

☐ 我了解被動態的意義，以及在描寫過程時為什麼用被動態是很重要的。

☐ 在寫作過程當中，我知道如何使用被動態。

PART
1

☐ 我知道一些有用的情態被動動詞。

☐ 我知道 made of、made from、made by 和 made in 之間的差異。

☐ 我知道如何描寫在過程裡一個動作的 result，以及過程裡一個動作的 purpose。

☐ 我已經學了許多有助於描述過程的詞彙。

☐ 我已經練習了很多寫作。

EXAM TIP BOX

✓ 避免寫出像這種簡單子句的字串：X is done … and then Y is done … and then Z is done … and then A is done …. 這樣寫得不到高分。

✓ 思考一下你可以將過程裡的哪些階段描述成另一個之前或之後階段的目的或結果，並且寫出複句或複合句：X is done, in order to Y, resulting in Z。

✓ 這樣可以幫你得到更高的分數。

NOTES

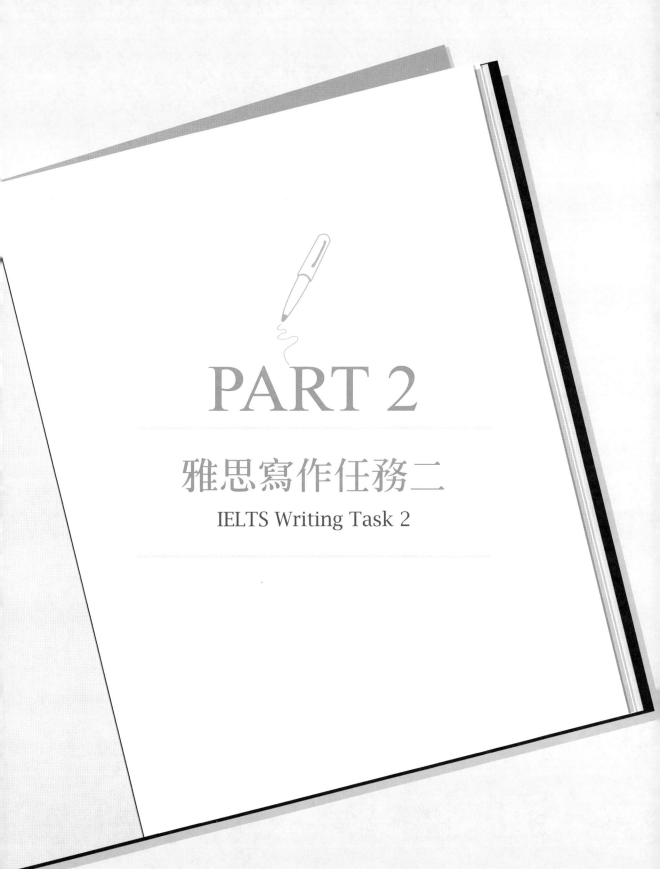

PART 2

雅思寫作任務二

IELTS Writing Task 2

Unit 8

寫作任務二介紹

Introduction to Task 2

任務描述 Task Description

正如我們在「雅思寫作概論」中學到的，Task 2 基本上是個論述性任務。題目會要你根據一個觀點、問題或議題提出論述。而根據不同情況，你可能需要針對問題提出解決方法、論述和證明一個看法、評價和反駁一個論點或觀點。這裡的重點是用語的說服力和組織的清晰度。

如果你以前做過 IELTS 測驗，就會知道 Task 2 的提示有兩個部分。

1. 一則聲明。這則聲明可能有兩種形式：「一個觀點」或是「一個問題／解決方法」。

> 觀點
>
> In recent years, many countries have become extremely concerned about the increase in crimes against immigrants. Better enforcement of the law and stricter punishments are necessary.

在這個觀點的範例中，你可以看到第一個句子描述了某一個狀況，第二個句子則針對該狀況提出一個觀點。

> 問題／解決方法
>
> Global warming has recently become the most urgent long term issue the world faces, and many people think not enough is being done to solve this problem.

2. 一個指示。

> 觀點
>
> Write an essay expressing your point of view.

在觀點的情況下，你必須同意或反對該觀點，並提出論述以表達反對或支持它的原因。

問題／解決方法

What problems are the effects of global warming causing us now, and what can we do to solve them?

在問題的狀況下，你必須針對該問題舉出更多例子，然後提出解決辦法。

　　這兩類題目都要求你透過論證來說服他人。其中很重要的是，你必須知道題目要求你寫的是哪一種類型的文章。爲了幫助你了解這一點，我們要進行一些練習，把重點放在說明文字上。

Practice 1

請閱讀在 **IELTS Writing Task 2** 中常見的說明文字，並將它們分類放進下方的表格。

- Discuss both of these views and give your own opinion.
- Discuss possible ways of Ving ….
- Discuss the advantages and disadvantages of this.
- Do you believe that v.p. …?
- How do you think v.p. …?
- Identify the problems and suggest ways to V….
- To what extent do you agree or disagree?
- What are some ways to V…?
- What can governments do to V…?
- What should be done to V …?
- Which do you consider to be the best n.p. …?
- Write an essay expressing your point of view.

argument / opinion	problem / solution

請研究表格，並且閱讀下方說明。

argument / opinion	problem / solution
• To what extent do you agree or disagree? • Write an essay expressing your point of view. • Do you believe that v.p. …? • Discuss the advantages and disadvantages of this. • Discuss both of these views and give your own opinion. • Which do you consider to be the best n.p. …?	• How do you think v.p. …? • What should be done to V …? • Discuss possible ways of Ving …. • Identify the problems and suggest ways to V …. • What are some ways to V …? • What can governments do to V …?

☆ 請仔細確認 argument / opinion 的說明文字，題目可能只要你提出觀點，或還要你討論相反意見。事實上，就算只寫一句相反的意見，你都應該正反意見並陳。

☆ 請注意，在 problem / solution 的說明文字中，有許多用語是用來建議作法，例如：ways to, What can X do to, should be done to 等等。另外也需留意 What do you think（你的意見）和 How do you think（你的建議）之間的差異。

　　整個寫作測驗的時間只有一小時，所以你必須非常嚴格地控制時間。建議花在 Task 2 的寫作時間不能超過 45 分鐘，其中包括 10 分鐘用來分析題目和規劃你的答案，30 分鐘用來寫作，5 分鐘檢查並修改文章。

高分寫作標準 Criteria for Success

根據 IELTS 官方考試中心提供的資訊，寫作測驗 Task 2 的評分標準有六個。

1. Argument 論證

第一個標準是「論證」，所以這是最重要的標準。它指的是你組織想法的方式必須讓主考官覺得很有邏輯。你的想法必須有邏輯才能說服讀者。在接下來的單元裡，我會教你英文資訊的基本邏輯，以及該如何妥善的運用它。

2. Ideas 想法

第二個標準是想法的品質和關連度。你的想法必須讓人感覺明智又合理，並且有事實根據。假如他們讓你當主管，而你可以馬上解決某個問題的話，把這樣的解決方法直接寫出來可不好。主考官會假設你是一個明智且受過良好教育的人，至少在某種程度上已經認真考慮過這些問題。所以你的想法必須和主題有關。

3. Evidence 證據

這個標準和上一個標準，強調的是依據「由廣而專」的原則來組織文章，在下一個單元將可以學到更多相關細節。總之，你必須為你的意見舉出一些具體的例子，不管它是來自於你對這個世界的常識，或是自己個人的經驗。運用你的常識來舉例會比較好，因為這些知識可以說明比較高層次的思考和語言能力。主考官對你的個人故事沒什麼興趣，他們有興趣的是你的想法和思考能力。

4. Communicative quality 溝通品質

我們很難精確說明這個標準到底是什麼，但它實際的意思是指你的寫作內容帶給讀者的整體印象。這個印象來自兩方面：你用英文表達想法的能力，以及你思考彼此相關、有趣且組織這些論點的能力。在這個標準裡，你必須達到這兩者才能得到高分。

5. Vocabulary 字彙

這個標準和下一個標準主要涉及的是語言。主考官會特別注意你所用的語彙。他會想看到你使用精準的相關字、同義字、常用來對該主題表達想法的詞彙,以及和這個主題相關的特定用語。在寫作內容中是否使用了大量詞彙,是你得到 6 分(以下)或 7 分(以上)的差異關鍵,這一點不只寫文章的時候是如此,對整個測驗來說都是一樣的。如果你想要得到高分,就必須認真增進你的字彙能力。

6. Sentence structure 句子結構

在 Unit 1,我們知道如果把這個標準放在 Task 1,它是要你著重在精準度。精準度在這裡也很重要,但更重要的是你必須具說服力。這表示你要以正確的句構來表達想法,並使用正確的動詞。在接下來的單元裡,你會學到可以幫助你更有說服力地表達、組織想法的用語,但你可以自己決定是否要學習或完全正確地使用它們。

至此可以看出,前面三個標準的重點在於組織,後面三個則側重於用語。這表示不管你的文法和字彙能力有多好,如果你沒有好的想法,並且正確組織這些想法,你就無法得到高分。當主考官閱讀你的文章時,他或她會把重點放在這六個要點上,並據此判斷你的表現。

寫作的過程 The Process of Writing

　　在 Uint 1，我們談過寫作的三個過程：having ideas「產生想法」、organising ideas「組織想法」，以及 writing ideas「寫下想法」。你已經學過如何在寫作 Task 1 的過程中運用這些知識。而要在寫作 Task 2 時運用這些知識也是差不多的道理。如果你把這三個過程拆開，效果會比較好。在此我會簡短地說明一下該怎麼做。有時間的話，你可以再回到 Unit 1 的這個部分重讀一次。

1. Having ideas 產生想法

　　這是在寫作過程中腦力激盪的部分。一般來說，當你在做腦力激盪時，應避免組織你的想法，而是把重點放在產生想法。然而在 IELTS 測驗中，由於時間緊迫，你必須在一開始就有非常簡單的組織。所以，我建議依據文章的類型來組織你的想法。如果是 argument / opinion「論證／意見」類的文章，你可以先決定你的意見是什麼，然後把你的意見組織成兩種：支持你的意見的想法，以及反對你意見的想法。如果是 problem / solution「問題／解決方法」的文章，你可以把你的想法分成兩種：problem「問題」，以及 solution「解決方法」。我將在下一個單元說明該怎麼做。

2. Organising ideas 組織想法

　　在英文裡，所有資訊都要根據基本的結構組織起來。這個基本結構是：

> **general ideas come first, followed by specific examples**
> 先寫一般想法，再寫具體例子

　　General「一般想法」和 specific「特定想法」之間，永遠都有一條明顯的差異和界線。這個結構非常重要，重要到文法和字彙也是用這種方式組織。中文的組織結構則很不一樣。在中文，一般和特定之間的差異並不重要，所以它們的界線並不清楚。舉一個最簡單的例子，中文裡的名詞並不會因為東西是一個或多個而產生變化，但是在英文裡會在字的後面加上 s 來表示複數，沒有 s 則表示一般性的東西。再看一個例子：

Doctors are usually overworked. → 意思是指一般的醫生（複數）。這句話並沒有指是哪一個特定的醫生，所以我們知道它說的是一般所有的醫生。

The doctor is overworked. → 意思是指某個特定的醫生。我們可以從句子前後的語言和脈絡，知道句中說的是指哪一個特定的醫生。

你必須提升對英文這個重要部分的敏感度。而在下一個單元你將學到更多。

3. Writing ideas 寫下想法

在本單元前面的內容中有提到過，這在寫作過程裡是屬於語言學的部分。你將在 Unit 10-Unit 14 當中著重於學習英文的細節。許多細節都需要靠記憶及充足的練習量。我再強調一次，你必須在 IELTS 測驗裡花時間把這些過程分開。做過練習後，它可以幫助你得到最佳結果。在下一個單元裡，我會要你把重點放在組織思考，而在 Unit 10-Unit 14，重點則要放在語言思考。

在你結束這個單元之前，請將下列的清單看過，確定你能將所有要點都勾選起來。如果有一些要點你還搞不清楚，請回頭再次研讀本單元的相關部分。

□ 我已經了解 Task 2 的測驗內容以及我必須做些什麼。

□ 我已經學到 Task 2 有兩種類型的文章：argument / opinion「論證／意見」的文章，以及 problem / solution「問題／解決方法」的文章。

□ 我已經做過分辨這兩種文章說明文字的練習。

□ 我已經學會該如何安排寫作 Task 2 的時間。

□ 我已經知道主考官會用哪六個標準來評判我的文章。

□ 我已經看過寫作的三個過程，也知道當我在從事任何寫作時，很重要的是把這些過程分開。

□ 我已經知道 IELTS Task 2 裡的三種不同寫作過程。

□ 我現在已經準備好要開始更深入地進行 Task 2 的寫作練習。

EXAM TIP BOX

✓ 整個寫作測驗的時間只有一小時，所以你必須非常嚴格地控制時間。建議花在 Task 2 的寫作時間不能超過 45 分鐘，其中包括 10 分鐘用來分析題目和規劃你的答案，30 分鐘用來寫作，5 分鐘檢查並修改文章。

✓ 你可以從 Task 1 或 Task 2 開始都沒有關係，但一定要嚴格控管時間。

✓ 如果你從 Task 1 開始寫，即使寫了 15 分鐘後還沒寫完，也要開始寫 Task 2。

✓ 如果你從 Task 2 開始寫，即使寫了 45 分鐘後還沒寫完，也要開始寫 Task 1。

✓ 你必須兩個任務都做得好，才會得到高分。

Unit 9

分析題目並規劃你的答案

**Analysing the Title and Planning
Your Answer**

前言與暖身練習 Warm Up

　　在這個單元裡，你將學習如何分析題目並規劃你的答案。本單元有許多相關的練習，這些練習很重要，因為透過大量的分析題目及規劃答案練習，能幫助你在考試時更快速、輕鬆地完成這件事，不但節省時間，也會讓你更有自信地進行接下來的寫作。

　　你先前之所以無法在考試取到高分，原因之一可能是因為你沒有先規劃答案。在開始寫作前先規劃答案才能有邏輯地組織你的想法，而不是想到什麼就寫什麼。不管你的語言能力有多好，如果沒有把想法組織起來就很難取得高分。意即為了得到高分，你必須表現出你能夠根據特定的模式組織自己的想法：general / specific「一般／特定」。在本單元稍後將會有更詳細的解說。

　　好的，你準備好要開始了嗎？接下來，我們將從你在 IELTS 寫作 Task 2 可能產生的問題開始。

✎ Practice 1

請研究這兩個題目敘述，列出你在寫作文章時可能產生的問題。

Topic 1

> The mass media, including television, radio and newspapers, have a great influence in shaping people's ideas.
>
> To what extent do you agree or disagree with this statement?

Topic 2

> The destruction of rain forests to create land for agricultural use is a serious problem.
>
> What are some of the common problems, and what can be done to reduce them?

🔑 範例答案

我當然不知道你寫了什麼，但是這裡有一些考生們常見的問題。以下排列沒有特別的順序，也許你會認同其中一些問題。

Q1 我不知道該寫什麼，我沒有想法，因爲我從來沒想過這個題目。

Q2「我對這個題目有很多想法，但我不知道該從哪裡下手」，或是「我不知道該如何組織我的想法。」

Q3 文章裡有些字彙我不懂。

Q4 我不知道我該做什麼。我該針對題目提出自己的看法嗎？我該明確反對或同意嗎？或是，我可以說「在某些情況下，A 選項比較好；在其他情況下，B 選項比較好」嗎？

Q5 我不知道從哪裡開始，該如何結束？

Q6 我不知道該寫多少段。

Q7 我不知道該怎麼用英文寫出一個段落。

在這個單元裡，我們來看看該如何處理這些問題。在 Unit 8（以及 Unit 1 的第三部分，還記得嗎？）裡，你學過寫作的三個思考過程：having ideas「產生想法」、organising ideas「組織想法」，以及 writing ideas「寫下想法」。在這裡我們將探討前面兩個過程：「產生想法」和「組織想法」。首先，我們要把重點放在分析題目並產生想法，接著透過組織你的想法來規劃出答案。

分析題目 Analysing the Title

分析題目和說明文字

1. **題目：請將關鍵字彙畫上底線**。請把重點放在字串和配合的字彙上，這樣你比較容易在自己的寫作中使用這些字彙。舉例來說，在 Practice 1 的 Topic 1 題目中，除了特定的字彙像是 mass media、television、radio 和 newspapers，你可以在 have a great influence in Ving 這個字串及 shape ideas 這種搭配詞畫上底線。這樣做可以讓你比較容易使用 influence 這個字彙，而且你最少有一個動詞可以用來表達想法：shape。又例如在 Topic 2，你可以把搭配詞 agricultural use 和 serious problem 畫上底線，然後把這些字用在你的文章裡，不過在使用時要確定你知道這些關鍵字彙的意思。雖然這裡不太可能會出現你不知道的字彙，但若真的有不認識的字，就要運用你的常識，並且試著從脈絡裡猜出它們的意思。如果文章裡有很多字彙你不懂，這表示你的閱讀量實在不夠。請記得，增加字彙量最好的方法就是盡可能多閱讀。

2. **說明文字：請確定你知道該做些什麼**。在 Unit 8 裡，你已學到 Task 2 有兩種類型的文章題目：argument / opinion「論證／意見」的文章，以及 problem / solution「問題／解決方法」的文章。

   A. 在 argument / opinion essay（例如 Practice 1 的 Topic 1），你須針對一個題目表達自己的意見，並且用好的理由和例子來支持你的意見。我建議提出明確的意見，而不要說：「在某些情況下，A 選項比較好；在其他情況下，B 選項比較好」。重點不在於你是否真的同意或反對，因為沒有人真的在意你的想法，大家在意的是你是否能提出論證。此外，你必須闡述問題的另一面，並且說明你不支持的原因。有些 argument / opinion essays 可能會要你討論某件事的優點和缺點，並且要你表達自己的意見。

   B. 在 problem / solution essay（例如 Practice 1 的 Topic 2），你必須更詳細地描述問題，並且提出一些該如何解決問題的建議。在作答時有一點很重要，就是不能只是鉅細靡遺地描述問題或只是提出解決方法。你必須兩者都要著墨，因為主考官想知道你是否懂得表達問題和解決方法。在本單元稍後將會教你該使用哪些用語來表達。

   現在，你知道該如何分析題目，那麼就讓我們繼續往下看看該如何透過腦力激盪，為你要寫的文章產生想法。

規劃你的答案：產生想法
Planning Your Answer: Generating Ideas

🔍 腦力激盪

3. 把你腦力激盪出來的**想法整理成簡單的表格**，這樣可以得到非常基本的結構。我們稍後會練習這部分。

4. 當你在做腦力激盪時，請**避免寫完整的句子**。相反的，請把**重點放在字彙**，尤其是搭配字，並且把搭配字寫在表格裡正確的欄位。如果字很長，不要把它全部寫出來，只要寫前面一個音節來幫助你記憶即可。盡量多節省一些時間。專心讓想法湧現，然後在它消失之前把它寫下來！

5. 試著**幫你的想法思考出一些具體的例子**，並且試著**為你的建議想出一些結果**。

6. 試著**平衡你的想法**，讓你在「論證／意見」的文章裡，有三分之二的想法支持你的意見，三分之一的想法反駁你的意見；以及在「問題／解決方法」的文章裡，有三分之一的問題想法，三分之二的解決想法。

✏️ Practice 2

請針對 **Practice 1** 的 **Topic 1** 來做腦力激盪。把你的想法整理在下方的表格。

opinion: Agree	
reasons I agree with this statement	**reasons I disagree with this statement**

請參考表格內容，並且閱讀下方的說明。

opinion: Agree	
reasons I agree with this statement	**reasons I disagree with this statement**
• positive or negative influence • happens whether they want it or not • TV, radio, newspaper — traditional media • new media — facebook, social networking, go online, twitter, LINE • exposed to ideas from • virtually impossible - escape	• views shaped by other people's views • come into contact with other people • independent thinking • influence is exaggerated

☆ 在表格中可以看到我先決定好自己的意見是什麼，然後再把想法大致上組織成兩種類型：我贊成的原因，以及我反對的原因。

☆ 你可以看到我贊成題目的想法，所以贊成那一欄的內容比較多，但是請注意我也在反對那一欄放了一些內容。你必須稍微平衡兩方意見。

☆ 你可以看到我沒有寫完整的句子，並且主要是寫出搭配字或是片語。

☆ 此外，請注意我如何舉出具體的例子：new media examples: facebook, social networking, go online, twitter, LINE；以及 traditional media examples: TV, radio, newspapers.

☆ 現在，先不要擔心我如何組織這些字。當它們出現在我腦海時，我只是把它們寫下來，然後直接放進正確的欄位。

在我們開始討論如何組織這些字彙之前，先用「問題 / 解決方法」的題目來進行相同的任務。

✏ Practice 3

請針對 **Practice 1** 的 **Topic 2** 來做腦力激盪。把你的想法整理在下方的表格。

problem	solution

🔑 範例答案

請參考表格內容，並且閱讀下方的說明。

problem		solution
• local areas	• flora and fauna	• people eating meat all the time
		• government – urgently legislate
• groundcover is burnt	• the loss of	• prevent companies from stripping
• planet as a whole		the land
	• terrible air pollution	• enforce the laws – send a message
• causes	• logging	
• impacts	• soil erosion	
• affects	• flooding	
• contributes to	• global warming	
• loss of wildlife	• surrounding	
• natural habitat	countries	

☆ 針對這個「問題／解決方法」的文章，我把想法大致上組織成兩種類型：problem 和 solution。

☆ 當想法出現在我腦海時，我只是簡短把它寫下來。你可以看到我寫下可以在這篇文章裡使用的動詞：causes, impacts, affects, contributes to，並把它們放在 problem 欄位，但我大概也會在文章裡的 solution 部分使用它們。

☆ 你可以再次看到我沒有寫完整的句子，只是一些搭配字或是片語。

☆ 請注意，我也思考了解決方法的一些結果：enforce the laws – send a message。

☆ 再次提醒，在這個階段時，先不要擔心想法的組織。

　　在下一個部分，我們會討論如何組織你的想法，以及如何安排段落。現在這個部分很重要，你不應該跳過它。首先，我將說明在英文裡所有資訊都根據哪些基本結構組織起來。然後，我會告訴你如何把這些知識用在第一段的寫作上。

英文的資訊結構 Information Structure in English

在先前的單元裡，你已經學過 general 和 specific 之間的差異。為了幫你清楚了解一般資訊和特定資訊之間的清楚差異，我們要進行幾個任務。

Practice 4

請組織這些文字。

orange	green	colour	blue	yellow	purple
car	truck	motorbike	vehicle	bus	coach
table	chair	furniture	bed	closet	bench

範例答案

☆ 我希望你可以看到，組織文字最好的方式是這樣：colour 是一般性概念，orange、green、blue、yellow、purple 是具體的例子；vehicle 是一般性概念，car、truck、motorbike、bus、coach 是具體的例子；furniture 是一般性概念，table、chair、bed、closet、bench 是具體例子。另一種表達方式是 orange、green、blue、yellow 和 purple 是顏色的種類等等。

☆ 這裡很重要的是要看出這些字之間的 general-specific 的關係：vehicle、colour 和 furniture 是 general，其他字則是這些一般文字的 specific 例子。

我們再來試試看更複雜的資訊。

Practice 5

請將以下文字分類。注意，你須判斷出有哪些類別，以及有多少字。

Africa	brain	dog	government	lung	orange	professional
after	architect	doctor	horse	mammal	organ	Scarlatti
apple	cat	fruit	in	monarchy	pear	tyranny
Asia	composer		kidney	Europe	preposition	Beethoven
at	continent		lawyer			democracy
Bach						

請參考以下表格檢查你的答案，並且閱讀我的說明。

general							
mammal	composer	fruit	preposition	continent	government	professional	organ
specific							
horse dog cat	Bach Beethoven Scarlatti	apple orange pear	after in at	Asia Europe Africa	democracy monarchy tyranny	architect doctor lawyer	lung kidney brain

☆ 希望你可以看出這些字被組織成一般想法和具體例子。例如 horse、dog 和 cat 是 mammals 的例子。

至此，你應該很清楚一般和特定的概念，接著就來看看該如何運用這個知識寫出一個段落。

英文裡的段落通常先有一般性的陳述。這個一般性的陳述叫做主題句 (topic sentence)。主題句是用來告訴讀者這個段落的大意，之後，會有更多具體的資訊——通常是三個或四個句子——來支撐這個一般性的陳述。請看下圖。

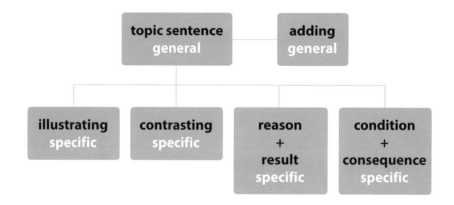

請注意，主題句之所以是主題句，並不是因為它是第一個句子，而是因為它含有最一般性的資訊。其他句子則都跟著主題句，而且其他句子之所以有意義，是因為它們都以某種方式指涉主題句。也就是說，如果我們把主題句從段落中剔除，就很難清

楚說明其他句子指涉的對象是誰，以及這個段落大致上在說些什麼。我們來進行一個任務，讓你可以更了解我的意思。

✎ Practice 6

請從下方清單選擇一個合適的主題句，以完成該段落。

_____. There are three main types of tax. The first is personal income tax, which is tax charged on the money which people earn from their jobs. Another kind of tax is corporation tax, which is a tax paid by businesses and corporations on the profits they make each year. Then there is value added tax, or sales tax, which is a tax paid by someone buying goods or services. This kind of tax is usually a percentage of the total cost of the purchased goods or services.

---

1. A filibuster is the process of delaying or preventing the passing or making of a new law by extending the discussion time about the new law and thus delaying the vote on the new law.

2. In recent years, the destruction of the rainforests in South East Asia and the Amazon basin has been increasing.

3. Microcredit, also known as microfinance, is the lending of money to poor people who live in the countryside, especially in developing countries.

4. Taxation is how the state raises money from its citizens to pay for the services the state offers to its citizens, and to pay for the costs of government.

5. Volcanoes are places where magma, which is a kind of melted rock below the earth's surface, pushes through to the surface of the earth in an eruption, or explosion.

🔑 範例答案

☆ 最適合這個段落的主題句是第 4 句。你也許有答對，因為 tax 這個字不斷出現在段落中。

☆ Taxation 是個一般性的字，意思是徵稅的過程；Tax 則是個具體的字眼。這裡的主題句說的是一般的徵稅，其他的句子則都說明具體的徵稅種類，就像 colour 是一般性的字眼，blue 則是顏色的一種。

☆ 所以，主題句之所以是主題句，是因為它含有最一般性的資訊，而不是因為它是第一個句子。實際上，主題句經常出現在段落的中間，或有時候出現在段落的後半

段，但讀者之所以知道那是主題句，靠的不是它的位置，而是因爲它和其他句子的一般性關係。

☆ 然而，在進行 IELTS 寫作時，你應該把你的主題句放在文章段落的開頭。

我們再來進行另一個任務，把這部分釐清。

Practice 7

請將句子正確排列。哪一句是主題句？

A. Corpus linguistics is useful because it allows researchers to study huge amounts of language very quickly.

B. Corpus linguistics is the term used to describe the analysis of language using computers.

C. In order to do corpus linguistics, or computational language research, you need two things: a large body of language, called a corpus, and a software program called a concordancer.

D. The bigger the corpus is, the more useful it is for this kind of research.

E. The concordancer can search through the corpus very quickly to find examples of language use the researcher is interested in.

F. The corpus is stored electronically on a computer and includes all kinds of samples of spoken and written language.

主題句：_____

第二句：_____

第三句：_____

第四句：_____

第五句：_____

第六句：_____

範例答案

請看看正確答案，並且閱讀下面的說明。

主題句：B
第二句：C
第三句：F
第四句：D
第五句：E
第六句：A

☆ 首先，如果你看不懂句子中的字彙，請不用擔心。你不是非得要知道這些字彙的意思才能了解一般／特定的模式，而這正是我要你在這裡特別注意的。

☆ B 是主題句，因為它是最一般性的句子：它介紹和說明了 corpus linguistics「語料語言學」這個詞。其他句子則提供了更多語料語言學的具體資訊。

☆ C 是下一個句子，因為它告訴我們 corpus linguistics 更具體的細節：我們需要的兩個東西。接著，F 是下一句，因為 corpus 是 C 句提到的第一個詞，而 D 句用更具體的細節說明 F 句。C 句的第二個詞是 concordancer，這個詞在 E 句有更多具體的說明和解釋。

☆ 最後，整個段落用 A 句概括。亦即如果我們沒有一開始就讀到其他資訊，我們不會知道為什麼語料語言學有用。

☆ 另一方面，你或許會把 A 句放在第二句，因為它更一般性。這樣做也可以。

☆ 這裡的重點在於，你必須開始用 general / specific 來作思考。如果你了解這一點，那就太棒了！

　　現在你已經學到英文組織資訊的方式，以及該如何安排段落，讓我們把這個知識應用在本單元稍早前練習的字彙上。

將想法組織成段落
Organising Ideas into a Paragraph

你已經學到如何腦力激盪出想法，現在你必須根據 general / specific 的思考模式來組織它們。

7. 先判斷你知道哪些字彙是一般性的，然後把那些字用在你的主題句。然後，判斷要將哪一個字彙加入主題句的具體資訊之中。就像你在組織字彙一樣，思考一下文章最後的形式，想一下你需要幾個段落。

現在用前面 Practice 1 的 Topic 1，讓你看看一個例子。

✎ **Practice 8**

請研究表格中的 **agree** 欄位，並且閱讀下方說明。

opinion: Agree	
reasons I agree with this statement	**reasons I disagree with this statement**
• **A3** positive or negative influence	• views shaped by other people's views
• **B1** happens whether they want it or not	• come into contact with other people
• **A1 ii** TV, radio, newspaper – **i** traditional media	• independent thinking
• **B** new media: facebook, social networking, go online, twitter, LINE	• influence is exaggerated
• **A2** exposed to ideas from	
• **A** virtually impossible – escape	

☆ 注意 A 和 B，以及 A1、A2 等等的標號。

☆ A 句和 B 句是主題句。我決定要寫三個段落當作這篇文章的主體，寫兩個段落來支持論述，以及一個段落來批評它。

☆ 句子 A1、A2 和 A3 針對 A 句提出了具體資訊，而 B 句也是一樣的狀況。

☆ 請注意，我還有 A1i 和 A1ii：我這樣做是因為我想要讓 A1i 先出現，因為它比較一般性。A1ii 會是 A1i 的具體例子。

來看看當我寫作時，這樣的計畫如何運作。

Practice 9

閱讀以下文章的段落，並且將 **Practice 8** 表格裡 **agree** 欄位的字彙畫上底線。請比較 **Practice 8** 的計畫和最後完成的段落。

It's virtually impossible in our day to escape any kind of contact with mass media. First, anyone who uses traditional media, for example watches TV, listens to the radio or reads the newspaper is going to be exposed to ideas, and those ideas are going to influence them either positively or negatively.

Secondly, even if you never watch TV or read a newspaper, anyone who goes online, logs into Facebook, or uses other social media such as twitter or LINE is also going to have their views shaped by those media, whether they want to be influenced or not.

範例答案

希望你有找到所有字彙，並且看出我在 Practice 8 規劃的結構，如何呈現在最後的段落文章中。

好的，現在換你來試試看。

Practice 10

請組織 **Practice 8** 表格裡 **disagree** 欄位裡的字彙。

範例答案

請看我如何組織 disagree 欄位的字彙，並且將它和下面的段落比較。和之前一樣，請將段落裡的字彙畫上底線。

opinion: Agree	
reasons I agree with this statement	**reasons I disagree with this statement**
• **A3** positive or negative influence	• **C2** views shaped by other people's views
• **B1** happens whether they want it or not	• **C3** come into contact with other people
• **A1 ii** TV, radio, newspaper – **i** traditional media	• **C1** independent thinking
• **B** new media: facebook, social networking, go online, twitter, LINE	• **C** influence is exaggerated
• **A2** exposed to ideas from	
• **A** virtually impossible – escape	

On the other hand, there are those who argue that this influence is exaggerated, and that our thinking is independent, or influenced more by the views of other people we come into contact with. I don't agree with this, because the views of the people we meet are just as likely to be formed by mass media as well.

☆ 請注意我把 C 句標號了，那是我的第三段。

☆ C 句是最一般性的，接著是針對 C 提出更具體細節的 C1、C2 和 C3 句。

☆ 希望你也是這樣標號。如果 C1、C2 和 C3 的順序不一樣，請不用擔心，但我希望你有看出 influence is exaggerated 是最一般性的句子，因此它應該是主題句 C。

☆ 希望你在段落中有找到所有字彙。如果沒有，請回頭繼續找！

　　到目前為止，我們討論的都是 argument / opinion 的文章，但你還必須學會在 problem / solution 文章中使用一樣的方法來組織段落。接下來我要用前面 Practice 1 的 Topic 2 來說明該怎麼做。

Practice 11

請研究表格中的 **problem** 欄位，並且閱讀下方的說明。

problem		solution
A local areas & planet as a whole	**A2** flora and fauna	people eating meat all the time
	the loss of	government – urgently legislate
B groundcover is burnt	**B1** terrible air pollution	prevent companies from stripping the land
causes	**C** logging	
impacts	**C1** soil erosion	
affects	**C2** flooding	enforce the laws – send a message
contributes to	**D** global warming	
		all of us
A1 loss of wildlife	**B2** surrounding	
A3 natural habitat	countries	

☆ 我決定要寫兩個大段落當作這篇文章的主體、寫一個段落來說明問題，最後再用一個段落來說明解決方法。

☆ 在這裡，A 句是我的主題句，B、C 和 D 句，則是我的支持句。

☆ 我沒有把動詞 causes、impacts、affects、contributes to 和片語 loss of 標號，因為在這個階段，我還不確定自己會如何用這些詞。我只知道當我寫作時，我會大量使用這些字彙。

　　現在就來看看當我寫文章時，這樣的規劃會有什麼效果。

Practice 12

閱讀以下文章的段落，並且將 Practice 11 表格裡 problem 欄位的字彙畫上底線。請比較 Practice 11 的計畫和最後完成的段落。

Destroying rainforests causes many problems, not only for the areas where the destruction is taking place, but also for the planet as a whole. In local areas, logging causes loss of wildlife, as many species of flora and fauna lose their natural habitat. When the rainforest is destroyed, the groundcover is often burnt to clear the land quickly. This causes terrible air pollution for the surrounding countries. In addition, the loss of groundcover as a result of logging causes soil erosion, which leads to flooding. Not only this, but rain forest destruction also contributes to global warming.

🔑 範例答案

希望你有找到所有的字彙，並且看出我在 Practice 11 規劃的結構，如何呈現在最後的段落文章中。

好的，現在換你來試試看。

✎ Practice 13

請組織 Practice 11 表格中 solution 欄位裡的字彙。

🔑 範例答案

請看我如何組織 solution 欄位的字彙，並且將它和下面的段落比較。和之前一樣，請將段落裡的字彙畫上底線。

problem		solution
A local areas & planet as a whole	**A2** flora and fauna	**B1** people eating meat all the time
B groundcover is burnt	the loss of	**A** government – urgently legislate
causes	**B1** terrible air pollution	**A1** prevent companies from stripping the land
impacts	**C** logging	
affects	**C1** soil erosion	
contributes to	**C2** flooding	**A2** enforce the laws – send a message
	D global warming	
A1 loss of wildlife	**B2** surrounding	**B** all of us
A3 natural habitat	countries	

The first solution must come from government. Governments in the countries impacted by this problem must urgently legislate to prevent companies stripping the land. Not only must they legislate, but they must also enforce the laws as well. This will send a message to potential businesses that the law should be obeyed. The second solution must come from the people, all of us. We should not be so keen to eat meat with every meal. This will affect the demand for meat, and then hopefully the practice of deforestation will slow down.

☆ 請注意我在本段又用了 A 和 B 句。A 會是我的第一個解決方法,而 B 是我的第二個方法。

☆ A 和 B 是最一般性的,接著 1、2 和 3 是比較具體的結果。

☆ 希望你也是這樣標號。如果 A 和 B 的順序不一樣,請不用擔心,但希望你有看出它們是最一般性的句子。

☆ 希望你在段落中已經找到所有字彙。如果沒有,請回頭繼續找!

好了,在這個單元中已經學了很多東西。現在,我們用一張清單來做個簡單的摘要。

分析題目並規劃你的答案:重點清單
1. 把題目的關鍵字彙畫上底線。 2. 請確定你知道該做些什麼:argument / opinion 或 problem / solution。 3. 請決定你的意見,然後把腦力激盪出的想法整理進兩個欄位之中。 4. 請避免寫下完整的句子,而是要在腦力激盪時把注意力放在字彙上。 5. 請思考具體的例子 (a/o) 和結果 (p/s)。 6. 請平衡你的想法。 7. 請用標號的方式組織你的想法,然後把它們寫下來。請思考主題句和支持主題的細節。

PART 2

為了幫助你學習和記得這張清單,接下來會多給你兩篇文章做練習。這個練習不會提供範例答案,但你還是應該花點時間來練習。就像在本單元一開始說的,這個過程在一開始時看似困難,但你練習過越多次,在考試時的表現就會越好,自信心也會越高。

Practice 14

請參考上面的清單,用以下兩個題目來練習你在這個單元中所學之「分析題目並規劃答案」的過程。

Further education institutions should be forced to accept the same numbers of male and female students in every subject.

Write an essay expressing your point of view.

The internet has changed the way we share and use information, but it has also created new problems.

Identify the problems and suggest ways to solve them.

　　在你結束這個單元之前，請將下列的清單看過，確定你能將所有要點都勾選起來。如果有一些要點你還搞不清楚，請回頭再次研讀本單元的相關部分。

☐ 我了解該如何在英文裡組織資訊。
☐ 我了解一般 (general) 和具體 (specific) 的差異。
☐ 我已經學到如何組織段落。
☐ 我已經學到如何分析文章題目和說明文字。
☐ 我完全了解如何重複使用文章題目裡的關鍵詞字彙。
☐ 我知道如何腦力激盪出想法，並規劃我的文章。
☐ 我知道如何進行腦力激盪、組織我的想法，並規劃我的文章。
☐ 我已經大量練習過如何規劃我的答案。
☐ 我已經練習過很多 IELTS Writing task 2 的範例。

EXAM TIP BOX

✓ 在介紹的部分大約要寫 70 個字。
✓ 在文章主體部分大約寫 130 字，並把它分成兩個大段落，或是三個比較小的段落。
✓ 結論部分大約要寫 50 個字。
✓ 請確保段落之間的斷行很清楚，讓你的文章更容易閱讀。

Unit 10

寫下你的答案——
寫作「介紹」

**Writing Your Answer–
Writing the Introduction**

內容和組織 Content and Organisation

在前面的單元裡，我們學到如何分析題目、如何腦力激盪出想法，以及如何規劃你的答案。在這個單元裡，你將學到如何撰寫文章的「介紹」，無論文章類型是 argument / opinion 或 problem / solution。首先，我們會先把重點放在組織內容和介紹上。為了得到高分，你該寫什麼？該如何組織你的想法？接著，我們會看一些你可以用在介紹的用語。雖然大部分你要學的東西是用在 argument / opinion 文章，但只要稍微調整一下，它們也可以用在 problem / solution 文章。我會告訴你兩種文章的調整策略和用語。

現在先來看看範例。

Practice 1

閱讀以下題目和三個介紹範例。你認為哪一個介紹寫得比較好，為什麼？請試著列出理由清單。

> Plans to give prisoners computers with access to the internet so that they can study while they are in prison have been criticized for wasting government money.
>
> Write an essay expressing your point of view.

介紹一

Plans to give prisoners computers with access to the internet so that they can study while they are in prison have been criticized for wasting government money. I agree with this and think that the government should spend the money on other things. There are two main reasons.

介紹二

There is no doubt that giving inmates computers with internet access will help many convicted criminals to educate themselves for a better life after they leave prison. On the other hand, this will also cost a lot of public money, money which could be used for other things. It's my opinion that the benefits of this plan far outweigh the costs. There are many reasons why I think so.

178

介紹三

Some prisoners can study to get a higher degree such as law or medicine while they are in prison. It cannot be denied that prisoners have lots of time, so studying is one way to pass the time, and it will also help convicts to find work after they leave if they learn some skill they can use. Yes, it will cost some money but the benefits to society are higher in my opinion. For example, society could train prisoners to do menial jobs while they are in prison. Everyone will benefit from this, including the prisoners, the prisons and the government, which could use the workforce to do jobs others outside don't want to do.

🔑 **範例答案**

希望你有看出介紹二寫得最好。為什麼呢？

☆ 介紹二從描述背景的句子開始。Background「背景句」重複使用題目裡的字彙，但卻不是整個題目照抄。你已經在 Unit 3 裡學過如何在寫作 Task 1 的第一句時重複使用題目裡的字彙。在本單元稍後，我會告訴你在寫作 Task 2 的介紹時又要如何運用這個寫作技巧。

☆ 介紹二有 balancing「平衡句」，也就是提出另一個與題目和背景句相反的可能看法。這篇文章是 argument / opinion 類型，所以你必須在介紹中寫論證。

☆ 介紹二的背景句和平衡句都很一般性。它們表達一般的看法，不會談論具體細節，或是提出具體例子。

☆ 介紹二有清楚的 opinion「意見句」。

☆ 介紹二包含 signposting「路標句」，說明了文章其餘的篇幅會更詳細討論意見。這種句子的功能在於描述文章其餘篇幅的組織。

☆ 介紹二相當簡短，不會超過四個句子。

☆ 雖然介紹一有表達清楚的意見，並且有一句路標句，但它寫得並不好，因為它只是把題目重新抄一遍。不要照抄文章的題目，這麼做只是在浪費寶貴的時間，而且一旦主考官知道你只是照抄，他可能連讀都不會讀。此外，介紹一沒有提出平衡的論證，而且長度也太短了。

☆ 介紹三更糟糕，因為它雖然有清楚的意見，但卻缺乏平衡句和路標句，寫了太多細節，而且寫得太長了。

所以，我們可以從中整理出什麼結論？

寫作「介紹」的清單
1. 重複使用題目的字彙，但不要照抄。
2. 從背景句開始寫。
3. 用平衡句來寫你的論證。
4. 請寫一個意見句。
5. 用路標句當作結尾。
6. 請表達一般性的內容，不要提出具體的例子或細節。

用語 Language

現在我們就來看看，該如何在介紹裡重複使用題目的字彙，而且不是直接照抄。

在上一個單元裡有提過，你應該先將題目裡的字彙畫上底線，然後可以針對字彙進行幾個變化。現在我們來研究一個例子，比較一下 Practice 1 的題目說明以及介紹二。

✎ Practice 2

請研究這張表格和下方的說明。

文章題目	介紹二	摘要
prisoners	inmates convicted criminals	請注意使用同義詞
access to the internet	internet access	請注意你可以如何改變字彙的順序
study	educate themselves	請注意同義詞的使用
wasting government money	cost a lot of public money	請注意同義詞的使用

☆ 你可以用同義字，但使用時必須非常謹慎。因為它們用起來並不如你想的那麼單純。請確定你使用的同義字都是你知道字義的字。

☆ 你可以改變字的順序，形成搭配字。例如，relations between people 可以改成 human relations。

☆ 你還可以改變詞性，例如將動詞改成名詞。

我們來練習這個部分。

✎ Practice 3

閱讀文章題目，然後將可使用在介紹中的替代字彙填入下方表格。

Governments should legislate to ensure that women have the same opportunities as men in the market for labour.

Write an essay expressing your point of view.

文章題目	介紹
legislate	
ensure	
same opportunities	
market for labour	

🔑 範例答案

請看這個表格。

文章題目	介紹
legislate	pass laws
ensure	make sure
same opportunities	equal opportunities / same chances
market for labour	labour market / job market

　　希望你有做出相同的改變，而且也思考過同義字。這一點要看你的字彙量是否充足，所以我一再強調，多學一些字彙來準備 IELTS 考試非常重要。學字彙最好的方法，就是大量閱讀。

　　我們現在要來看看，如何在介紹裡寫「背景句」和「平衡句」。

✏️ Practice 4

請將以下 set-phrases 分類放進表格中。

- Although this may be true in some cases, v.p.
- However, there are two sides to this statement.
- In recent years v.p.

- It cannot be denied that v.p.
- It is true to say that v.p.
- Many people believe that v.p.
- However, this is surely not the only way to look at the question.
- Many people consider that v.p.
- There is no doubt that v.p.
- However, while this may be true to some extent, v.p.
- On the other hand, v.p.

background	balancing

🔑 範例答案

請仔細研究這張表格，以及下方的說明。

background	balancing
• In recent years v.p.	• Although this may be true in some cases, v.p.
• It cannot be denied that v.p.	• However, there are two sides to this statement.
• It is true to say that v.p.	• However, this is surely not the only way to look at the question.
• Many people believe that v.p.	
• Many people consider that v.p.	• However, while this may be true to some extent, v.p.
• There is no doubt that v.p.	• On the other hand, v.p.

☆ 你可以在 problem / solution 的文章中使用背景句。但是不該在這類文章中使用平衡句。

☆ 注意，這些 set-phrases 大部分是以 v.p. 結尾，所以請確定在描述背景時，你使用的是 v.p.。如果你不確定 v.p. 是什麼，請回到 Unit 3，然後重新研讀那個部分。

☆ 請留意 in recent years。在 v.p. 中必須使用現在完成式，例如：In recent years, there has been a drop in the birth rate in my country.，不可使用現在簡單式或過去簡單式。

☆ 如果你要用 become 這個動詞，不可用在現在簡單式，要用在現在完成式。

☆ 就其他 set-phrases 來說，你應該在接下來的 v.p. 用現在簡單式。

☆ 請不要寫沒有用的東西，例如：In recent years, vegetarianism has been on the increase. 或 In recent years, gender equality has become a big issue.。因為早在你還沒出生之前，Vegetarianism「素食主義」和 gender equality「性別平等」就已經是個重要議題！為了得到高分，你的寫作必須合理，要表現出你的智慧，並反映真實世界的樣貌。

☆ 當你在寫 balancing 的句子時，請確保你的想法的確和第一個句子不同。

☆ 在學這些 set-phrases 時，請確定你已完全正確地理解它們的用法。須注意小細節，尤其是標點符號，例如，請注意哪些有逗號，以及這些逗號在哪裡。

⊠ 錯誤

- In recent years, <u>globalization</u> has become a big issue.
- In recent years, <u>there was</u> a lot of talk about democracy.
- In recent years, plastic waste in the sea <u>becomes</u> a big problem.
- On the other <u>hand it</u> is not always the case.

☑ 正確

- In recent years, <u>anti - globalization</u> has become a big issue.
- In recent years, <u>there has been</u> a lot of talk about democracy.
- In recent years, plastic waste in the sea <u>has become</u> a big problem.
- On the other <u>hand, it</u> is not always the case.

✎ Practice 5

請回到 **Practice 1** 的介紹範例，並且將前述這些 **set-phrases** 的例子都畫上底線。

🔑 範例答案

你應該找到三個 set-phrases 的例子，兩個在介紹二：

• There is no doubt that

• On the other hand

一個在介紹三：

• It cannot be denied that

　　接下來，我們把焦點放在 set-phrases 的細節，協助你確認自己是否已正確地理解它們的用法。

Practice 6

請看這些句子，找出 set-phrases 裡的錯誤並且修正它們。我們來看看範例。

EX. Many people believed that prison is only for punishment and not for deterrent.

Many people believe that prison is only for punishment and not for deterrent.

1. There is not doubt that giving prisoners opportunities to study in prison is a good idea

　→ _____

2. It cannot be denied giving prisoners computers with internet access.

　→ _____

3. It is true saying that the plan will cost a lot of public money.

　→ _____

4. In recent years the number of prisoners increases.

　→ _____

5. Many people consider that giving prisoners computers with internet access.

　→ _____

6. However, while this may be true to extent, there are other ways of considering the question.

　→ _____

7. Although this may be true in some case, some prisoners might become rehabilitated if they can study in prison

→ _____

🔑 範例答案

1. There is no doubt that giving prisoners opportunities to study in prison is a good idea.
2. It cannot be denied that giving prisoners computers with internet access is controversial.
3. It is true to say that the plan will cost a lot of public money.
4. In recent years the number of prisoners has been increasing.
5. Many people consider that giving prisoners computers with internet access is a waste of money.
6. However, while this may be true to some extent, there are other ways of considering the question.
7. Although this may be true in some cases, some prisoners might become rehabilitated if they can study in prison.

☆ 請注意 2. 和 5. 的 n.p. 和 v.p. 都錯了，其他則遺漏一些東西，或是稍微改變一些字。
☆ 4. 的 set-phrase 後面的 v.p. 動詞時態有一個錯誤。
☆ 請注意哪些句子少了標點符號。
☆ 請務必確認自己已正確地學習並使用這些 set-phrase，特別是小細節。

現在，我們來看你可以使用哪些用語表達自己的意見，以及為 signposting 提出你文章的概要。

✏️ **Practice 7**

請將以下 **set-phrases** 分類放進表格中。

- I (dis)agree with the view that v.p.
- There are many reasons why I think so.
- I do not believe that v.p.
- It's my opinion that v.p.
- There are many ways to solve this problem.
- I (dis)agree with this, and think that v.p.

- This essay will look at some of the common problems and will then suggest two solutions.
- I can think of two solutions to this problem.
- There are two/three main reasons.
- I firmly believe that v.p.
- There's no doubt in my mind that v.p.

opinion set-phrases	signposting set-phrases

🔑 範例答案

請仔細研究這張表格，以及下方的說明。

opinion set-phrases	signposting set-phrases
• I firmly believe that v.p. • It's my opinion that v.p. • I (dis)agree with the view that v.p. • There's no doubt in my mind that v.p. • I do not believe that v.p. • I (dis)agree with this, and think that v.p.	• There are many reasons why I think so. • There are two/three main reasons. • I can think of two solutions to this problem. • This essay will look at some of the common problems and will then suggest two solutions. • There are many ways to solve this problem.

☆ 你當然可以用 In my opinion 來表達意見，但這樣寫並不高明，無法讓你得到高分。請嘗試用一些其他的 set-phrases。

☆ This essay will argue that v.p. 是非常學術和客觀的陳述方式。

☆ 你可以在 problem / solution 的文章使用以下三個 set-phrases：I can think of two solutions to this problem. / There are many ways to solve this problem. / This essay will look at some of the common problems and will then suggest two solutions.。在稍後將會看到更多範例。

☆ 請記得，當你學習和使用這些 set-phrases，要確定自己完全正確地了解所有小細節，尤其是字尾和小詞。

☒ 錯誤

- I disagree the view that governments should legislate on gender equality.
- I firm believe that governments should legislate on gender equality.
- There are many reason why I think so.
- There are many way to solve this problem.

☑ 正確

- I disagree with the view that governments should legislate on gender equality.
- I firmly believe that governments should legislate on gender equality.
- There are many reasons why I think so.
- There are many ways to solve this problem.

✎ **Practice 8**

請回到 Practice 1 的介紹範例，並且將前述這些 set-phrases 的例子都畫上底線。

🔑 範例答案

你應該找到四個 set-phrases 的例子，兩個在介紹一：

- I agree with this and think that …
- There are two main reasons.

還有兩個在介紹二：

- It's my opinion that …
- There are many reasons why I think so.

　　現在，我們來看一個 problem / solution 的題目，我將告訴你該如何把用語調整成適合 problem / solution 的文章。

問題／解決方法的文章 Problem / Solution Essay

✎ Practice 9

請閱讀文章題目、介紹範例，以及下方的說明。

Rising sea levels caused by global warming is one of the biggest problems humanity faces, both now and in the future.

What other problems are associated with this, and what are some possible solutions?

🔑 介紹範例

In recent years, rising sea levels have threatened many low-lying parts of the world. This has caused serious flooding and other problems for some of the world's major cities and industrial zones. It's my opinion that national governments alone can not solve this problem, and that it needs an international response. I can think of two solutions to this problem, one long term, and one short term.

☆ 請注意句子的順序是 background、opinion、signposting。你不應該在這種文章使用平衡句，因為題目並未要你提出論證，也沒有要你探討問題的正反面。題目只是要你描述一個問題，並提出解決方法。

☆ 請注意前面學到的 set-phrases 用法。

☆ 請注意 can 和 need 這兩個助動詞的用法。你將必須在 problem / solution 的文章使用這樣的助動詞，而且會在稍後學到更多使用它們的方法。

☆ 文章其餘的篇幅，可能會先用一個簡短的段落提出例子，討論其他因海平面上升所引發的問題，然後再寫兩個段落來描述一些長期的解決方法，最後是一個簡短的結論。

強化 Consolidation

✏ Practice 10

請閱讀下面針對 **Practice 3** 文章題目所做的介紹，然後將你在本單元學到的所有用語都畫上底線。

> There is no doubt that women should have the same chances to find jobs as men. On the other hand, some companies might find it difficult to recruit men and women in equal numbers, due to the nature of the labour market, or due to the kind of work being offered. I do not believe that it's the job of government to pass laws to make sure companies recruit equal numbers of men and women. There are two main reasons why I think so.

☆ 請注意句子的順序是 background、opinion、signposting。
☆ 請注意題目中的字彙如何被改變。
☆ 請注意 set-phrases。
☆ 請注意內容長度。
☆ 請注意內容有多一般。
☆ 文章其餘的篇幅，可能會討論為什麼政府不應該用通過法律的方式，確保性別平等的兩個原因。

　　好的，現在換你來練習寫作。

✏ Practice 11

請閱讀下面的 **argument / opinion** 寫作題目，然後用你在本單元學到的方法和用語寫一篇介紹。

> Some people believe that children are naturally competitive, and that this should be encouraged in order to prepare them for the adult world. Others think that children should be taught to cooperate instead.
>
> Discuss both these views and give your own opinion.

🔑 範例答案

請閱讀我的參考答案和下面的說明。

There is no doubt that children like to compete against each other, and that they like to win. However, while this may be true to some extent, in the real world, cooperation is just as important. It's my opinion that children need to learn how to compete fairly and how to cooperate usefully, in order to prepare them for the world they will face as adults. There are three main reasons why.

☆ 我當然不知道你寫了什麼，但希望你寫了一些和參考答案相仿的內容。
☆ 請注意句子的順序是 background、opinion、signposting。
☆ 請注意題目中的字彙如何被改變。
☆ 請注意意見中表達同意兩者看法的方式。

✏️ Practice 12

閱讀下面的 problem / solution 寫作題目，然後用你在本單元學到的方法和用語寫一段介紹。

> Overpopulation of urban areas is causing many problems for citizens.
>
> What are some of the most serious ones, and what can individuals and governments do to solve these problems?

🔑 範例答案

請閱讀我的參考答案和下面的說明。

It cannot be denied that one of the most serious problems inhabitants of big cities face is the problem of overcrowding. Too many people are crowding together in spaces that were not designed or built for so many people. I firmly believe that citizens and city governments have the responsibility to look for solutions to this problem. This essay will suggest two solutions.

☆ 根據 Practice 9 中所提供的範例，希望你寫了一些相仿的內容。

☆ 請注意句子的順序是 background、opinion、signposting。

☆ 請注意 set-phrases 的使用。

☆ 文章其餘的篇幅可能會先用一個簡短的段落討論其他因人口過剩所引發的問題，然後再寫一個段落描述從個人層次出發的解決方法，最後用一個段落描述從政府層次出發的解決方法。

　　在你結束這個單元之前，請將下列清單看過，確定你能將所有要點都勾選起來。如果有一些要點你還不清楚，請回頭再次閱讀本單元的相關部分。

□ 我已經學到如何針對 argument / opinion 和 problem / solution 的文章撰寫介紹。

□ 我已經學到如何讓介紹維持一般性，內容不要有太多細節，我也學到介紹的合適長度。

□ 我學到如何藉由改變文法、字彙和同義字，以使用文章題目的用語。

□ 我已經學到句子的順序：在 argument / opinion 文章裡，順序是 background、balance、opinion、signposting；在 problem / solution 文章裡，順序是 background、opinion、signposting。

□ 我已經學到許多可以用在介紹裡的 set-phrase。

□ 我已經看過並學到許多範例。

□ 我已經練習寫過兩個介紹。

EXAM TIP BOX

✓ 如果題目使用名詞片語，那麼就在介紹使用動詞片語；如果題目使用動詞片語，那麼就在介紹使用名詞片語。

✓ 這樣做可以讓主考官知道你能夠掌握基本的語言，也可以幫助你得到更高的分數。

Unit 11

寫作段落——
增加、闡述、對比
**Writing a Paragraph—
Adding, Illustrating, Contrasting**

前言與暖身練習 Warm Up

在接下來的幾個單元裡，你必須根據在 Unit 9 學到有關組織想法的知識來寫作文章，並且將學習如何透過把想法加入主題句來寫作段落。

你可以用以下方法發展出主題句。

1. 在相同的層次上將其他想法加入主題句，內容不要更一般，也不要更具體。
2. 將例子加入主題句，藉此說明具體的細節。
3. 將反對意見加入主題句，藉此製造對比。
4. 將你支持某個意見的原因加入主題句。
5. 將和你的想法有關之結果資訊加入主題句。
6. 將和你的想法相關之條件資訊加入主題句。
7. 將和你的想法可能產生之後果相關資訊加入主題句。

以上方法的寫作要領將在接下來的各單元中告訴你。首先，在本單元裡除了告訴你 adding「加入意見」、illustrating「闡述意見」和 contrasting「對比意見」的用語，還會訓練你的思考能力。你將會在此學會使用 argument / opinion 文章和 problem / solution 文章的用語。

✎ **Practice 1**

請針對以下的文章題目規劃你的答案，然後閱讀範例文章。

The government should not support the arts. The money will be better spent on other things.

To what extent do you agree or disagree?

Many people believe that art is something which only a few people are interested in, and that because of this the government should not spend public money on it. However, while this may be true to some extent, nonetheless, the arts play a significant role in public life. I firmly believe that the government should support the arts. There are two main reasons why I think so.

First, (1) _____. Actors, dancers, musicians and theatre and film technicians, for example, often have highly developed skills which take years of training to develop. However, without state support, the institutions where such people train will not survive, and the people who work in those institutions will also be out of work. Also, opera houses and theatres which receive state funding employ many people, not only in the big cities, but also when they tour outside the cities.

Second, (2) _____, such as education, health and defence. Although the benefits of spending on the arts may be difficult to measure, that doesn't mean that there are no tangible benefits for the nation as a whole. Take my country (UK) for example. The theatre industry in London is world famous and millions of tourists go to see a musical or visit museums when they come to London. This kind of tourist attraction brings in revenue for the state. Without initial government funding, many of the sights the tourists come to see would never have been created.

To summarize, it is my opinion that the arts are important for everyone, and the benefits of the state supporting them far outweigh the costs.

Practice 2

請在下列句子選出適當主題句以完成 **Practice 1** 每個段落的填空。

A. Actors need to train in voice, movement, and stagecraft.
B. Musicians need to train for years before they can reach the level required to play some of the most difficult pieces audiences love to hear.
C. Some people think that the government should only spend money on things which

benefit the whole of society,

D. The arts provide employment to lots of people who have highly specialised skills.

E. The best musical I have ever seen is *Cats*, which I saw in London when I was a student.

F. The highest achievement of a society is its arts.

G. The most famous training institution for actors in the world is in London.

H. We can measure the benefits of spending on things society needs by using statistics.

🔑 範例答案

請看看我的答案,並且閱讀底下的說明。

(1) D　　(2) C

☆ 我們已經學過主題句是段落裡最一般性的句子,其他句子則都跟著主題句。在範例中可以看到 D 是第二段中最一般性的想法,而 C 則是第三段中最一般性的想法。這些段落的其他句子都指向這兩個主題句。

☆ A 和 B 都太具體了。它們在第二段的作用是支持句,而不是主題句。

☆ E 和 G 也太具體了。你可能認為 G 和主題不相關。這樣想也許是對的,但它是否真的與政府資助藝術這個主題無關呢? E 的意見則太個人化了。主考官其實並不在乎你的個人經驗。

☆ H 也與主題不相關。這句也許適合放在講與統計學好處相關的段落,但不適合放在這裡。

☆ 大多數錯誤句子談的內容都太具體或不相關,而 F 則是太一般性了。

　　現在,你將會學習如何透過在 general / specific 的層次上加入 (adding) 其他意見發展你的主題句;如何透過具體例子闡述 (illustrating) 你的主題句;以及如何提出對比 (contrasting) 意見,或是反對主題句。當你加入想法時,必須確定要加入主題句的想法不是具體的例子,也不是對比或反對的意見。同樣的,當你在闡述主題句時,必須確定要加入的是例子,而不是對比或其他在相同層次的句子。當你提出與主題句對比的意見時,也必須得確定有真正的反差出現。接下來將透過練習來讓你更了解我的意思。

 **Practice 3**

根據主題句，選出可用於為主題句加入、闡述或對比想法的句子，填入表格中。

EX. Smoking is bad for your health.

adding	illustrating	contrasting
E	G	H

1. Exercise is good for your physical health.

adding	illustrating	contrasting

2. The arts teach us how to be true to ourselves.

adding	illustrating	contrasting

3. Social media has many benefits.

adding	illustrating	contrasting

A. Exercise makes you feel happy.

B. Exercise often hurts and can cause physical problems.

C. Facebook is the most popular social media site for my generation.

D. It is also good for your mental health.

E. It is bad for the health of the people around you.

F. It is very popular.

G. Smoking causes shortness of breath and high blood pressure.

H. Smoking is very enjoyable and helps to relax people.

I. Social media has many dangers.

J. The arts simply help us to pass the time and they have no usefulness.

K. The theatre unites the individual with society because we are part of an audience.

L. They teach us how to be good citizens.

請研究表格及下方的說明。

1. Exercise is good for your physical health.

adding	illustrating	contrasting
D	A	B

2. The arts teach us how to be true to ourselves.

adding	illustrating	contrasting
L	K	J

3. Social media has many benefits.

adding	illustrating	contrasting
F	C	I

☆ E、G 提出具體的例子說明抽菸的危險性；H 則提出反對或對比的看法。

☆ D、A 具體說明為什麼運動有益於你的心理健康——因為運動會影響你的情緒；B 則是對比意見。

☆ L、K 是一種藝術型式的具體例子；J 則是主題句的對比意見。

☆ F、C 是社群媒體網站的一個具體例子；I 則是主題句的一個對比意見。

　　看過這些意見後，我們來看看用語。首先從加入想法 (adding) 開始，然後看如何闡述意見 (illustrating)，最後再看如何提出對比意見 (contrasting)。要提醒很重要的一點是，你必須確實做每一個練習，而且當你在做練習的時候，請想一想在這個單元已經學到了什麼。

加入意見 Adding Ideas

Practice 4

請研究表格裡的用語、例句和下方的說明。

adding ideas	
• A further point to consider is n.p. • Also, • Another good thing about n.p. is that v.p. • Another good thing is that v.p. • Another n.p. is that v.p.	• Another reason why v.p. is that v.p. • In addition to this, v.p. • In addition, v.p. • Not only that, but also v.p. • … not only n.p., but also v.p. • On top of that,
sample sentences	
• Smoking has many dangers for the smoker. Another danger of smoking is that it has the same negative affects on bystanders. • Social media helps families to stay in touch. In addition to this, it also helps people stay informed. • The arts are important for a civilized society. A further point to consider is the employment that the arts offer to many people.	

☆ 在台灣，人們常用 moreover 和 furthermore 來新增資訊。可惜的是，在英文裡它們很少出現，甚至很少被使用。因為這些字聽起來很不自然，所以最好盡可能避免使用它們。相對的，請盡量用上方表格中列出的字。

☆ 請注意，當你用 Another n.p. is that v.p. 的句型時，一定要重複上一個句子的名詞片語。請看上面的第一個例句。

☆ 在使用這些用語時，你必須非常小心 n.p. 和 v.p. 之間的差異。

☆ 此外，請務必小心一切的細節：小詞、字尾，確定你完整使用了 set-phrase，並且注意每一個標點符號。

☆ 請確保你要寫的想法不是具體的例子，也不是對比的意見。

⊠ 錯誤

- On top of that <u>reason</u>, there is another benefit.
- Another good thing about the arts is that <u>social benefits</u>.
- Cycling is good for your physical health. <u>In addition</u>, it helps your blood circulation.

☑ 正確

- <u>On top of that</u>, there is another benefit.
- Another good thing about the arts is that <u>there are many social benefits</u>.
- Cycling is good for your physical health. In addition, <u>it helps to keep the environment clean</u>.

✎ Practice 5

請完整閱讀 Practice 1 的範例答案，並且把你能找到的新增用語都畫上底線。

🔑 範例答案

你應該在第二段找到共兩個用語。

- Also,
- … not only n.p. but also

☆ 請注意，在 Also 之後的句子新增了其他論點至主題句，但是並沒有提出例子或與它對比。

☆ in the big cities 和 outside the cities 是同一個層次上的意見，它們不是具體的例子，也不是對比。

✎ Practice 6

請在 Practice 3 的主題句中用新增用語的方式將 D、L、F 加入。來看看範例。

EX. Smoking is bad for your health. <u>Not only that, but also it is bad for the health of the people around you.</u>

1. Exercise is good for your physical health.

2. The arts teach us how to be true to ourselves.

_____

3. Social media has many benefits.

_____

🔑 範例答案

請研究我的範例，並確定你了解它們是怎麼寫出來的。

1. Exercise is good for your physical health. <u>Another good thing about exercise is that it is good for your mental health.</u>
2. The arts teach us how to be true to ourselves. <u>In addition to this, they teach us how to be good citizens.</u>
3. Social media has many benefits. <u>Also, it is very popular.</u>

闡述想法 Illustrating Ideas

 Practice 7

請研究表格裡的用語、例句及下方的說明。

illustrating ideas	
• Take for example the way that v.p. • Take n.p. for example, • For example, • For instance, • A good example here is n.p., which v.p.	• A good example here is the way that v.p. • In my country, • In my situation, • On a personal level, • …, such as … • …, like …
sample sentences	
• Smoking is very bad for your health. Take cancer for example, it is known that the number one cause of lung cancer is smoking. • The arts provide employment for many people. A good example here is the way that even a small opera house or theatre provides employment for many technicians and others. • Social media is great for keeping people informed about events. A good example here is Facebook, which can be used in the event of an emergency to let people know you are ok.	

☆ 你可以在句子中間使用 for example 和 for instance，也可以在一系列例子的前面或後面使用。但是若你這樣做，請記得不要用大寫，並確定標點符號正確。

☆ Such as 只會出現在句子中間，和 like 一樣。不要用 such like。

☆ 務必留意標點符號和 set-phrase 的其他細節，並確保你已正確使用它們。

☆ 此外，請注意你何時必須使用 n.p. 和 v.p.。

☒ 錯誤

- The benefits include <u>For example,</u> low cost, high visibility, and ease of access.
- There are many social media platforms in my country, <u>such like</u> LINE, Whatsapp, and Facebook.
- Cycling has many health benefits. Take for example the way that <u>increased heart rate</u>.

☑ 正確

- The benefits include, <u>for example,</u> low cost, high visibility, and ease of access.
- There are many social media platforms in my country, <u>such as</u> LINE, Whatsapp, and Facebook.
- Cycling has many health benefits. Take for example the way that <u>it increases</u> your heart rate.

✎ Practice 8

請完整閱讀 Practice 1 的範例文章，並且把你能找到的闡述用語例子都畫上底線。

🔑 範例答案

你應該找到三個用語：

第二段：for example
第三段：… such as … / Take my country for example.

☆ 請注意 for example 的標點符號，以及它在句子裡的位置應該是例子清單的後面。
☆ 請注意 such as 的標點符號，以及它在句子裡的位置應該是例子清單的前面。
☆ 請注意 Take my country for example. 是一個完整的句子，後面接著一個軼聞或一個具體的案例。

 **Practice 9**

請運用闡述用語將 **Practice 3** 中的 **A**、**K**、**C** 句加入句子裡。來看看範例。

EX. Smoking is bad for your health. Not only that, but also it is bad for the health of the people around you. <u>A good example here is the way that smoking causes shortness of breath and high blood pressure.</u>

1. Exercise is good for your physical health. Another good thing about exercise is that it is good for your mental health. _____

2. The arts teach us how to be true to ourselves. In addition to this, they teach us how to be good citizens. _____

_____

3. Social media has many benefits. Also, it is very popular. _____

_____

🔑 範例答案

請研究我的範例,並確定你了解它們是怎麼寫出來的。

1. Exercise is good for your physical health. Another good thing about exercise is that it is good for your mental health. <u>For example, it makes you feel happy</u>.
2. The arts teach us how to be true to ourselves. In addition to this, they teach us how to be good citizens. <u>A good example here is the way that the theatre unites the individual with society because we are part of an audience.</u>
3. Social media has many benefits. Also, it is very popular. <u>A good example here is Facebook, which is the most popular social media site for my generation.</u>

對比意見 Contrasting Ideas

✏ **Practice 10**

請研究表格裡的用語、例句和下方的說明。

contrasting ideas
• However,
• While it is true that v.p., nonetheless, v.p.
• While this may be true to some extent, nonetheless, v.p.
• On the other hand,
• Still,
• On the contrary,
• Although v.p., v.p.
• By contrast,
• Then again,

sample sentences
• Smoking is very bad for the health. However, many people still smoke in spite of this knowledge.
• While it is true that social media keeps us connected, nonetheless, it is also very isolating as well.
• Although exercise is generally good for you, there are some forms of exercise which must be done carefully.

☆ 注意，on the other hand 是一個慣用語，所以你不能對它進行任何改變。例如不能寫成 on the other side 或是 on the other foot。

☆ 在使用這些用語時，你必須非常了解 n.p. 和 v.p.。

☆ 使用 Although 時請十分小心，你絕對不可以在從屬子句裡使用它。

☒ 錯誤

- Skydiving is a great sport with great benefits. On the other <u>side</u>, you need a lot of expensive equipment.
- The arts are very expensive to support. While this may be true, nonetheless, <u>great benefits</u>.
- <u>Although</u> everyone enjoys listening to music, <u>but</u> not many people are prepared to pay a lot of money for doing so.

☑ 正確

- Skydiving is a great sport with great benefits. On the other <u>hand</u>, you need a lot of expensive equipment.
- The arts are very expensive to support. While this may be true, nonetheless, <u>there are great benefits</u>.
- <u>Although</u> everyone enjoys listening to music, not many people are prepared to pay a lot of money for doing so.

✎ Practice 11

請完整閱讀 Practice 1 的範例文章，並且把你能找到的對比用語的例子都畫上底線。

⚷ 範例答案

你應該找到四個用語：

介紹：However, / while this may be true to some extent, nonetheless.
第二段：However
第三段：Although

☆ 請注意，在介紹裡這兩個用語是在一起的：However, while this may be true to some extent, nonetheless,

☆ 請特別注意有 although 的句子，裡面沒有 but。

Practice 12

請運用對比用語將 **Practice 3** 中的 **B、J、I** 句加入句子裡。來看看範例。

EX. Smoking is bad for your health. Not only that, but also it is bad for the health of the people around you. <u>However, smoking is very enjoyable and helps to relax people.</u>

1. Exercise is good for your physical health. Another good thing about exercise is that it is good for your mental health. _____

_____

2. The arts teach us how to be true to ourselves. In addition to this, they teach us how to be good citizens. _____

_____

3. Social media has many benefits. Also, it is very popular. _____

_____

🔑 範例答案

請研究我的範例，並確定你了解它們是怎麼寫出來的。

1. <u>While it is true that</u> exercise is good for your physical health, <u>nonetheless, there are some sports which can be very dangerous.</u>
2. The arts teach us how to be true to ourselves. In addition to this, they teach us how to be good citizens. <u>Still, the arts simply help us to pass the time and they have no usefulness.</u>
3. Social media has many benefits. Also, it is very popular. <u>Then again, social media has many dangers.</u>

　　最後，我們來把你在這個單元學到的內容都練習一次。請花一點時間規劃下方文章題目的答案，然後寫一篇介紹和兩個段落。請將你在前幾個單元學到的所有內容都練習過。

請針對以下題目規劃你的答案,並且寫一篇文章。

> Traditional values like trust, honour and kindness don't seem important these days. A person's worth seems to be judged according to material possessions and social status.
>
> To what extent do you agree or disagree with this opinion?

　　在你結束這個單元之前,請將下列清單看過,確定你能將所有要點都勾選起來。如果有一些要點你還不清楚,請回頭再次閱讀本單元的相關部分。

□ 我知道該如何圍繞著包含一般性意見的主題句寫出一個段落。

□ 我知道該如何透過 adding 其他想法至主題句的方法,發展主題句的觀點;透過一些具體例子 illustrating 主題句;或是用相反意見 contrasting 主題句。

□ 我清楚知道 adding 意見、illustrating 意見和 contrasting 意見的差異。

□ 我對 general / specific 的結構已有更深入的了解。

□ 我已經學到可以用來 add 意見、illustrate 意見或 contrast 意見的用語。

□ 我已經看過許多這些用語的例子。

□ 我已經看過這種用語的常見錯誤用法。

□ 我已經大量練習過如何使用這些用語。

□ 我已經練習過很多寫作。

EXAM TIP BOX

✓ 如果你實在激盪不出任何想法,請試著思考你既有想法的對比意見,或是就既有的想法思考相關的例子,這是讓你思考出新東西的好方法。

✓ 盡量讓你的例子和一般性知識有關,而不是寫你的個人經驗。

Unit 12

寫作段落——
原因和結果

**Writing a Paragraph—
Reason and Result**

現在，你必須根據在前面單元學到的知識來寫作段落。這個單元的學習重點是用來描述狀況或問題之 reason「原因」的用語，以及用來描述狀況或建議之 result「結果」的用語。和之前的單元一樣，這個單元也會訓練你的思考力。我們將把焦點放在 problem / solution 的文章，但你也可以在這個單元學會在 argument / opinion 文章裡使用這些用語。

Practice 1

請針對以下文章題目規劃你的答案，然後閱讀範例文章。

Global overpopulation is a serious problem which will get worse in the future.

What are some of the problems, and what can individuals and governments do to solve them?

The global population currently stands at around 7.5 billion. There is no doubt that this is a serious problem. This essay will look at some of the common problems caused by overpopulation and will then suggest two solutions.

(1) _____. Food, clean water and agricultural land is fast running out due to overpopulation. We live on a finite planet, but we live as though we have unlimited resources at our disposal. A large and growing population causes environmental damage and pollution. The destruction of rainforests and other natural habitats to create enough land for agricultural use is the result of the pressure of a large population and the necessity to provide enough food for everyone. The earth's resources are being used up faster as a result of our expectation that every person on the planet can have a first world lifestyle.

In my opinion, (2) _____. This may cause some people to miss out on having a large family, but individuals should not think that having large families is a human right. Not only individuals but also governments have to act. Single and childfree people should be given tax concessions, and people with large families should be penalised by the government. The result of this will be a slowdown in the rate of population growth.

In the last analysis, if we are all going to share this planet in the future, we will need to be less selfish about our desires and expectations.

Practice 2

請在下列句子選出適當主題句以完成 **Practice 1** 每個段落的填空。

A. Birth control in the form of education and free condoms should be encouraged.

B. By the year 2100 the population of the world will be 11.2 billion.

C. India, China and Brazil have the biggest populations in the world today.

D. One of the most serious problems is scarcity of resources.

E. Only governments and NGOs can solve this problem.

F. Only private citizens can solve this problem.

G. The main solution to this problem is birth control, which should be encouraged by individuals and governments.

H. The population of the world is bigger now than it has ever been.

🔑 範例答案

請看看我的答案，並且閱讀底下的說明。

(1) D　　(2) G

☆ 你可以看到文章的結構和題目相關。第二段描述問題，第三段提出解決方法。

☆ 你已經學過主題句是段落裡最一般性的句子，其他句子則都跟著主題句。在範例中可以看到 D 是第二段中最一般性的想法，因為它包含 problem 這個字，而且這裡的主題句需要 problem 這個字。這些段落裡的其他句子，都是針對資源稀少提出進一步細節。

☆ B 和 C 分別提出預估的人口成長數字及高人口國家的例子，因為太具體了而不適合當作主題句。

☆ G 是第三段中最一般性的意見。本段的其他句子都針對個人和政府雙方如何協助解決問題，提出進一步的細節說明。

☆ 句子 E 和 F 不是第三段的主題句，因為 E 只描述了政府和非政府組織，而 F 只描述了個人，但主題句應該兩者都描述。

☆ A 太過具體而不是主題句，因為它提出一個解決方法的例子。

☆ H 因為太過一般性而不是這兩個段落的主題句。

　　接下來，我們會從「原因」開始談起，先看想法，然後再探討用語。

原因 Reason

在現實生活中，原因 (reason) 總是出現在狀況之前，它是狀況的成因。然而，我們陳述它們之間的關係時，未必會依照實際生活的關係。在中文，原因出現在動作或狀況之前——在中文裡，我們常以「由於」作為句子開頭。但是在英文裡，更常見的寫法是把動作或狀況放在前面，然後才描述它的成因。

實際生活
overpopulation   →   scarce resources 【原因】   【狀況】
中文
overpopulation   →   scarce resources 【原因】   【狀況】
英文
scarce resources   →   overpopulation 【狀況】   【原因】

PART 2

在英文裡，我們會在主要子句（第一個子句）描述狀況，然後把狀況的成因放在從屬子句（第二個子句）。例如：Resources are scarce now because of overpopulation.，而主考官認為你應該知道要這樣寫，且認為你會遵循這個規則。把從屬子句放在前面並不是錯的，但這樣寫很不專業，也不符合學術習慣。所以，你必須清楚知道行動或狀況的原因。為了幫助你了解這點，我們來進行一個練習。

✎ Practice 3

請將左邊的狀況和右邊的原因進行配對。

狀況
Overpopulation has happened
Unemployment has increased in the developing world

原因
now most people can afford to buy a car
the internet

People are becoming more anti social	the rise of automation
Traffic congestion is getting worse	everyone is watching their smartphone screen all the time
Obesity is on the rise	there has been an increase in life expectancy among all ages.
It's now easier to share information	our sedentary lifestyle

範例答案

請看看我的答案，並確保你已了解其中的因果關係。

☆ 請注意，最後一個適合用在 argument / opinion 的文章。

狀況	原因
Overpopulation has happened	there has been an increase in life expectancy among all ages
Unemployment has increased in the developing world	the rise of automation
People are becoming more anti social	everyone is watching their smartphone screen all the time
Traffic congestion is getting worse	now most people can afford to buy a car
Obesity is on the rise	our sedentary lifestyle
It's now easier to share information	the internet

現在，我們來看看可以使用哪些用語描述一個狀況或問題的原因。

 **Practice 4**

請研究表格裡的用語、例句和下方的說明。

reason	
… because of n.p. … … because v.p. … … as v.p. … … since v.p. …	… due to n.p. … … due to the fact that v.p. … … v.p. as a result of n.p. … … n.p. is the result of n.p. …
sample sentences	
• The forest has been cleared because the company wanted to use the land to raise cattle. • The water has been polluted due to the waste from the nearby factory. • The infant mortality rate has decreased since the introduction of universal healthcare.	

☆ 在每一個句子裡，你會看到狀況先出現，接著是造成該狀況的原因。

☆ 注意，你絕對不可以在同一個句子裡使用 so 和 because。

☆ 即使 as a result of 和 is the result of 都用了 result 這個字，但它們實際的意思是在講原因，不要被搞混了。你使用它們的方式，應該和使用 because of 一模一樣，而且它們的意思都一樣。

☆ 注意，在 is the result of 的前面，絕對不可以用 v.p.。

☆ 請留意 is the result of 和 as a result of 之間的細微差異。

☆ 需特別注意哪些字後面接 n.p.，以及哪些字後面接 v.p.。

> ☒ 錯誤
> • As the company wanted to raise cattle, <u>the forest was cleared</u>.
> • <u>Because</u> extreme weather is increasing, <u>so</u> people are afraid of living near the sea.
> • People are getting fatter due to <u>they have</u> too much sugar in their diet.
> • <u>People are getting fatter</u> is the result of too much sugar in their diet.

> ☑ 正確
> • <u>The forest was cleared</u> as the company wanted to raise cattle.
> • People are afraid of living near the sea <u>because</u> extreme weather is increasing.
> • People are getting fatter <u>due to the fact that</u> they have too much sugar in their diet.
> • <u>Increased obesity</u> is the result of too much sugar in people's diet.

請完整閱讀 Practice 1 的範例文章，並且把你能找到的原因用語都畫上底線。

🔑 範例答案

你應該在第二段找到三個用語。

• due to
• is the result of
• as a result of

☆ 注意，在每個句子中，第一個子句描述狀況，第二個子句描述狀況的原因。
☆ 注意 n.p. 的使用，due to 的後面不能接 v.p.。

✏️ **Practice 6**

請用原因的用語來寫作與 Practice 3 中「狀況」有關的句子。來看看範例。

EX. Overpopulation has happened because there has been an increase in life expectancy among all ages.

🔑 範例答案

請研究我的範例，並確定你了解它們是怎麼寫出來的。

1. Unemployment has increased in the developing world because of the rise of automation.
2. People are becoming more anti social due to the fact that everyone is watching their smartphone screen all the time.
3. Traffic congestion is getting worse because now most people can afford to buy a car.
4. Rising obesity is the result of our sedentary lifestyle.
5. It's now easier to share information as a result of the internet.

到目前為止，這種用語還算容易學。但是，來看看當我們把重點放在「結果」時，會有什麼狀況。

結果 Result

　　使用結果用語（及這種用語背後的觀念）的一個困難之處在於：什麼是原因，什麼又是結果，取決於你如何看待這件事，因為任何狀況都是前一個狀況的結果 (result)，也是下一個狀況的原因，所以這是某種因果關係鏈。一般在英文中的規則是，你必須把你想強調的資訊放在第一個子句。我們稱之為 topic position「主題位置」。

現實		
overpopulation 【原因】	→	scarce resources 【結果】
英文例句 1		
scarce resources 【topic position 主題位置】	→	overpopulation 【原因】
英文例句 2		
overpopulation 【topic position 主題位置】	→	scarce resources 【結果】

例句 1 Resources will become scarce due to overpopulation.

例句 2 Overpopulation is out of control. As a result, resources will become scarce.

　　你可以從這兩個例子看到，透過更改放在 topic position「主題位置」的資訊，我們可以改變句子的重點，但整個句子的意思和現實生活的關係仍未改變。也就是在現實生活裡，人口過剩仍然是資源稀少的原因，而不是相反的狀況。這樣你了解了嗎？

　　在 problem / solution 的文章裡，當你提出解決一個問題的方法，你也應該思考這個建議所產生的結果會是什麼。為了幫助你了解這一點，我們來進行一個練習。

Practice 7

請將左邊的建議和右邊的結果進行配對。

建議	結果
The government should restrict the number of children each couple can have	a drop in obesity

Certain industries should be forbidden to automate	a slowdown in the unemployment rate
People should be encouraged to interact more with each other	communities will be stronger
There should be a very high tax on car sales	it's very difficult for governments and corporations to keep secrets
Physical exercise should be made a part of every schoolchild's day	reduce the number of cars on the road
The internet now reaches into most homes	the birthrate will go down

🔑 範例答案

請看看下面的答案，並確保你已了解這裡的因果關係。

☆ 注意，最後一個適合用在 argument / opinion 的文章。

建議	結果
The government should restrict the number of children each couple can have	the birthrate will go down
Certain industries should be forbidden to automate	a slowdown in the unemployment rate
People should be encouraged to interact more with each other	communities will be stronger
There should be a very high tax on car sales	reduce the number of cars on the road
Physical exercise should be made a part of every schoolchild's day	a drop in obesity
The internet now reaches into most homes	it's very difficult for governments and corporations to keep secrets

現在，我們來看看可以使用哪些用語描述建議或解決方法將產生的結果。

 **Practice 8**

請研究表格裡的用語、例句和下方的說明。

result	
• The effect of this will be n.p.	• The effect of this will be to V
• This may cause s/o to V	• As a result, v.p.
• This could lead to n.p.	• The effect of this could be to V
• This will lead to n.p.	• The result of this will be that v.p.
• This could result in n.p.	• The effect of this could be n.p.
• The result of this could be that v.p.	• This will result in n.p.
• This may cause n.p.	• The result of this could be n.p.
• The result of this will be n.p.	• This means that v.p.
	• … so, v.p.

sample sentences
• Universal healthcare was introduced, so infant mortality went down.
• Everyone has a smartphone now. As a result, it's easier for companies to target advertising.
• The government should give everyone a basic income. This will result in a fairer distribution of wealth.
• Parents should teach their children to be more polite. This could lead to a better society.

☆ 注意，so 表示結果。請將它和 Practice 4 的 because 一起比較。

☆ 務必留意 As a result（結果）和 Practice 4 中的 as a result of n.p. 還有 n.p. is the result of n.p.（原因）之間的差異，以及小詞之間的微小細節，例如逗點和大寫。

☆ This means that 和 so 更適合用在 argument / opinion 的文章裡。

☆ 這些 set-phrases 大部分是從一個句子開始。所以你應該在第一個句子描述你的建議或解決方法，接著在下一個句子描述可能的結果。不要把它們寫成一個長的句子。

☆ 請注意，這裡的主詞常常是 this。你也可以用 that，但絕對不應該用 it。It 指的只有前一個句子的特定一個字，而 this 或 that 指的則是前面整個句子，或是前面句子的一組字。

☆ 須特別小心 v.p.、n.p. 和 V。

☒ 錯誤

- People should be prevented from living by the sea, <u>as a result</u> of they will not suffer so much from flooding.
- Governments should do more to help poor people, <u>this could result in</u> a drop in poverty.
- The laws against pollution should be more strictly enforced. <u>It</u> will lead to a better environment for everyone.
- Companies should enforce a lunchtime nap on their workers. This will lead to <u>people will</u> be more productive in the afternoon.

☑ 正確

- People should be prevented from living by the sea. <u>As a result,</u> they will not suffer so much from flooding.
- Governments should do more to help poor people. <u>This could result in</u> a drop in poverty.
- The laws against pollution should be more strictly enforced. <u>This</u> will lead to a better environment for everyone.
- Companies should enforce a lunchtime nap on their workers. This will lead to <u>increased productivity</u> in the afternoon.

✎ Practice 9

請完整閱讀 Practice 1 的範例文章，並且把你能找到的結果用語都畫上底線。

🔑 範例答案

你應該在第三段找到兩個用語。

- This may cause
- The result of this will be

☆ 請注意，在每個句子裡，第一個子句是描述建議，第二個子句則描述建議可能產生的結果。

☆ 請注意 n.p. 和 v.p. 的使用。

現在，請用結果的用語來寫作 **Practice 7** 的相關建議。來看看範例。

EX. The government should restrict the number of children each couple can have. As a result, the birthrate will go down.

範例答案

請研究我的範例，並確定你了解它們是怎麼寫出來的。

1. Certain industries should be forbidden to automate. This could lead to a slowdown in the unemployment rate.
2. People should be encouraged to interact more with each other. The result of this could be that communities will be stronger.
3. There should be a very high tax on car sales. The effect of this will be to reduce the number of cars on the road.
4. Physical exercise should be made a part of every schoolchild's day. The effect of this could be a drop in obesity.
5. The internet now reaches into most homes. This means that it's very difficult for governments and corporations to keep secrets.

　　最後，我們來把你在這個單元學到的內容都練習一次。請花一點時間規劃下方文章題目的答案，然後寫一篇介紹和兩個段落。請將你在前面幾個單元學到的所有內容都練習過。

Practice 11

請針對以下題目規劃你的答案，並且寫一篇文章。

> Social media has totally changed the way we start and maintain relationships. However, this has created many new problems.
>
> What are the most serious problems associated with social media and what can we do to solve them?

在你結束這個單元之前，請將下列清單看過，確定你能將所有要點都勾選起來。
如果有一些要點你還不清楚，請回頭再次閱讀本單元的相關部分。

□ 我知道該如何圍繞著一個問題或一些解決方法來寫出一個段落。
□ 我清楚知道 reason「原因」和 result「結果」的差異。
□ 我知道該如何透過描述狀況或問題的 reason，來發展主題意見。
□ 我知道該如何透過建議或解決方法可能產生的 result，來發展主題觀點。
□ 我對 general / specific 的結構已有更深入的了解。
□ 我已經學到可以用來描述 reason 和 result 的用語。
□ 我已經看過許多這些用語的例子。
□ 我已經看過這種用語的常見錯誤用法。
□ 我已經大量練習過如何使用這些用語。
□ 我已經練習過很多寫作。

EXAM TIP BOX

✓ 在寫作 problem / solution 的文章時，你應該用合理的用語描述所有
  你要描述的問題的「原因」。

✓ 在寫作 argument / opinion 的文章時，如果你描述一個狀況，試著思
  考造成該狀況的原因，並且用這些用語描述它。

Unit 13

寫作段落——
語態、條件和後果
Writing a Paragraph–
Modals, Conditions and Consequences

前言與暖身練習 Warm Up

在這個單元裡，你將學習如何透過提出造成某個狀況的 condition「條件」，以及可能產生的 consequences「後果」之相關資訊來發展你的主題句。這個單元的目的是告訴你可以用來描述這些條件和後果的用語。我們將看一些你可以用在文章裡的重要「情態助動詞」，這些情態助動詞可以讓你的文章有變化，並且幫你得到較高的分數。在本單元學習到的用語對於 problem / solution 的文章比較有幫助，但你也可以把它們用在 argument / opinion 的文章。

Practice 1

請針對以下文章題目規劃你的答案，然後閱讀範例文章。

> Cybercrime – crime involving computers – is becoming more common as we put more of our personal information online.
>
> What are the problems associated with cybercrime, and what can be done to solve them?

It cannot be denied that cybercrime is becoming more frequent. It's my opinion that this is a very serious problem that will only get worse in the future. This essay will look at some of the common problems and will then suggest a solution.

(1) _____. Take for example the way that personal banking information is now all stored on the cloud. It is very easy for criminals to access this information and steal money from ordinary citizens' bank accounts. The financial industry should have foreseen this problem, and banks ought to have taken action to prevent this kind of crime. If banks were more careful about security, they wouldn't have this problem.

(2) _____. Banks must be forced to improve their security systems so that hackers cannot access them. They should be made to refund any money stolen from their customers' accounts, and they ought to be forced to pay a fine when a theft occurs. If we force banks to be more careful about security, this kind of crime might not be so common. Another solution is to make customers more aware of the importance of changing their passwords frequently. If people change their passwords regularly, it will make it more difficult for criminals to access their information.

In conclusion, cybercrime causes great harm to private citizens and public institutions. Overall, it's clear that both banks and customers have a role to play in preventing it.

Practice 2

請在下列句子選出適當主題句以完成 **Practice 1** 每個段落的填空。

A. Another problem is banks losing money.
B. It is becoming easier for criminals to access personal information for their own uses.
C. Crime is when bad people break the law.
D. For example, my bank refused to pay me back when I had my money stolen.
E. I had money stolen from my bank account.
F. Nowadays it's becoming common for lots of information to be stored on the cloud.
G. Prevention is the best deterrent.

H. The solution is to make banks and individuals responsible.

🔑 範例答案

請看看我的答案，並且閱讀底下的說明。

(1) B   (2) H

☆ 你可以看到文章的結構和題目相關。第二段描述問題，第三段提出解決方法。

☆ 你已經學過主題句是段落裡最一般性的句子，其他句子則都跟著主題句。在範例中可以看到 B 是第二段裡最一般性的意見，因為它為接下來兩個具體說明的例句，提供了更一般性的想法。

☆ H 描述一般性的解決方法，所以我們可以看出文章被分成兩個部分：問題和解決方法。

☆ A 不是主題句，因為它很明顯是一個新增的句子：another problem ...。

☆ C 對關鍵字提出解釋，但它太一般性了；G 針對解決方法提出一般性的格言，但在這裡卻不夠具體。

☆ D 和 E 都太具體了。D 很明顯不是主題句，因為它以一個例子開頭。E 也不是第二段的主題句，因為接下來的句子會變得不合理。

☆ F 不是第二段的主題句，因為它包含的資訊在第二句裡重複了。

　　我們接下來將開始看看如何使用 modal verbs「情態助動詞」來提出解決方法，以及如何描述過去的錯誤所導致的問題。你也可以在 argument / opinion 的文章中，使用情態助動詞來表達你的意見。

情態助動詞 Modal Verbs

✎ **Practice 3**

請研究表格、例句和下方的說明。

非過去時間	
用語	意思和用法
should V shouldn't V ought to V ought not to V	這些情態助動詞是用於表達現在或未來應做卻未做的事情。should 和 ought to 的意思和用法並沒有差異。
must V mustn't V	這個情態助動詞與 should 和 ought to 有非常相似的意思,但我們會用這個情態助動詞來表達對某個處境的急迫性。
例句	

- The government should impose fines for companies who pollute the environment.
- There ought to be heavy fines for companies who break the law.
- Companies shouldn't think they can get away with breaking the law.
- People ought not to be so selfish.
- We must act fast, otherwise it will be too late.
- We mustn't ignore this problem, otherwise future generations will never forgive us.

☆ 所有例句都用現在或未來的時態來表達問題的解決方法。你可以在寫文章中的解決方法時使用這些用語。

☆ 請注意只有 ought 的後面接 to。人們常寫 must to,但這完全是錯的。如果你犯了這個錯誤,一定拿不到好分數。

☆ 請留意否定的形式,特別注意撇號的位置。

☆ Shouldn't 和 mustn't 通常是縮寫,但 ought not to 通常不縮寫。

☆ 有時我們會用 have to 而不用 must,因為在現實生活的狀況裡,它們的意思常常是一樣的。但是在 **IELTS 測驗裡,不要用 have to 會比較好。**

☒ 錯誤

- Governments should to listen to their people more.
- This problem must'nt be ignored.
- We have to take action now.
- Companies oughtn't to break the law.

☑ 正確

- Governments should listen to their people more.
- This problem mustn't be ignored.
- We must take action now.
- Companies ought not to break the law.

這些情態助動詞指涉的是現在、未來或是沒有指涉時間。因此,我們可以稱它們為 non-past modals「非過去情態助動詞」。你也可以用 should 和 ought to 來指涉過去,尤其是當你想要對過去的錯誤表達批判。在這種情況下,你必須加 have 和 past participle (p.p.),也就是動詞的過去分詞。

✎ **Practice 4**

請研究表格、例句和下方的說明。

過去時間	
用語	**意思和用法**
• should have p.p. • shouldn't have p.p. • ought to have p.p. • ought not to have p.p.	這些情態助動詞用來表達對過去犯的錯誤之批判。
例句	
• The government should have acted sooner. = 它們太晚採取行動。 • This company should not have broken the law. = 它們違法了。 • The criminals ought to have received stricter punishments. = 罪犯受到的懲罰太輕。 • They ought not to have committed the crime. = 他們犯了罪。	

☆ 所有例句都用來表達對過去所犯錯誤的批判。你可以在文章的問題部分使用這類用語。

☆ 必須用情態助動詞搭配 have + p.p. 來表達過去的時間。這表示你必須小心地使用正確的 p.p.，尤其當動詞是不規則動詞的時候。

☆ 請注意否定的 shouldn' have 是縮寫，但 ought not to 不用縮寫。

☆ 注意，你不應該用 must have p.p.。這樣寫的意思完全不一樣，而且你不應該在 IELTS 寫作中這樣寫。

⊠ 錯誤

• He should has told his boss about the problem sooner.
• They shouldn't have forgot the regulations.
• The government should'nt have ignored the whistleblower.

☑ 正確

• He should have told his boss about the problem sooner.
• They shouldn't have forgotten the regulations.
• The government shouldn't have ignored the whistleblower.

✎ **Practice 5**

請完整閱讀 **Practice 1** 的範例文章，並且把你能找到的情態助動詞都畫上底線。

🔑 範例答案

第二段

• should have foreseen
• ought to have taken

第三段

• must be forced
• should be made to
• ought to be forced

☆ 注意，第二段的情態助動詞全部指涉對過去的批判。

☆ 第三段的情態助動詞都指涉針對未來或現在的解決方法。

☆ 此外，請注意第三段的情態助動詞後面，都接被動態的不定詞：be forced、be made to。

我們來練習這些情態助動詞。

Practice 6

請重新正確排列這些句子中的字。第一個字是正確的。來看看範例。

EX. The companies who punish the government should severely pollute water.
The government should severely punish companies who pollute the water.

1. Factories discharge the river ought been not allowed to to have their waste into.

———————————————————————

2. Traffic to ought be controls pollution and factory prevent controls implemented to air.

———————————————————————

3. Diesel banned ago cars should a long have been time.

———————————————————————

4. Whistleblowers by protected law be should.

———————————————————————

5. We must buying change our companies business so that polluting go habits out of.

———————————————————————

6. We must generations action think future take of and now.

———————————————————————

🔑 範例答案

1. Factories ought not to have been allowed to discharge their waste into the river.
2. Traffic controls and factory controls ought to be implemented to prevent air pollution.
3. Diesel cars should have been banned a long time ago.
4. Whistleblowers should be protected by law.
5. We must change our buying habits so that polluting companies go out of business.
6. We must think of future generations and take action now.

✏️ Practice 7

承上題,請判斷各句分別指涉的是非過去時間還是過去時間。請在句子的旁邊為非過去時間寫 **NP**,過去時間寫 **P**。

🔑 範例答案

1. P   2. NP   3. P   4. NP   5. NP   6. NP

我們現在要繼續討論,看看應如何描述條件和後果。

條件和後果 Conditions and Consequences

在 IELTS 寫作任務中，你可能會想透過描述一個建議的條件和後果以發展自己的主題句，這部分在 Practice 1 範例文章的第三段可以看到。在 IELTS 測驗裡，有兩種條件和後果你可以用：the First Conditional「第一類條件」，和 the Second Conditional「第二類條件」。首先，我們來看看它們的意思以及相關用語。

The First Conditional「第一類條件」是指真實的條件。這表示如果第一個子句描述的情況真的發生了，第二個子句描述的情況也會自然成為第一句的結果而發生。你應該用這種條件句來描述在現實生活中，確實可能在現在或未來發生的情況

Practice 8

請研究表格中的例句和其下的說明。

The First Conditional
• If I get a high score in my IELTS test, I will be admitted to university abroad.
• If the government enforces the law, fewer companies will break it.

☆ 這些都有真實的可能性。
☆ 只要句子第一個部分的條件成立了，句子第二部分也會自然發生而成為結果。
☆ 第一個句子表達只要你用功，你就沒有理由得不到高分。
☆ 第二個句子表達政府沒有理由無法執法。

相反的，**The Second Conditional**「第二類條件」指的是某個狀況永遠都不會發生，因為它完全違背現實，因為它完全不是真實的。

Practice 9

請研究表格中的例句和其下的說明。

The Second Conditional
• If I got a high score in my IELTS test, I would be admitted to university abroad.
• If the government enforced the law, fewer companies would break it.

☆ 這些句子是假設性或不真實的，完全違反現實。

☆ 第一個句子表達你不打算考 IELTS，你沒有報名，而且你也不打算準備這個測驗。

☆ 第二個句子表達政府永遠不會執法，而且它們也不打算執法。

　　這裡很重要的是了解第一類和第二類條件句之間的差異，不在於時間，而在於現實性。如果你選擇寫第一類條件句，這表示你因為一些原因而相信條件有可能成真，它可能真的發生。如果你選擇第二類條件句，這表示你想要表達這個條件完全不可能成真，而且也完全不可能在現實發生。

✐ Practice 10

請研究表格中的例句和其下的說明。

The First Conditional
If I become the president of my country, everyone will be very happy.
☆ 這表示你有一些從政經驗，你也打算競選，而且你有贏的機會：這件事真的有可能發生。
The Second Conditional
If I became the president of my country, everyone would be very happy.
☆ 這表示你對從政完全沒有興趣，你永遠也不會變成總統，這件事不可能發生，是完全沒有事實根據的異想天開：這件事不可能發生。

　　就我的經驗來說，母語是中文的人常常很難了解第一類和第二類條件句的差異，因為中文不會刻意區分一個條件可能發生或不可能發生。了解兩者差異的關鍵，在於記得**第二類條件句永遠指的是與現實完全相反**。

　　現在，你已經知道這兩種條件的差異，我們繼續來看它的用語。

第一類條件句 First Conditionals

✎ **Practice 11**

請研究表格、例句和底下的說明。

真實	
條件子句	後果子句
If v.p. (present simple),	(will/won't V) (may/may not V) (might/might not V) (can V) (will probably V …)
例句	
• If there are more traffic police on the roads, motorists might drive more carefully. • Future generations will be in serious trouble if we continue to ignore climate change. • If the government introduces a higher road tax, fewer people will buy cars. • If we don't do something about global warming now, future generations might not have a good life.	

☆ 注意，所有句子都表達現在或未來可能成真的狀況。

☆ 所有句子都有兩個子句，而且如果句子用條件子句開頭，該句就有逗號；如果用後果子句開頭，就沒有逗號。主考官會看這些小細節，所以請確保你寫得正確。

☆ 你必須在條件子句使用現在簡單式，並在後果子句使用 will 或其他情態助動詞。注意，絕對不能在條件子句用 will。

☆ 可以把後果子句放在前面，但如果你這樣做，請小心動詞時態。

☆ 注意你在後果子句可以用哪一個情態助動詞。may 和 might 表達句子裡描述的後果只是眾多可能性的其中一個，亦即還有其他可能性是你沒有描述的。

☆ 不要擔心 may 和 might 的差異，這些情態助動詞的意思和用法都相同。

⊠ 錯誤
• If we take action <u>now it</u> won't be too late.
• If we <u>will</u> cut carbon emissions, it will help the environment.

☑ 正確

- If we take action <u>now, it</u> won't be too late.
- If we <u>cut</u> carbon emissions, it will help the environment.

✎ Practice 12

請完整閱讀 **Practice 1** 的範例文章，並且把你能找到的 **First Conditionals** 都畫上底線。

🔑 範例答案

第三段

- If we force banks to be more careful about security, this kind of crime might not be so common.
- If people change their passwords regularly, it will make it more difficult for criminals to access their information.

☆ 這個段落使用真實的 First Conditionals，表達這些事很容易發生。

現在我們就來練習 First Conditionals。

✎ Practice 13

請用 **Practice 11** 的用語擴展下面的資訊。來看看範例。

真實	
條件	後果
government and individuals share responsibility	solve problem
put up speed cameras	reduce speeding
good education	find a better job
increase tax on fuel	people think twice before using private car
invest in renewable energy	less pollution
stop hunting whales	increase in whale population

EX. If government and individuals share their responsibility, together we can solve this problem.

🔑 範例答案

很顯然，我不會知道你寫了什麼，但請研究我的範例，並確定你了解它們是怎麼寫出來的。

1. If they put up speed cameras everywhere, this will reduce speeding.
2. If people have a good education, they can find a better job.
3. If the government increases the tax on fuel, people might think twice before using private cars.
4. There will be less pollution if the government invests more in renewable energy.
5. If we stop hunting whales now, there might be an increase in the whale population in a few years.

在本單元的最後，我們來練習 Second Conditionals。

第二類條件句 Second Conditionals

✏️ Practice 14

請研究表格、例句和底下的說明。

非真實	
條件子句	後果子句
If v.p. (past simple),	(would/wouldn't V) (would probably V …) (could V)
例句	
• If people were not so greedy, they wouldn't consume so many of the earth's resources. • If corporations cared more about people and less about profits, their employers would probably be happier. • I could do more to prevent bad things from happening if I had more power. • If I didn't have Facebook, I would not be able to stay in touch with my parents so easily while I'm abroad.	

☆ 所有句子都表達現在或未來不可能成真的狀況，亦即都與事實相反。也就是人們確實貪婪、企業不在乎人們等等。

☆ 和 First Conditional 句子一樣，所有句子都有兩個子句。而且如果句子用條件子句開頭，該句就有逗號；如果用後果子句開頭，就沒有逗號。

☆ 注意，你必須在條件子句使用過去簡單式。這點讓人很混淆。這裡的過去簡單式不是表示過去的時間，而是表示非真實的過去時間。過去簡單式有兩個意思：真實的過去時間，例如 I went, and I came back，以及非真實的過去時間，例如 If I went, I would never come back.。

☆ 此外，你在後果子句必須使用 would 和 wouldn't，但不能用 couldn't。然而在條件子句中則絕對不可以用 would。

☆ 你可以把後果子句放在前面，但如果你這樣做，請小心動詞時態。

☒ 錯誤

- If we all <u>obey</u> the laws, social problems <u>disappear</u>.
- If governments <u>would rule</u> for everyone, not just for a privileged few, our country <u>is</u> a better place.

☑ 正確

- If we all <u>obeyed</u> the laws, social problems <u>would disappear</u>.
- If governments <u>ruled</u> for everyone, not just for a privileged few, our country <u>would be</u> a better place.

✎ Practice 15

請完整閱讀 Practice 1 的範例文章，將你能找到的 Second Conditionals 畫上底線。

🔑 範例答案

第二段

- If banks were more careful about security, they wouldn't have this problem.

☆ 這段是非真實或第二類條件句。它表達在現實裡，銀行並不在意它們的安全性。

✎ Practice 16

請用 Practice 14 的用語擴展下面的資訊。來看看範例。

非真實	
條件	後果
no media	people's general knowledge of world lower
government supply houses for everyone	high quality of living for all
no foreign workers in Taiwan	a lot of jobs not get done
I am prime minister	solve this problem
everyone is honest and not so selfish	social problems disappear
stop manufacturing cars	economy collapse

EX. If there were no media, people's general knowledge of the world would be a lot lower.

🔑 範例答案

再一次地，我顯然不會知道你寫了什麼，但請研究我的範例，並確定你了解它們是怎麼寫出來的。

1. If the government supplied houses for everyone, there would be a higher quality of living for all.
2. A lot of jobs would not get done if there were no foreign workers living in Taiwan.
3. If I were/was prime minister, I would solve this problem immediately.
4. If everyone was honest and not so selfish, a lot of social problems would disappear overnight.
5. If they stopped manufacturing cars, the economy of many countries would totally collapse.

　　最後，我們來把你在這個單元學到的內容都練習一次。請花一點時間規劃下方文章題目的答案，然後寫一篇介紹和兩個段落。請將你在最後幾個單元學到的所有內容都練習過。

✏️ Practice 17

請針對以下題目規劃你的答案，並且寫一篇文章。

> Globalisation has brought many benefits to the way we do business and communicate. But it has also caused many problems.
>
> What are the most serious problems associated with globalisation, and what can we do to solve them?

　　在你結束這個單元之前，請將下列清單看過，確定你能將所有要點都勾選起來。如果有一些要點你還不清楚，請回頭再次閱讀本單元的相關部分。

□ 我知道該如何圍繞著主題句寫出一個段落。

□ 我知道該如何使用情態助動詞來表達我的意見、提出問題的解決方法、表達我對過
　去錯誤的批判，以及表達一個解決方法的急迫性。

□ 我知道該如何寫條件和後果。

□ 我很清楚 First Conditionals「第一類條件句」和 Second Conditionals「第二類條件
　句」之間在意義和文法上的差異。

□ 我已經看過許多情態助動詞和條件句的例句。

□ 我已經看過這種用語的常見錯誤用法。

□ 我已經大量練習過如何使用這些用語。

□ 我已經練習過很多寫作。

EXAM TIP BOX

✓ 如果你在文章裡使用了多個條件句，請在其中一個先寫條件子句，
　另一個先寫後果子句。

✓ 這樣寫可以讓主考官知道，你能夠把兩種寫法都寫得正確。

✓ 不要忘記逗號！

Unit 14

寫作段落——
時態、複雜性和結論
**Writing a Paragraph—
Tenses, Complexity, and Conclusion**

前言與暖身練習 Warm Up

　　我們在本書 Part 1 中針對動詞時態做過許多討論。在 Unit 5，你學到描寫比較時該如何使用動詞時態；在 Unit 6，你學到在描寫地圖時，又該如何使用動詞時態。而在這個單元裡，你將學到在寫 Task 2 的「論證／意見」文章，以及「問題／解決方案」文章時，該如何使用動詞時態以改善寫作。我還要告訴你如何用 which 這個字寫出更複雜的句子。使用多樣的動詞時態和較複雜的句子結構，可以幫你得到較高的分數。最後，我們在這個單元也要學習如何寫「結論」。

✎ Practice 1

請針對以下文章題目規劃你的答案。然後閱讀範例文章。

> People are now living longer than at any time in human history. Longer life expectancy is a great blessing for humanity. What are the causes of increased life expectancy, and what is your opinion about it?
>
> Write an essay expressing your opinion.

範例文章

In recent years, life expectancy has increased in most developing countries. There are several causes for this, such as more sanitary living conditions and improvements to medical science. On the other hand there are those who say that increased life expectancy has drawbacks. In my opinion, increased life expectancy is a good thing. There are many reasons why I think so.

(1) _____. Most people have clean drinking water, and there are many people who are now enjoying better sewage arrangements. In the developing world, these conditions are also improving. We have learnt from the lessons of the past, that clean water and proper sewage treatment are the keys to better public health.

(2) _____. Our understanding of the causes of diseases and how to treat them has recently advanced rapidly, and it is still improving. For example, one hundred years ago, people did not understand that mosquitos carried malaria, and penicillin, which was discovered in 1928, meant that many diseases that were once considered incurable can now be cured quite easily. The result is a longer life and a higher quality of life for everyone.

(3) _____. We are already putting a heavy financial burden on the younger generation, and we are piling more pressure on the limited resources of the planet. But, in my view, these are more problems of wealth inequality and sustainability.

In conclusion, increased life expectancy is one of the benefits of modernity, and it's my opinion that it is something all human inhabitants of the planet will soon enjoy.

Practice 2

請在下列句子選出適當主題句以完成 Practice 1 每個段落的填空。

A. Although higher life expectancy is a blessing that should not be withheld from anyone, it does have some negative effects.

B. Cholera is a disease that used to cause many deaths globally.

C. Living conditions have improved immeasurably for the last hundred years, at least in the developed world.

PART 2

D. People must keep themselves clean if they want to live longer.

E. The developed world usually means the countries of Western Europe and North America.

F. Medical science has also improved.

G. There are many other problems besides life expectancy.

H. We now know that many diseases are caused by viruses and bacteria.

🔎 範例答案

請看看我的答案，並且閱讀底下的說明。

(1) C   (2) F   (3) A

☆ 你可以看到文章的結構按照介紹中鋪陳的三個要點：前面兩段為 sanitary living conditions「衛生生活條件」和 improvements to medical science「改善醫療科學」，而第四段則為 negative effects of higher life expectancy「較長壽命的負面影響」。其他在這些段落裡的句子，都分別為句子 C、F 和 A 提供更多具體例子。

☆ B 是「幾乎要被醫療科學根除之疾病」的一個具體例子，但是因為該句太具體，它不適合當作第三段的主題句。

☆ D 是「為了保持衛生生活條件，人們可以做什麼事」的一個例子，但該句太過具體而不能當作一般性的主題句，而且因為它用 must，故比較適合當作 problem / solution 文章的解決方法，不適用於 argument / opinion 的文章。

☆ E 太過一般性，而且和三個段落裡的其他句子都不太有關係。

☆ G 超過文章的範圍。這篇文章要你探討平均壽命，所以不要描述其他問題。在第四段，作者說龐大的財務負擔及地球資源面臨的壓力，是平均壽命增加導致的問題，而不是因為其他我們必須解決的問題。

☆ H 用稍微具體的方式，陳述第三段第二句所說的內容。但是請記得，一個段落應該以最一般性的意見開頭，因此 H 不適合放在這裡，它太具體了，而且太重複。

動詞時態 Verb Tenses

　　到目前為止，在 Part 2 前面的單元裡，你已經學過使用現在簡單式來表達想法，因為你大部分都是在描述事實和意見。而在接下來的部分，我將告訴你如何透過變化動詞時態，讓寫作的句子更複雜。基本上，在 Task 2 的文章中有五種時態可以用，這些時態的用法取決於你文章中所指的時間。

✎ **Practice 3**

請研究表格、例句和下方的說明。

時態和時間	
present simple 現在簡單式	這個時態是用來描述和時間無關的事情，例如：事實和意見。它也可以用在用來描述狀態的動詞，例如 be 和 have。
• The arts play a significant role in public life. • The theatre industry in London is world famous. • Actors have highly developed skills.	
present continuous 現在進行式	這個時態是用來描述在現在尚未結束的時間下，進行的趨勢或活動。如果沒有結果，或是你不想把重點放在結果上，請使用這種時態。
• The problem is getting worse all the time. • The gaming trend among young people is increasing. • Climate change is having a catastrophic effect on many lives around the world.	
present perfect simple 現在完成式	這個時態是用來描述在現在尚未結束的時間下，行動的結果。
• There has been a great improvement in living standards. • The situation has worsened in the last few years. • Climate change has had a catastrophic effect on many lives around the world.	

past simple 過去簡單式	這個時態是用來描述過去已經結束的行動或狀態。

- Many people died of the plague.
- The situation was very bad before the government started doing something about it.
- Scientists did not know what caused the problem, until they discovered the virus.

will V 未來簡單式	請用 will V 來描寫你很確定未來會發生的行動或狀態。

- The situation will only get worse.
- More people will die.
- Antibiotics will eventually become useless.

☆ 現在簡單式通常用來表達和時間無關的事情。比方說，Taiwan is an island 這個句子和現在的時間無關，因為它說的在昨天和明天也一樣成立。如果和現在的時間有關，它未必在昨天和明天也成立。

☆ 當 have 表示 possess，它是一種狀態，而且不能用在現在進行式，例如我們可以說 My country has a huge international debt，但是不能說 My country is having a huge international debt.。Have 也可以用來表示 get 或 eat，例如 I am having lunch.，在這種情況下，have 可以用現在簡單式。然而，在 IELTS 寫作裡，這種用法十分罕見。

☆ 現在進行式和現在完成式，描述的都是現在向未結束的時間。它們的差異在於你怎麼看待一個情況。你可能會想把重點放在一個持續的趨勢：Global warming is having a catastrophic effect on many lives around the world. 或是放在一個已經達成的結果：Global warming has had a catastrophic effect on many lives around the world.，它們在表達時間上意思都一樣，都是指現在，但要表達的觀點卻是不同的。

☆ 當你使用現在完成式，請確保動詞和主詞一致。是 It has improved，不是 it have improved.

☆ 當你使用現在進行式，請確保動詞和主詞一致。是 It is improving，而不是 it are improving.

☆ 許多人認為（或者有人教他們）現在完成式描述的是過去的時間，這是不正確的。它表示行動已經結束（perfected「已完成」），但動作發生的時間還沒結束（present「現在」）。不要把動作和時間搞混。

☆ 請用過去簡單式描述歷史事件，或是從你的自身經驗提出個人案例。

☆ 在 IELTS 寫作測驗裡，你不需要寫 be going to，這樣寫表示那是你的個人計畫，而在考試裡請不要寫有關你的個人計畫。

☆ 在 IELTS 測驗裡，你不需要用過去完成式。

☒ 錯誤

• Many people in the developed world are having two cars.
• People has learned how to cope.
• Governments is taking action to solve the problem.
• Last year my country has had an earthquake.
• I had experienced this situation personally a few years ago.

☑ 正確

• Many people in the developed world have two cars.
• People have learned how to cope.
• Governments are taking action to solve the problem.
• Last year my country had an earthquake.
• I experienced this situation personally a few years ago.

✎ Practice 4

請回到 **Practice 1** 的範例文章，並且將所有動詞都畫上底線。接著，請將它們分別填入下方表格的正確欄位。

動詞時態				
無時間動詞 present simple	現在時間動詞 （活動或趨勢） present continuous	現在時間動詞 （結果） present perfect	過去時間動詞 past simple	未來時間動詞 will V

請研究這張表格,以及我在下面的說明。

動詞時態				
無時間動詞 present simple	現在時間動詞 (活動或趨勢) present continuous	現在時間動詞 (結果) present perfect	過去時間動詞 past simple	未來時間動詞 will V
• there are • say • has • is • can	• are enjoying • are improving • is improving • are putting • are piling	• has increased • have improved • have learnt • has improved • has advanced	• did not understand • meant • was discovered • were	• will

☆ 注意,你可以在兩個動詞之間放像 still、also 之類的副詞。

☆ 請留意用來描述狀態而非條件的 stative verb「靜態動詞」,使用時你要用現在簡單式,例如 increased life expectancy has dangers.。

☆ 請注意範例文章如何使用現在簡單式表達意見、事實,以及用 set-phrases 來組織想法:… increased life expectancy is a good thing. There are many reasons why I think so.。

　　當使用這些動詞時態,請務必確保你使用的是正確的時間字串。這樣說的意思是,你用的時間字串應該和動詞時態有一樣的意義。我們在 Unit 6 學過時間字串,你也許會想快速去回顧一下。

Practice 5

請研究表格、例句和底下的說明。

時間 chunks			
present perfect simple		**present continuous**	
so far	since X	at present	still
yet	recently	nowadays	currently
now	lately	now	
just	never	at the moment	
for X	ever	these days	
already	for ages	already	
	in recent years		
sample sentences			
• So far, the situation has not improved.			
• Nowadays many people are becoming addicted to online gaming.			
• We have never had this problem before.			
• We are still trying to understand how this process works.			

☆ 使用這些字的時候，你絕對不能用 present simple「現在簡單式」，因為這些表達時間的字表示現在的時間，而我們在前面學過，現在簡單式表示是和時間完全無關的事情。

☆ 請注意哪些時間用語可以用在這兩種時態。

☆ 使用時，你必須把 just、already、recently、lately、never 和 still 放在兩個動詞中間。

☆ 只可以在問句使用 ever。不要在肯定句使用 ever。

☆ For 的後面必須寫一段時間，而在 since 後面你可以寫一個時間點。

⊠ 錯誤

• Since the start of the last century, scientists <u>find</u> many new drugs.

• So far scientists <u>are finding</u> cures for many diseases.

• Governments <u>have ever tried</u> to solve this problem.

• Technology has improved <u>for 2010</u>.

• Medical science has advanced <u>since ten years</u>.

☑ 正確

- Since the start of the last century, scientists <u>have found</u> many new drugs.
- So far scientists <u>have found</u> cures for many diseases.
- Governments <u>have tried</u> to solve this problem.
- Technology has improved <u>since 2010</u>.
- Medical science has advanced <u>for ten years</u>.

✎ Practice 6

請回到 **Practice 1** 的範例文章,找出所有時間用語的例子,並且注意它們使用的時態。

🔑 範例答案

你應該找到這些用語,以下根據它們出現的順序列出:

In recent years, / for the last hundred years / now / recently / still / now / already

☆ 請注意,我們把 ago 和過去簡單式一起用:one hundred years ago, people did not understand ...。

　　現在,一起來練習你學到與時態和時間用語有關的知識。

✎ Practice 7

請將句子改寫成正確的時態。來看看範例。

EX. Already many antibiotics become useless.
Already many antibiotics have become useless.

1. At the moment people live longer.

_____

2. Currently we face a problem of global overpopulation.

_____

3. Humanity never has such a high life expectancy.

_____

4. Medical science improve nowadays.

_____

5. Recently scientists discover a cure for this disease.

_____

6. Since the start of the 20 century, antibiotics are used to treat common illnesses.

_____

7. These days many people question whether a high life expectancy is a good thing.

_____

🔑 範例答案

1. At the moment people <u>are living</u> longer.
2. Currently we <u>are facing</u> a problem of global overpopulation.
3. Humanity <u>has never had</u> such a high life expectancy.
4. Medical science <u>is improving</u> nowadays.
5. Recently scientists <u>have discovered</u> a cure for this disease.
6. Since the start of the 20 century, antibiotics <u>have been used to</u> treat common illnesses.
7. These days many people <u>are questioning</u> whether a high life expectancy is a good thing.

寫複雜的句子 Writing Complex Sentences

　　現在來看如何透過使用 which 這個字，讓你的句子變得更複雜。我們將探討兩種使用這個字的方法，這兩種方法對 IELTS 考生來說普遍都覺得困難。首先，我們會先看如何將 which 和 there is/are 結構一起用，接著是將 which 和 non-defining relative clauses「非限定關係子句」一起用。

✎ **Practice 8**

請比較以下兩個句子和底下的說明。

簡單的句子	Many drugs can now cure this disease.
複雜的句子	There are many drugs which can now cure this disease.

☆ 這個表格告訴你一個包含主詞、動詞、受詞 (SVO) 結構的簡單句，可以透過加入一個介紹詞短語 (There is) 以及一個關係子句，把它改成比較複雜的兩個 SVOs。

☆ There is 的確非常簡單，但你一定要記得用 wh- 字彙。

☆ 如果句子的主詞是東西，請用 which；如果主詞是人，請用 who；如果句子的主詞是原因，請用 why。

☒ 錯誤

- There are many <u>drugs can</u> now cure this disease.
- There are many people <u>which</u> think the internet is unsafe for children.

☑ 正確

- There are many drugs <u>which</u> can now cure this disease.
- There are many people <u>who</u> think the internet is unsafe for children.

✎ **Practice 9**

請回到 **Practice 1** 的範例文章，並且找出這類句子的所有例子。

🔑 範例答案

你應該在前面兩段找到三個例子：

- there are those who say that increased life expectancy has drawbacks
- There are many reasons why I think so.
- there are many people who are now enjoying

✎ Practice 10

請用你剛才學到的文法改寫下列句子。

1. Many illnesses have been cured.

_____

2. A number of studies show that health is related to emotional wellbeing.

_____

3. Many cities in the developing world still do not have adequate sewage arrangements.

_____

4. Many people still do not have access to clean drinking water.

_____

🔑 範例答案

1. There are many illnesses which have been cured.
2. There are a number of studies which show that health is related to emotional wellbeing.
3. There are many cities in the developing which still do not have adequate sewage arrangements.
4. There are many people who still do not have access to clean drinking water.

　　到目前為止，我希望你覺得很簡單。現在，我們來看更複雜一點的。你可以用這種 wh- 子句來連結兩個不同的想法，或兩個不同的簡單句子，把它們融合成一個複雜的句子。

Practice 11

請比較以下兩個句子和底下的說明。

簡單的句子	This problem is very bad. It affects many people.
複雜的句子	This problem, which affects many people, is very bad.

☆ 首先，請注意使用這種文法結構時，兩個意見之間要有清楚的關連。如果想法之間沒有這種關連，寫出來會很奇怪。請記得要思考意義，不要只著重文法。

☆ 你必須將第二個想法緊接在第一個句子主詞的後面，接著用 which（或如果是人的話，用 who），而不是用第二句原本的主詞或受詞。

☆ 你必須省略第二個句子原本的主詞或受詞。

☆ 請注意你必須使用兩個逗號，一個就在第一句主詞的後面，第二個在內嵌子句的後面。

☒ 錯誤

- This problem, <u>which looks really nice when it's finished</u>, affects many people.
- The president <u>is, who</u> is usually elected by the people, serves for five years.
- The climate, which used to be quite stable, <u>it</u> is becoming more unstable.
- The scientist, <u>which</u> won the Nobel Prize, was discredited.
- The <u>virus which</u> probably originated in <u>Africa has</u> already killed millions of people.

☑ 正確

- This problem, <u>which seems to be getting worse</u>, affects many people.
- The <u>president, who</u> is usually elected by the people, serves for 5 years.
- The climate, which used to be quite <u>stable, is</u> becoming more unstable.
- The scientist, <u>who</u> won the Nobel Prize, was discredited.
- The <u>virus, which</u> probably originated in <u>Africa,</u> has already killed millions of people.

Practice 12

請回到 **Practice 1** 的範例文章，並且找出這類句子的所有例子。

🔑 範例答案

你應該在第三段找到一個例子：

penicillin, which was discovered in 1928, meant that ….

就像前面說過的，在使用這種文法時，你一定要確保兩個想法彼此相關。接下來我們會進行兩個練習來讓你更加了解相關用法。首先把重點放在意思，然後是用語。

✏️ Practice 13

請將欄位裡的想法加以配對。

主要想法	支援想法／額外想法
Infant mortality has been increasing	we know this from our experience in other countries
The illness has recently been conquered all over the world	it is usually a positive thing
The discoverer of the cure won the Nobel prize	it usually only affects people living in the developing world
A high life expectancy can also lead to problems	it used to claim many lives
The most effective solution is education	she tried for many years before she succeeded

🔑 範例答案

1. Infant mortality has been increasing. It usually only affects people living in the developing world.
2. The illness has recently been conquered all over the world. It used to claim many lives.
3. The discoverer of the cure won the Nobel prize. She tried for many years before she succeeded.
4. A high life expectancy can also lead to problems. It is usually a positive thing.
5. The most effective solution is education. We know this from our experience in other countries.

請用 Practice 11 的文法將前一個練習中的兩個句子合併成一句。來看看範例。

EX. 1. Infant mortality has been increasing. It usually only affects people living in the developing world.

   Infant mortality, which usually only affects people living in the developing world, has been increasing.

2. _____

3. _____

4. _____

5. _____

🔑 範例答案

2. The illness, which used to claim many lives, has recently been conquered all over the world.

3. The discoverer of the cure, who tried for many years before she succeeded, won the Nobel Prize.

4. A high life expectancy, which is usually a positive thing, can also lead to problems.

5. The most effective solution, which we know from our experience in other countries, is education.

☆ 請注意在第五句，which 指的是動詞 know 的受詞，也就是原本句子的 this。

結論 Conclusion

最後，我們要學習如何寫結論。基本上，寫結論非常簡單。你最多只需要用一句或兩句寫結論。這裡有一張清單可以協助你。

寫作「結論」的清單
1. 用一個句子總結你的論證 2. 重申你的意見 3. 保持一般性 4. 不要提出具體的例子或細節 5. 不要提出新意見

現在，我們來看看一些你可以用在結論的用語。

PART
2

Practice 15

請看看這些用來總結論證的片語。

總結用的 set-phrases	
In conclusion, In the last analysis, To sum up, To summarize,	On balance, Overall, it is clear that v.p. I would recommend that v.p.

☆ 請使用這些用語來總結你的論證。

☆ 你可以從 Unit 10 的 Practice 7 中選用一個表達意見的 set-phrases 來重申你的意見。

☆ 不要使用你在「介紹」用過的 set-phrase。請試著用不同的 set-phrase，讓主考官知道你懂更多的 set-phrases。

Practice 16

請看 **Practice 1** 範例文章的結論，注意它如何遵循上面的 **checklist**，並使用了 **Practice 15** 中的哪一個 **set-phrase**。

現在，請回顧一下 Unit 11-Unit 13 中範例文章的結論，注意它們如何遵循上面的 checklist，並使用了 Practice 15 中的哪些 set-phrases。

最後，我們還是用一個寫作練習來作為本書的結束。

📝 **Practice 18**

請針對以下題目規劃你的答案，並且寫一篇文章。

> Many people don't eat animal products. They believe that veganism is better for their health and also better for the environment.
>
> To what extent do you agree or disagree?

在你結束這個單元之前，請將下列清單看過，確定你能將所有要點都勾選起來。如果有一些要點你還不清楚，請回頭再次閱讀本單元的相關部分。

☐ 我更實際理解了一個段落如何以一個一般性的主題句，外加具體細節組織而成。

☐ 我知道如何正確使用動詞來描述無時間、現在的時間、過去的時間以及未來的時間。

☐ 我知道如何用現在的時間和過去時間的趨勢來描述結果。

☐ 我知道如何用 there is/are 和 which / who 來寫複雜的句子。

☐ 我知道如何使用 non-defining relative clauses「非限定關係子句」讓我的寫作更複雜。

☐ 我已經看過許多使用不同動詞時態的例句。

☐ 我已經看過許多使用關係子句的例句。

☐ 我已經看過這種用語的常見錯誤用法。

☐ 我已經大量練習過如何使用這些用語。

☐ 我已經練習過很多寫作。

EXAM TIP BOX

✓ 最好廣泛使用不同時態，讓主考官知道你能夠正確使用動詞。

✓ 盡可能讓你的結論越短越好！

以下彙整本書 PART 2 各單元的寫作 Task 2 範例題目，請根據你在書中學到的寫作技巧，實際進行寫作練習。

Unit 8

Topic 1

In recent years, many countries have become extremely concerned about the increase in crimes against immigrants. Better enforcement of the law and stricter punishments are necessary.

Write an essay expressing your point of view.

Writing Your Answer	
Introduction	
Paragraph ①	
Paragraph ②	
Paragraph ③	
Conclusion	

Global warming has recently become the most urgent long term issue the world faces, and many people think not enough is being done to solve this problem.

What problems are the effects of global warming causing us now, and what can we do to solve them?

	Writing Your Answer
Introduction	
Paragraph ①	
Paragraph ②	
Paragraph ③	
Conclusion	

Topic 1

The mass media, including television, radio and newspapers, have a great influence in shaping people's ideas.

To what extent do you agree or disagree with this statement?

Writing Your Answer	
Introduction	
Paragraph ①	
Paragraph ②	
Paragraph ③	
Conclusion	

附錄

1

The destruction of rain forests to create land for agricultural use is a serious problem.

What are some of the common problems, and what can be done to reduce them?

Writing Your Answer	
Introduction	
Paragraph ①	
Paragraph ②	
Paragraph ③	
Conclusion	

Further education institutions should be forced to accept the same numbers of male and female students in every subject.

Write an essay expressing your point of view.

Writing Your Answer	
Introduction	
Paragraph ①	
Paragraph ②	
Paragraph ③	
Conclusion	

附 錄

1

The internet has changed the way we share and use information, but it has also created new problems.

Identify the problems and suggest ways to solve them.

Writing Your Answer	
Introduction	
Paragraph ①	
Paragraph ②	
Paragraph ③	
Conclusion	

Topic 1

Plans to give prisoners computers with access to the internet so that they can study while they are in prison have been criticized for wasting government money.

Write an essay expressing your point of view.

	Writing Your Answer
Introduction	
Paragraph ①	
Paragraph ②	
Paragraph ③	
Conclusion	

附錄

1

Governments should legislate to ensure that women have the same opportunities as men in the market for labour.

Write an essay expressing your point of view.

Writing Your Answer	
Introduction	
Paragraph ①	
Paragraph ②	
Paragraph ③	
Conclusion	

Rising sea levels caused by global warming is one of the biggest problems humanity faces, both now and in the future.

What other problems are associated with this, and what are some possible solutions?

Writing Your Answer	
Introduction	
Paragraph ①	
Paragraph ②	
Paragraph ③	
Conclusion	

Some people believe that children are naturally competitive, and that this should be encouraged in order to prepare them for the adult world. Others think that children should be taught to cooperate instead.

Discuss both these views and give your own opinion.

Writing Your Answer	
Introduction	
Paragraph ①	
Paragraph ②	
Paragraph ③	
Conclusion	

Overpopulation of urban areas is causing many problems for citizens.

What are some of the most serious ones, and what can individuals and governments do to solve these problems.

	Writing Your Answer
Introduction	
Paragraph ①	
Paragraph ②	
Paragraph ③	
Conclusion	

附錄

1

 **Unit 11**

Topic 1

The government should not support the arts. The money will be better spent on other things.

To what extent do you agree or disagree?

Writing Your Answer	
Introduction	
Paragraph ①	
Paragraph ②	
Paragraph ③	
Conclusion	

Traditional values like trust, honour and kindness don't seem important these days. A person's worth seems to be judged according to material possessions and social status.

To what extent do you agree or disagree with this opinion?

Writing Your Answer	
Introduction	
Paragraph ①	
Paragraph ②	
Paragraph ③	
Conclusion	

附錄

1

Topic 1

Global overpopulation is a serious problem which will get worse in the future.

What are some of the problems, and what can individuals and governments do to solve them?

Writing Your Answer	
Introduction	
Paragraph ①	
Paragraph ②	
Paragraph ③	
Conclusion	

Social media has totally changed the way we start and maintain relationships. However, this has created many new problems.

What are the most serious problems associated with social media and what can we do to solve them?

Writing Your Answer	
Introduction	
Paragraph ①	
Paragraph ②	
Paragraph ③	
Conclusion	

附錄
1

Topic 1

> Cybercrime – crime involving computers – is becoming more common as we put more of our personal information online.
>
> What are the problems associated with cybercrime, and what can be done to solve them?

	Writing Your Answer
Introduction	
Paragraph ①	
Paragraph ②	
Paragraph ③	
Conclusion	

Globalisation has brought many benefits to the way we do business and communicate. But it has also caused many problems.

What are the most serious problems associated with globalisation, and what can we do to solve them?

	Writing Your Answer
Introduction	
Paragraph ①	
Paragraph ②	
Paragraph ③	
Conclusion	

Topic 1

> People are now living longer than at any time in human history. Longer life expectancy is a great blessing for humanity. What are the causes of increased life expectancy, and what is your opinion about it.
>
> Write an essay expressing your opinion.

Writing Your Answer	
Introduction	
Paragraph ①	
Paragraph ②	
Paragraph ③	
Conclusion	

Many people don't eat animal products. They believe that veganism is better for their health and also better for the environment.

To what extent do you agree or disagree?

	Writing Your Answer
Introduction	
Paragraph ①	
Paragraph ②	
Paragraph ③	
Conclusion	

附錄
1

　　爲方便複習，以下彙整本書學過的重要用語。若在用法上有不清楚的部分請再回頭閱讀該單元的相關部分。

Unit 2

分析資訊及組織答案的用語〈參照 P.44〉

organising your response	interpreting the data
• Significantly, … • On the other hand, … • Another point to notice is that v.p. … • Generally, … • Also, … • Another thing to note is that v.p. … • What's interesting is that v.p. … • … v.p. while v.p. …	• This means that (clearly) v.p. … • The reasons for this are that v.p. … • The reasons for this are unclear. • A possible reason for this might be that v.p. … • Clearly, … • This might be due to the fact that v.p. … • This suggests that v.p. …

Unit 3

表達插圖類型的字彙〈參照 P.52〉

general	specific	
graphic	bar chart	diagram
graph	flow chart	line chart
illustration	map	pie chart
visual	table	

shows 的同義字〈參照 P.53〉

shows n.p. shows wh- v.p.	displays n.p. illustrates n.p. presents n.p. represents n.p.	displays wh- v.p. illustrates wh- v.p. presents wh- v.p. represents wh- v.p.

常用來和 **n.p.** 連用的連接短語 〈參照 **P.58**〉

why	where	when
… the reasons for … … the relative 　 importance of …	… the location(s) of … … the origin(s) of … … the source(s) of …	… the start of … … the end of … … the (different) period(s) of … … the time(s) of …

how	how often / how soon	how much / how many
… the methods of … … the ways of …	… the frequency of …	… the numbers of … … the amount of … … the percentage of … … the proportion of … … the demand for … … the consumption of … … the rate of … … the decrease of … … the increase of …

which / what
… the types of …   … the kinds of …   … the categories of …

Unit 4

描述變動的動詞片語 〈參照 **P.66**〉

unfinished time	adverb
has increased	dramatically
has decreased	rapidly
has risen	sharply
has fallen	
has dropped	significantly
has gone down	considerably
has gone up	enormously
has remained steady	
has stabilized	noticeably
	markedly

finished time	adverb
increased	gradually
decreased	steadily
rose	
fell	modestly
dropped	slightly
went up	
went down	fivefold
remained steady	tenfold
stabilized	

描述變動的名詞片語〈參照 **P.70**〉

verb	adjective		movement noun
be	a dramatic	a modest	increase (of # in s/th)
have	a rapid	a slight	decrease (of # in s/th)
experience	a sharp	a small	rise (of # in s/th)
see	a sharper	a smaller	fall (of # in s/th)
show			drop (of # in s/th)
enjoy	a significant	a steady overall	
suffer	a considerable	an overall	
	an enormous	a net	
	a major		
		a fivefold	
	a noticeable	a tenfold	
	a marked		
	a gradual		
	a steady		

描述變動中的最高點或最低點〈參照 **P.73**〉

type of movement	verb phrase	noun phrase
/\	peaked (at #)	reached a peak (at #)
\/	troughed (at #)	reached a trough (at #)
—	stabilized (at #) remained steady (at #)	- -

280

描述數字的兩種方式〈參照 **P.74**〉

distance		point	
X points/units	by X percent/%	to X	be at X
X percent/%	from X to Z	from X	at X
by X points/units	of X %		
of X points/units			

可作為「模糊標記」的字彙〈參照 **P.75**〉

preposition	vagueness marker	number
	roughly	
	around	
	just over	
	just under	
	approximately	

Unit 5

比較「相異處」的寫法 (1)〈參照 **P.86**〉

describing differences 1			
be	much	higher (n.p.)	than n.p.
have	slightly	lower (n.p.)	than v.p.
do	x%	more (n.p.)	
		less (n.p.)	
		fewer (n.p.)	
		___ er (n.p.)	

比較「相異處」的寫法 (2)〈參照 **P.87**〉

describing differences 2			
There were/was	much	higher (n.p.)	than n.p.
	slightly	lower (n.p.)	
	x%	more (n.p.)	
		less (n.p.)	
		fewer (n.p.)	

附錄
2

比較「相似處」的寫法 (1)〈參照 P.91〉

describing similarities 1			
be have do	(just) (almost) (not)	as much (n.p.) as many (n.p.) as (adjective) the same (n.p.)	as n.p. as v.p.

比較「相似處」的寫法 (2)〈參照 P.92〉

describing similarities 2			
There were/was	(almost) (not)	as much (n.p.) as many (n.p.)	as n.p. as v.p.

描述「最高級」〈參照 P.96〉

regular	irregular
the highest n.p. the lowest n.p. the biggest n.p. the most n.p. the least n.p. the fewest n.p. the smallest n.p. the _____est n.p.	the best n.p. the worst n.p. the most (adjective) n.p.

Unit 6

描述一般性的變化：動詞片語〈參照 P.108〉

describing general changes: verb phrase		
finished time verb	**unfinished time verb**	**adverb**
changed was developed was transformed	has changed has been developed has been transformed	dramatically spectacularly considerably significantly radically

描述一般性的變化：名詞片語〈參照 P.109〉

describing general changes: noun phrase			
verb		**adjective**	**noun**
finished time	**unfinished time**		
saw	has seen	dramatic	changes
experienced	has experienced	spectacular	developments
underwent	has undergone	considerable	transformations
witnessed	has witnessed	significant	
		radical	

描述「改變」的字彙〈參照 P.112〉

verbs: changes					
constructive changes		**destructive changes**		**no change**	
English	**中文**	**English**	**中文**	**English**	**中文**
add (sth) to	添加	chop down	砍倒	remain as it is/was	保持原樣
build	建立	clear	清除	remain untouched	保持不變
construct	建造	cut down	降低	leave (s/th) untouched	保持不變
convert (s/th) into	轉換為	destroy	破壞	leave (s/th)	未開發
develop	發展	demolish	拆除	undeveloped	
establish	建立	divert	轉移	leave (s/th) alone	讓某人獨處
expand	擴大	drain	排出	spare	騰出
extend	延伸	flatten	整平		
modernize	現代化	knock down	擊倒		
open	打開	remove	移除		
plant	栽種	ruin	毀壞		
reconstruct	重建	pave over	鋪平		
relocate	搬遷				
renovate	修復				
replace	取代				
set up	建立				
turn (s/th) into	擴大				
widen					

描述「時間」的字串〈參照 **P.116**〉

finished time chunks	unfinished time chunks
over the period	during this time
from X to Y	during the X year period
during that time	so far
during the X year period	recently
between X and Y	
X years ago	

描述「位置」的字串〈參照 **P.118**〉

location chunks	
to the north/south/east/west	next to the X
to the north/south/east/west of the X	beside the X
to the north east/north west/south east/south west of the X	near the X
to the right/left of the X	by the X
in the north/south/east/west	… nearby.
in the north/south/east/west of the X	north
between the X and the Y	south
among the Xs	east
in the middle/centre of the X	west
through the middle/centre of the X	north east/north west
on the other side of the X	south east/south west
across from the X	by the edge of the X
opposite the X	at the edge of the X
on the north/south/east/west/side of the X	from north to south
	from east to west
	outside the X

「序列標記」的寫法〈參照 P.129〉

sequence markers	
The process of X starts with n.p.	in the next stage
The process of making X starts when v.p.	in this stage
First,	in the final stage
Second,	in the second stage
Next,	during the next stage
After that,	during the second stage
After this,	during this stage
Then,	during the final stage
Finally,	
While this has been happening, v.p.	
Meanwhile,	
At the same time,	
It's during this stage that v.p.	

不同時態中，動詞的主／被動用法〈參照 P.133〉

passive verb chunks		
verb tense	active	passive
present simple	they make X	X is/are made
present continuous	they are making X	X is/are being made
present perfect	they have made X	X has been/have been made
past simple	they made X	X was/were made
past continuous	they were making	X was/were being made
past perfect	they had made X	X had been made
will future	they will make X	X will be made

情態動詞的主／被動用法〈參照 P.135〉

active modal verbs	passive modal verbs
They **can** check X	X **can** be checked
They **have to** check X	X **has** to be checked
They **need to** check X	X **needs** to be checked

附錄
2

285

| They **should** check X | X **should** be checked |
| They **allow** X to cool down | X is **allowed to** cool down |

描述「過程」的動詞字串〈參照 P.137〉

English	中文	English	中文
be added to	被加到	be lengthened	被加長
be adjusted to	調整為	be mixed together	被混合
be altered to	被改為	be mixed with Y	被與 Y 混合
be applied to	被應用於	be packaged	被包裝
be assembled	被組裝	be packed into	被包裝成
be bent (into X)	被彎曲成	be prepared	做好準備
be cast	被施放	be pressed	被按下
be chosen	被選中	be pumped out	被抽出來
be classified (into X)	被分類為	be put together	被放在一起
be combined with	與……結合	be released	被釋出
be cooled	被冷卻	be removed	被移除
be crushed	被粉碎	be rolled	被滾動
be cut into	被切成	be separated into X and Y	被分成 X 和 Y
be designed	被設計	be shipped	被運送
be developed	被開發	be shortened	被縮短
be discarded	被丟棄	be sieved	被篩過
be divided into	被分成	be sorted (into)	被排序成
be dried	被烘乾	be stored	被儲存
be evaluated	被評估	be stretched	被延展
be extracted	被提取	be transported	被運送
be flattened	被整平	be thrown away	被丟掉
be ground into	被磨成	be used to V	被用於
be hardened	被硬化	be washed	被洗
be heated	被加熱	be welded together	被焊接在一起
be inserted into	被插入	be left to V	被留給

描寫動作的「目的和結果」〈參照 P.140〉

purpose	to V, in order to V
result	Ving, resulting in n.p.

寫作「介紹」〈參照 P.183、P.187〉

background
• In recent years v.p.
• It cannot be denied that v.p.
• It is true to say that v.p.
• Many people believe that v.p.
• Many people consider that v.p.
• There is no doubt that v.p.

balancing
• Although this may be true in some cases, v.p.
• However, there are two sides to this statement.
• However, this is surely not the only way to look at the question.
• However, while this may be true to some extent, v.p.
• On the other hand, v.p.

opinion set-phrases
• I firmly believe that v.p.
• It's my opinion that v.p.
• I (dis)agree with the view that v.p.
• There's no doubt in my mind that v.p.
• I do not believe that v.p.
• I (dis)agree with this, and think that v.p.

signposting set-phrases
• There are many reasons why I think so.
• There are two/three main reasons.
• I can think of two solutions to this problem.
• This essay will look at some of the common problems and will then suggest two solutions.
• There are many ways to solve this problem.

附錄

2

加入意見〈參照 P.199〉

adding ideas	
• A further point to consider is n.p. • Also, • Another good thing about n.p. is that v.p. • Another good thing is that v.p. • Another n.p. is that v.p.	• Another reason why v.p. is that v.p. • In addition to this, v.p. • In addition, v.p. • Not only that, but also v.p. • … not only n.p., but also v.p. • On top of that,

闡述想法〈參照 P.202〉

illustrating ideas	
• Take for example the way that v.p. • Take n.p. for example, • For example, • For instance, • A good example here is n.p., which v.p.	• A good example here is the way that v.p. • In my country, • In my situation, • On a personal level, • …, such as … • …, like …

對比意見〈參照 P.205〉

contrasting ideas
• However,   • While it is true that v.p., nonetheless, v.p.   • While this may be true to some extent, nonetheless, v.p.   • On the other hand,   • Still,   • On the contrary,   • Although v.p., v.p.   • By contrast,   • Then again,

描述「原因」〈參照 **P.215**〉

reason	
… because of n.p. … … because v.p. … … as v.p. … … since v.p. …	… due to n.p. … … due to the fact that v.p. … … v.p. as a result of n.p. … … n.p. is the result of n.p. …

描述「結果」〈參照 **P.219**〉

result	
• The effect of this will be n.p. • This may cause s/o to V • This could lead to n.p. • This will lead to n.p. • This could result in n.p. • The result of this could be that v.p. • This may cause n.p. • The result of this will be n.p.	• The effect of this will be to V • As a result, v.p. • The effect of this could be to V • The result of this will be that v.p. • The effect of this could be n.p. • This will result in n.p. • The result of this could be n.p. • This means that v.p. • … so, v.p.

情態助動詞〈參照 **P.227-228**〉

附錄
2

非過去時間	過去時間
should V shouldn't V ought to V ought not to V	should have p.p. shouldn't have p.p. ought to have p.p. ought not to have p.p.
must V mustn't V	

第一類條件句〈參照 P.234〉

真實：First Conditional	
條件子句	後果子句
If v.p. (present simple),	(will/won't V)
	(may/may not V)
	(might/might not V)
	(can V)
	(will probably V …)

第二類條件句〈參照 P.237〉

非真實：Second Conditional	
條件子句	後果子句
If v.p. (past simple),	(would/wouldn't V)
	(would probably V …)
	(could V)

Unit 14

五種動詞時態的用法〈參照 P.245〉

時態和時間	
present simple 現在簡單式	這個時態是用來描述和時間無關的事情，例如：事實和意見。它也可以用在用來描述狀態的動詞，例如 be 和 have。

- The arts play a significant role in public life.
- The theatre industry in London is world famous.
- Actors have highly developed skills.

present continuous 現在進行式	這個時態是用來描述在現在尚未結束的時間下，進行的趨勢或活動。如果沒有結果，或是你不想把重點放在結果上，請使用這種時態。

- The problem is getting worse all the time.
- The gaming trend among young people is increasing.
- Climate change is having a catastrophic effect on many lives around the world.

present perfect simple 現在完成式	這個時態是用來描述在現在尚未結束的時間下，行動的結果。

- There has been a great improvement in living standards.
- The situation has worsened in the last few years.
- Climate change has had a catastrophic effect on many lives around the world.

past simple 過去簡單式	這個時態是用來描述過去已經結束的行動或狀態。

- Many people died of the plague.
- The situation was very bad before the government started doing something about it.
- Scientists did not know what caused the problem, until they discovered the virus.

will V 未來簡單式	請用 will V 來描寫你很確定未來會發生的行動或狀態。

- The situation will only get worse.
- More people will die.
- Antibiotics will eventually become useless.

時間字串〈參照 P.249〉

present perfect simple		present continuous	
so far	since X	at present	still
yet	recently	nowadays	currently
now	lately	now	
just	never	at the moment	
for X	ever	these days	
already	for ages	already	
	in recent years		

寫複雜的句子 (1)〈參照 P.252〉

簡單的句子	Many drugs can now cure this disease.
複雜的句子	There are many drugs which can now cure this disease.

寫複雜的句子 (2) 〈參照 P.254〉

簡單的句子	This problem is very bad. It affects many people.
複雜的句子	This problem, which affects many people, is very bad.

寫結論 〈參照 P.257〉

總結用的 set-phrases	
In conclusion, In the last analysis, To sum up, To summarize,	On balance, Overall, it is clear that v.p. I would recommend that v.p.

國家圖書館出版品預行編目(CIP)資料

IELTS 高點：雅思制霸 7.0⁺ 說寫通 / Quentin Brand 作；
周群英, 戴至中譯. -- 初版. -- 臺北市：波斯納, 2019.04
　　面：　公分

　ISBN: 978-986-96852-8-3（平裝附光碟片）

　1. 國際英語語文測試系統　2. 考試指南

805.189　　　　　　　　　　　　　　　　108004012

IELTS 高點：雅思制霸 7.0⁺ 說寫通 〈寫作強化篇〉

作　　者／Quentin Brand
譯　　者／周群英、戴至中
執行編輯／朱曉瑩

出　　版／波斯納出版有限公司
地　　址／台北市 100 館前路 26 號 6 樓
電　　話／(02) 2314-2525
傳　　真／(02) 2312-3535
客服專線／(02) 2314-3535
客服信箱／btservice@betamedia.com.tw
郵撥帳號／19493777
帳戶名稱／波斯納出版有限公司

總 經 銷／時報文化出版企業股份有限公司
地　　址／桃園市龜山區萬壽路二段 351 號
電　　話／(02) 2306-6842

出版日期／2019 年 4 月初版一刷
定　　價／580 元
I S B N／978-986-96852-8-3

貝塔網址：www.betamedia.com.tw

本書之文字、圖形、設計均係著作權所有，若有抄襲、模仿、冒用情事，依法追究。
如有缺頁、破損、裝訂錯誤，請寄回本公司調換。

喚醒你的英文語感！

對折後釘好，直接寄回即可！

廣 告 回 信
北區郵政管理局登記證
北 台 字 第 14256 號
免 貼 郵 票

100 台北市中正區館前路26號6樓

貝塔語言出版 收
Beta Multimedia Publishing

寄件者住址 □ □ □

貝塔語言出版
Beta Multimedia Publishing

讀者服務專線（02）2314-3535　　讀者服務傳真（02）2312-3535
客戶服務信箱　btservice@betamedia.com.tw

www.betamedia.com.tw

謝謝您購買本書！！
貝塔語言擁有最優良之英文學習書籍，為提供您最佳的英語學習資訊，您可填妥此
表後寄回（免貼郵票）將可不定期收到本公司最新發行書訊及活動訊息！

姓名：_____　性別：□男 □女　生日：_____年_____月_____日

電話：(公)_____(宅)_____(手機)_____

電子信箱：_____

學歷：□高中職含以下　□專科　□大學　□研究所含以上

職業：□金融　□服務　□傳播　□製造　□資訊　□軍公教　□出版
　　　□自由　□教育　□學生　□其他

職級：□企業負責人　□高階主管　□中階主管　□職員　□專業人士

1.您購買的書籍是？_____

2.您從何處得知本產品？(可複選)
　　　□書店 □網路 □書展 □校園活動 □廣告信函 □他人推薦 □新聞報導 □其他

3.您覺得本產品價格：
　　　□偏高 □合理 □偏低

4.請問目前您每週花了多少時間學英語？
　　　□ 不到十分鐘 □ 十分鐘以上，但不到半小時 □ 半小時以上，但不到一小時
　　　□ 一小時以上，但不到兩小時 □ 兩個小時以上 □ 不一定

5.通常在選擇語言學習書時，哪些因素是您會考慮的？
　　　□ 封面 □ 內容、實用性 □ 品牌 □ 媒體、朋友推薦 □ 價格□ 其他_____

6.市面上您最需要的語言書種類為？
　　　□ 聽力 □ 閱讀 □ 文法 □ 口說 □ 寫作 □ 其他_____

7.通常您會透過何種方式選購語言學習書籍？
　　　□ 書店門市 □ 網路書店 □ 郵購 □ 直接找出版社 □ 學校或公司團購
　　　□ 其他_____

8.給我們的建議：_____
_____

喚醒你的英文語感！

Get a Feel for English !

喚醒你的英文語感！

Get a Feel for English !